OTTO PENZLER PRESE
AMERICAN MYSTERY CL/

RIM
OF THE PIT

HAKE TALBOT is a pen name of the American writer Henning Nelms (1900-1986). Nelms reserved his real name for writing non-fiction about showmanship (his chief occupation was as a stage magician), but wrote several mysteries and stories under the Talbot moniker.

RUPERT HOLMES is a two-time Edgar award-winner and the *New York Times* best-selling author of *Murder Your Employer*, volume one in *The McMasters Guide to Homicide*.

RIM
OF THE PIT

HAKE
TALBOT

Introduction by
RUPERT
HOLMES

AMERICAN
MYSTERY
CLASSICS

Penzler Publishers
New York

Published in 2023 by Penzler Publishers
58 Warren Street, New York, NY 10007
penzlerpublishers.com

Distributed by W. W. Norton

Cover image: Andy Ross
Cover design: Mauricio Diaz

Paperback ISBN 978-1-61316-465-5
Hardcover ISBN 978-1-61316-464-8
eBook ISBN 978-1-61316-466-2

Library of Congress Control Number: 2023908315

Printed in the United States of America

9 8 7 6 5 4 3 2 1

INTRODUCTION

From the very first sentence . . . we are into the realm of nightmare. Miracles gather and explode. A dead man returns—or does not return. A flying ghost, apparently, swoops down and attacks. No angels, but goblins and wizards seem to dance on a pin. *Rim of the Pit* is a beauty.

—John Dickson Carr

THIS MAY be the first you've heard of *Rim of the Pit* and its author Hake Talbot. But as indicated by the above quote from his review of Talbot's 1944 gem, it was held in high esteem by John Dickson Carr, acknowledged master of the locked room mystery. In the early nineteen-eighties, a panel of experts selected by Edward D. Hoch—no stranger himself to impossible murders in hunting lodges and snowbound cabins—voted it second only to Carr's own masterpiece *The Hollow Man* (known to American readers as *The Three Coffins*) as landmarks of that sub-genre.

But to call *Rim of the Pit* a locked room mystery barely begins to describe this *outré* and unrelenting "long night's journey into Hades." For while it contains many components of a Golden Age classic—relatives and relative strangers are sequestered at a remote lodge in the wilderness during a fiendish blizzard and one of them is brutally murdered—there is nothing even remotely cozy about this avalanche of impossible events. Enough plasma is spilled to satiate the most hematophagous reader, topped off by the discovery of a body fully drained of blood. Both demonic possession and the flesh-eating "Windigo" (mythological winter monster of indigenous tribes of North America) are given serious consideration as the agents of murder. Rarely has the supernatural been accommodated so credibly and articulately in a mystery, to such an extent that you may find yourself agreeing with the characters that a deceased person might qualify as an ongoing suspect.

At times teetering on the brink of horror, Talbot further lends his mystery the pernicious aura of a textbook of Forbidden Arts with the epigraphs that commence each chapter, several times quoting Eliphas Levi, a nineteenth-century occultist who wove his *Doctrine and Ritual of High Magic* around the tarot deck and alchemy. The book begins to feel dangerous in one's hands as the unholy implausible transmutes into the wholly feasible, especially if you're reading *Rim of the Pit* in "those hours of darkness when the powers of evil are exalted"—quoting Conan Doyle and *The Hound of the Baskervilles* . . . and, of course, a supernaturally-attuned black hound named Thor figures in the story just for good measure.

If a whodunit is a mystery, then a howdunit is a magic act, and *Rim of the Pit* is a howdunit written by a magician. "Hake Talbot" was the pen name of Henning Nelms, a *bona fide* Renaissance man: attorney, advertising expert, college drama professor, and author of tomes on the stagecraft of magic, set design, and old-fashioned melodrama. His *Magic and Showmanship: A Handbook for Conjurors* was not a book of magic tricks but a serious guide for professional magicians seeking to infuse their performances (or staged séances) with the same approaches and techniques used in legitimate theatre.

Thus, it's hardly surprising if, while reading *Rim of the Pit*, one might envision a bravura stage thriller, its cast of ten trapped by the elements in an impressively handsome two-level cabin set. The plot hits the ground running for dear life with the memorable first sentence: "I came up here to make a dead man change his mind." And when we immediately learn that these Ten Little Individuals have assembled to hold a séance—not a harmless parlor game for an evening's diversion but a concerted attempt to make contact with someone from beyond the grave—we expect the evening may quickly go south . . . assuming the pit of Hell is a compass point.

There are indications that Hake Talbot, who was forty-four when *Rim* was published, knew his John Dickson Carr, who specialized in impossible crimes that often bore the stage dressing of the preternatural until well into his detective's final summation. In *The Hollow Man*, published ten years before *Rim*, a Professor Charles Grimaud is murdered in inexplicable fashion; in Talbot's tale, a character central to the mystery bears the name Grimaud Désanat—*please also note the last name is an anagram of "de Satan."* Talbot's Grimaud may or may not be dead but, in his macabre tale, it matters little: dead or alive, he's still a suspect!

And just as in *The Hollow Man* there is a legendary chapter devoted to a discussion of the genre by detective Gideon Fell himself, *Rim* contains several fascinating sidebars about the mechanics of magic, with particular emphasis on phony séances; these play out not as digression but informed discourse among the characters relevant to the nightmarish events unfolding. Yet even this discussion of the fakery behind some phony mediums' ghostly effects only makes us more seriously ponder if *genuine* supernatural elements are at play here . . . much like the magician's device of "exposing" to the audience how a miraculous feat was accomplished, only to repeat the trick minus the revealed flummery and miraculously achieving the same results.

Finally, both *Hollow* and *Rim* feature corpses discovered upon a field of unblemished snow, the apparent victims of gunshot wounds; how could they have been wounded when there are no footprints anywhere near the body? Rest assured the explanations offered are as wildly divergent in both books as are the two author's voices throughout.

It will not betray any secrets to reveal that the role of detective in this extraordinary mystery is taken by one Rogan Kincaid, although for the first few chapters you might have considered him a suspect until a footnote reveals that he was central to the author's previous mystery, *The Haunted Hangman*—this being the only other novel penned by "Hake Talbot."

Kincaid is introduced as a professional gambler, adventurer, and apparent rake (the novel boasts not one but two surprisingly amenable young women who may have raised readers' eyebrows or pulses in the years just prior to Mickey Spillane). As the mystery deepens, Kincaid at times blends into the background, more like another "man who explained miracles," G.K. Chesterton's Father Brown, who could go unnoticed amid impossible crimes until quietly weighing in with an observation that sends the scenery crashing down upon the stage. But once the snowstorm and deaths subside, Kincaid takes charge to offer a way out of the abyss for those who have survived the night, as well as an explanation of the night itself for an audience of one (plus you, of course).

In his textbook *Magic and Showmanship*, Henning Nelms asserts that "the art of conjuring consists in creating illusions of the impossible." Under the *nom de plume* of Hake Talbot, he conjured up the grand illusion that is *Rim of the Pit*. And before you begin reading his *tour de force*, let me hijack one of Sherlock Holmes' most famous observations by way of advice: when you have eliminated all which is impossible, you may have eliminated too much.

Hey, it's really snowing up a blizzard, isn't it? Better toss another log on the fire . . . and if you must step outside, make sure to bundle up. You could catch your death out there.

—RUPERT HOLMES

RIM
OF THE PIT

I

Dead of Winter

There are dead people whom we mistake for living beings.
—ELIPHAS LÉVI, *Dogme de la Haute Magie*

"I came up here to make a dead man change his mind."

There was earnestness behind the quiet statement.

It was growing dark. The blaze in the huge fireplace flickered on the face of the speaker and made its expression difficult to read. The fingers of his left hand moved restlessly over the smooth coat of the great dog that lay on the sofa beside him. Round-faced, round-bodied, in worn hunting clothes that gave no hint of his wealth, Luke Latham stared belligerently up at his tall house guest.

"Well, go on. Why don't you laugh?"

"Not until I'm sure it's funny."

Latham hunched his shoulders. "It isn't. It's plain Hell."

The black Dane pricked his ears, then sprang to the floor and stood with head erect, growling softly. His master looked at him in surprise. A moment later his own ears caught the crunch of feet on snow. Latham moved around the corner of the fireplace into the hall wing of the low L-shaped room, and opened the door.

The girl outside wore ski togs that took advantage of slim hips and brought out the long lines of her figure. The wind had tinted her cheeks, but her face looked pale against her blue-black hair, and her gray eyes were troubled.

Before Latham could speak, the man with him said, "Hello, Sherry Ogden," and fresh color leaped in the girl's face.

"Rogan Kincaid!" She held out both hands. "Jeff told me he drove you up this morning, but I couldn't imagine anything dragging you this far from civilization."

"I wasn't dragged. I was attracted."

Sherry tilted her head to one side and looked at him. "By a chance to take Luke's hide at poker?"

"Lots of men have had cracks at my hide," Latham chuckled, "but I'm still wearing it. Truth is, Rogan was in Quebec, headed south. Jeff met him and offered him a ride this far. But where did you see that nephew of mine, Sherry? He was in such a rush to go hunting, he grabbed his gun and left while the pie we had for lunch was still sticking out the corners of his mouth."

"Jeff didn't need a gun," Sherry confided. "The game he's after has baby-blue eyes and answers to the name of 'Barbara.' As a matter of fact, there's some doubt about who's doing the hunting. Either way, the betting is you're going to acquire a niece. They're over at my place now, swapping coos."

Latham took the girl's parka and they strolled to the fire, where the Dane greeted her by thrusting a cold muzzle into her gloved hand. She curled on one end of the sofa and sat looking up at Rogan. Tall, lean, enigmatic, with strong unsymmetrical features, he was in such striking contrast to his host's dumpy rotundity that for a moment a smile touched the corners of her lips. Then she caught the older man's shrewd eyes and her glance dropped. The color had gone from her cheeks, and the hand that pushed back her black curls trembled.

"This isn't just a social visit, Sherry." Latham's voice was kindly. "What's bothering you?"

Her fingers locked together in her lap. She twisted them apart, and drew a long breath before she spoke.

"Luke, are you certain my father is dead?"

Rogan read surprise in his friend's face, but there was none in the voice that answered.

"I saw his body."

"Are you absolutely sure it was Father?" the girl insisted. "I mean, they said he was . . . Besides, it was all so impossible."

A puzzled expression puckered the corners of Latham's eyes. "Lots of men get lost in the snow, my dear."

"I know, but not Father. He'd spent half his life outdoors. And that other man . . . Everyone told me he was a regular old woman about marking a trail. They said he *never* took any chances. A person like that couldn't wander away."

"I'm sorry, Sherry." Rogan spoke softly. "I didn't realize. . . . Jeff said nothing about Mr. Ogden's—"

"Frank Ogden isn't my father," she interrupted. "He isn't even my stepfather."

"When Sherry was born her mother died," explained Latham. "Her father married again."

"I was about twelve when Father . . . was lost." She began pulling off her gloves with little nervous gestures. "Then my stepmother married Frank. They adopted me, and I've called myself 'Ogden' ever since. Father was French—from Provence. My real name is Seré Désanat."

Mr. Kincaid was puzzled. "But if your father died ten years ago . . . ?"

The girl flashed him a smile. "It was fourteen, but thanks. I know I'm being a fool . . . only . . . only . . ." Her lips began to tremble and she huddled back on the sofa. "I'm scared."

"Don't see what's troubling you," said Latham. "Never was any doubt about his death. Made the funeral arrangements myself. That's how I happened to see the body. Some fool may have told you he was pretty badly . . . changed by exposure. He was. Recognized him, though . . . No question at all."

"I know," Sherry admitted doubtfully, "and you couldn't have made a mistake about his left hand. But"—she gave a little gesture of helplessness—"he couldn't have gotten lost, either—not Father. He could find his way anywhere, like an animal . . . places he'd never been before. The lumberjacks used to make bets on him."

"That part of the Hudson Bay country is Hell's icebox, they tell me. Your father and that other man—Querns, wasn't that his name?—had never hunted it before. Top of that a storm came up—bad one. Fellow wrote me that even the guide got lost hunting your father. Said the poor devil wouldn't have come out alive himself if he hadn't run into some explorers." Latham moved closer to the fire. "Country like that does things to a man sometimes. Gets inside his mind—changes it around. Saw a trapper once who'd been lost for three days. He walked right across a railroad track without seeing it. Started to run away from us when we shouted at him."

"I know I'm being a fool . . . but . . ." Sherry broke off as the black dog moved over and put his head in her lap. She stared down at him. "Thanks, Thor. You don't think I'm crazy, do you?"

"We don't either," Latham grunted. "Can't help, though, unless you tell us what's wrong."

"It's . . . oh, so many things." Again the little helpless gesture. "Luke, why did Frank bring Mr. Vok here? Is it because of the séance?"

"What séance?" asked Kincaid. "And who is Mr. Vok?"

"Svetozar Vok," Latham informed him. "Frank Ogden picked him up in Quebec. Refugee from Czechoslovakia."

"He's more like a refugee from a horror movie." Sherry shuddered. "Wait till you see him, Rogan. He's a mile high and looks like the oldest inhabitant of a graveyard."

Her host chuckled. "Vok's not that bad, Sherry. Queer bird, but I like him. Struck me as rather witty."

"He gives me the creeps. He's like a mummy that's still smiling over one of the embalmer's jokes." She glanced up at Latham. "Besides, why is he at Cabrioun? It's not like Frank to pick up a refugee. Particularly a penniless one. Frank isn't the kind to help lame dogs over stiles."

"That's not fair, Sherry. I don't get along with Frank too well myself, but he can be generous when he likes. Practically pensioned Madore Troudeau by making him caretaker at Cabrioun. Frank didn't get any good out of that. None of the family's been up here for years."

The girl was not satisfied. "There are other things too, Luke. We haven't been here since Father died. Why did we come now? And why didn't we bring any of the servants? Why has Frank been so jumpy lately? And what has the séance got to do with it? And . . . and . . . lots of things."

Latham hesitated. "I know you're not a believer, Sherry. Though how you can help it after what you've seen your stepmother do time and time again . . ."

"I think it's mostly Irene who's kept me from believing. I admit queer things occur at her séances . . . things nobody's ever been able to explain. But she's such a fraud, I can't put faith in a thing she does. Everything about her is phony. That's why this . . ."

The words trailed off. Latham sat on the sofa and took Sherry's hand.

"Something's happened to you. You came here to tell us about it. Maybe we can help."

The girl stared into the fire. Then without looking at either of the men she said:

"Today I heard my father's voice."

There was a long silence after that. Thor stirred uneasily. Sherry put her hand on his head and crumpled his ears.

"I didn't have much to do this morning," she went on. "Frank was out hunting with Madore and that Professor Ambler who's staying with you. Irene locked herself in her room, like she's been doing since we came. Barbara was fixing her hair in case Jeff got here. At last I decided that even Mr. Vok's company was better than being left alone, so I screwed up my courage and took him skiing. He turned out to be pretty good at it. We went across the lake to slide down The Snake's Back. It was when we were coming home I heard Father. We were in the middle of the lake. There wasn't a soul within a quarter of a mile. There couldn't have been."

She stood and began walking back and forth before the fire.

"It was the song I heard first, an old Provençal thing. There's a high note in it Father could never reach. He used to make a funny little trill instead. The words were perfectly beastly. 'Pierre! Death comes for you; the toad digs your grave; the crows sound your knell . . .' I hated it," Sherry grimaced at the recollection. "It's been a long time since then. I'd even forgotten the tune until I heard it today."

"Sound travels pretty far over ice," Latham reminded her. "Wind plays tricks with it, too."

"Do you think I haven't told myself all that?" The girl turned and threw out her hands. "It wasn't only the song. Afterward a man's voice spoke. It was Father."

"Make out what he said?"

"There was a little echo, and I missed all but a few words. The only thing I could be positive of was . . . my own name."

"Sure you remembered your father's voice after all these years?"

Sherry bit her lip. "You don't forget things like that. Besides, who else could it have been? There's no one within miles of the lake this time of year. Jeff and Rogan hadn't come. Mr. Vok was with me. You wouldn't do a thing like that, and the other three men were all together hunting."

She broke off and resumed her pacing. Rogan watched her for a long minute.

"There's more yet," he declared. "You'd better let us have it all."

Sherry spun on her heel and flung back her head.

"All right, and it's this that's driving me frantic. The voice was loud enough even if it did sound far away, and I know Mr. Vok has good ears. But he didn't hear it!"

II

She Shall Have Music . . .

Pierre!
La mort te ven querre;
Le grapaut
Te fa le traue;
Les courbasses
Te sounoun lous classes;
L'escourpioun
Te reboun.
—*Chant populaire*

"FRANK OGDEN shouldn't have let you come up here." Latham's kindly face was troubled. "I wouldn't have had you worried for anything."

Sherry stared at him. "Luke! You mean you expected this?"

"Not exactly. Not surprised, either."

"That's it, then." Her eyes widened in comprehension. "That's why you came. That's why Irene's holding this séance. *You're trying to bring Father back!*"

"We aren't doing it for fun," Latham protested glumly. "This was the place for it—his country. He was a sort of king in these woods. That's why we brought him here to be buried"—he gestured with both hands—"right in the middle of his timber."

"It's the anniversary of his death, too."

"Reason we picked this time to come."

"But why are *you* doing this, Luke? Why is Irene doing it? She's been married to Frank over twelve years now. I don't think he cares much about her, but she's all wrapped up in him. Besides, why in the name of all that's reasonable is Frank so keen on it?"

"You ought to have been told before," Latham admitted. "You know the business arrangements between the Ogdens and my firm, don't you?"

"Vaguely." Sherry moved back to the sofa. "Frank's always looked after such things and I've never paid much attention. You buy most of the logs that come from our timber holdings. Your mill is really a special wood-processing plant. Frank owns a patent on the process, and you pay him a royalty. Isn't that right?"

"Close enough—or was until recently. Now we're in a queer kind of a jam. Part of it's complicated as a government questionnaire. It's all mixed up with the location of our mill, water rights, power plants—that sort of thing." Latham hunched back on the sofa. "What it amounts to is this. *All* our logs come from your forests. We're the only people who can handle your pulpwood at a profit. The combination of your kind of timber and our mill setup is what makes Frank Ogden's patent valuable."

"You mean each of us depends on the others. So that if one of us wouldn't play ball, the rest would be in the soup."

"Except that you and your stepmother own a lot of hardwood on the other side of the state. The pulp business doesn't mean as much to you as it does to Frank and me. We'd always figured on there being enough pulp-timber to last another twenty-five or thirty years. Two, three months ago we found we were almost finished logging Swamp River. That meant we'd have to go into Onawa. Your father left Onawa to your stepmother, so we weren't expecting trouble. We got it, though—plenty. Irene told us Grimaud willed her that property for a special reason. Said he didn't want it logged for twenty years. Made her promise not to let it be cut sooner."

"Sort of left you out on a limb, didn't it? But wasn't that a strange thing for Father to ask?"

"No. Sound sense then. All second-growth. Needed time to develop. Ogden's patent changed that. Small logs are worth as much per board foot as big ones. Your father's reasoning doesn't hold any more."

"I don't blame Irene for not daring to break a promise she made Father," said Sherry. "I wouldn't have risked it myself, even if he is dead. What are you trying to do now—get in touch with Father in the other world and ask him to let you log the timber?"

"It's a funny way of doing business," Latham confessed. "But we were in a funny fix. Had to find some way out. Frank thought of using Irene's powers as a medium. We tried in town. No luck. Then I suggested coming up here. Your hearing your father's voice makes me think I had a good idea."

"Maybe. Anyhow, it convinces me that Irene had a right to be scared to death."

In the past, Rogan had found the aberrations of his spiritual-ist friends mildly amusing. This was different. Calling back the dead to clear up a commonplace business arrangement was like trading in a second-hand magic carpet on the price of a new Ford. Nevertheless, if the spiritualistic premise were granted, the idea was as logical as a demonstration in geometry. The thought was unwelcome. In Mr. Kincaid's experience, logic applied to fantasy meant danger for someone.

"I don't know that what you've told me is any more comforting than the idea I came with," Sherry said. "But at least it isn't bottled up inside me." She took a compact from her pocket and started to powder her nose. "Good heavens, my hair's like the inside of a mattress. Why didn't one of you tell me?"

Rogan grinned. "I like 'em tousled."

"Quiet, you." Sherry stuck out her tongue at him. "Can I borrow a comb, Luke?"

Latham patted his bald head. "What would I do with a comb?"

"I have one," Rogan offered. "Shall I get it, or would you rather use it before a mirror?"

"The mirror, please. I can only see one eye in this thing."

"Second door on the right. The comb's on the bureau."

When she had disappeared at the head of the stairs, he turned to Latham.

"That was quite a testimonial to the father."

The older man nodded somberly. "Grimaud Désanat was a queer fish. French. Son of a shoemaker. Emigrated to Canada when he was eighteen. Picked up an education from his parish priest. Drifted across the border. Like Sherry said, he was a natural woodsman. Couldn't have learned that in France. It wasn't only finding his way. I've seen him take a million feet out of country no other logger would touch. Sherry's mother was Irish—Ellen O'Hara. When Grimaud married her, she looked just like Sherry does today."

Latham stared into the fire and his round eyes grew reminiscent.

"Ellen was the sort of woman you only meet once in a lifetime, and Grimaud knew it. Built Cabrioun for her—place we're having the séance tonight. Sherry was born there, first winter they were married. Ellen only had an Irish woman and a couple of *habitant* servants to look after her. It had started to snow. Grimaud left in plenty of time to fetch the doctor from Lynxhead. That's six miles. People around here still talk of that storm. Took Grimaud and old Doc Nesbit four days to get back. When they did, Ellen was dead."

He put a fresh log on the fire.

"Can't blame a man if a thing like that turns his brain. Peyton Ambler says people who live in the farm districts in France, and never see a decent-sized town more than once a year, develop a queer streak. It came out in Grimaud, queer—and cruel. Some ways he was sharper than ever. Started to make money by the bankful. But he hated Sherry because she'd killed her mother. Six months after she was born, he married again. Couldn't believe it at first, but when I saw Irene I knew why. She's starting to fall to pieces now, but in those days she was the image of Ellen. Only difference was she had brown eyes. Ellen's were gray. Character was different, too. I don't think Grimaud even noticed that. Irene wasn't Ellen. That was enough for him. Almost from the start he held it against her. He began drinking, too—raw brandy. I never told Sherry, but I think that's why he couldn't find his way back to camp the time he got killed."

Rogan grimaced. "You haven't picked a very pretty ghost to raise."

"I said it was Hell. No other way out. Million and a half tied up in my business. Won't be worth a counterfeit dime. Irene doesn't dare disobey Grimaud. Can't say I blame her."

"What are you going to do if your séance scheme doesn't work?"

"Go bust. Jeff and Frank Ogden were in Quebec trying to get logs from the other side of the border at a price we can afford."

"Doesn't Ogden have faith in the séance plan?"

"More than I have. He doesn't know Grimaud. Matter of fact, Frank felt the Quebec trip was a waste of time. That's why he quit and came back yesterday. Jeff kept plugging till last night. No go."

Rogan eyed his host shrewdly. "I don't suppose you've thought of fixing things yourself so you'll get the right answers?"

"Fake Grimaud's ghost, you mean?" Latham's voice rose in surprise. "Hell's clinkers, man! I'd be afraid to. He wasn't the sort to fool with while he was alive. Only an idiot would risk it now he's dead!"

Sherry came down the stairs. Whatever she might be feeling, her outward poise had returned. She stood before the fire and stretched, fully aware of how the gesture displayed firm, round breasts under the yellow sweater. Then the gray eyes clouded again. She turned to Kincaid.

"Do you mind going home with me? It's only a three-minute walk, but I don't think I'm quite up to facing the woods alone now that it's growing dark."

Latham rummaged in the closet and returned with a pair of ski boots, which he tossed to Rogan.

"These are Jeff's. Better wear 'em. Shoes'll get full of snow. Take Thor along. He needs a run. Maybe he can help you drag Jeff away from this prospective niece of mine. It'll take some doing. I've seen her. Tell Jeff he's got to come back here to the lodge and help cook dinner." Latham turned to Sherry. "Thought we could pick up a guide in Lynxhead, or a cook. No luck. All gone with hunting parties."

He bade them good-by and they set out, with Thor stalking majestically ahead. The long New England twilight had set in, and Gothic elms cast lean shadows over the snow. Sherry slipped her hand through Rogan's arm and drew her body close to him.

A man of cities, Kincaid found this winter-struck wilderness disquieting. The gray light, the naked trees—black against the snow-shrouded earth—the wind whispering in the dry branches, were all alien. Even the small wild things seemed unfriendly.

His uneasiness had begun that morning when Jeff turned off the main highway some twenty miles the other side of Lynxhead, and had increased with every slap of the chains against the mudguards. The woods suggested menace—menace that was no less disturbing because he knew it to be unreal. That he could find no basis for his misgivings only made matters worse.

Danger was the breath of life to Kincaid, but he liked odds that could be calculated. Here he was out of his element. Experience had taught him a healthy respect for his instincts, but he knew they were only mental short cuts, treacherous unless they could be tested by reason. In his normal surroundings he made such a test automatically. Always he found what he sought—the shadow, the trick of voice, the flicker of movement that had set his nerves on guard. Here in this gray-lit landscape he found nothing. He knew only that his whole being was braced against an attack that might come at any moment and from any side.

Suddenly the black dog stiffened. Sherry's grasp on Rogan's arm tightened. Then she relaxed with a little laugh.

"I should know better than to jump. Thor probably smells rabbits."

"More likely it's bears. A hound that size couldn't even work up an appetite over a rabbit." The incident annoyed Kincaid. I'm like the dog, he thought—sniffing something I can't see.

No hint of his mood was allowed to reach the girl. She saw nothing in the snow but its beauty. As they walked, the wind brought the color back to her cheeks. The pressure of her body against Rogan's no longer indicated a need for support, but became a token of intimacy.

She had, she told herself, no illusions about this man. A friend had pointed him out in a Palm Beach hotel the previous winter.

"He's not exactly a beauty, my dear, but so interesting-looking, don't you think? I met him five years ago in Egypt. Out there they tell the most frightful tales about him. Apparently he just travels around the world and makes his money by gambling. A Captain Everitt I knew in Cairo said he'd seen Mr. Kincaid kill a man in a brawl in Shanghai, or some such place. Apparently this Kincaid just bent the other man backward over the bar until his spine snapped. The captain said the dead man was a Japanese army officer and a famous jujitsu expert. But of course I don't believe *that*."

Sherry believed it. The next night she had witnessed a demonstration of a very different facet of Rogan's prowess, when she had visited a swank gambling house outside the city. She had noticed Kincaid as he entered and stood for a few seconds in the doorway. Then he had strolled to a poker table and pulled out a chair. One of the men already seated had jumped to his feet, proclaiming loudly that he had no intention of playing with a crooked cardsharp. Remembering Captain Everitt's story, Sherry had expected mayhem at the least. Instead Rogan had merely nodded and said:

"If you're quitting, you'd better leave the cards you've been holding out. I like to play with a full deck."

With that he had extended his hand and twitched two aces from under the other's vest.

Sherry never knew whether the man had really held out the cards, or whether she had witnessed some bit of legerdemain on

Rogan's part, but she felt he would always be like that—invulnerable, ready with the one perfect counterstroke for any attack that might come.

She knew there could be no constant companionship with such a man. Yet his physical nearness was an exhilarating experience. The week in Florida . . . the promise of the next few days up here. . . . Sherry had once seen a giant engine in a steel mill and had held her hand so that the great connecting rod, at the extreme end of its outward lunge, had tapped her fingers as lightly as a kitten. The nearness of that tremendous and perfectly controlled power which, had she moved an inch nearer, would have flung her across the room without noticing it, had held something of the same thrill—the same feeling of excitement.

It was working in her now. The fear that had filled her since morning was draining away. When they branched from the wagon track onto a footpath, a sudden glimpse of the lake brought a surge of remembered terror. But the moment passed, and by the time they rounded a huge pine and came within sight of her house she was almost gay.

"That's Cabrioun."

Like the lodge, it was a two-storied structure built of logs chinked with graying mortar. However, where Latham's house was low and rambling, Cabrioun was compact and vertical. Its eaves hung within ten feet of the ground, and its steep roof climbed past shallow dormers to loftly ridgepoles set in the form of a "T". The hint of medieval France given by its lines was obscured by a boxlike structure—obviously the kitchen wing—that had been built on the end from which Rogan and Sherry approached.

The house stood in a clearing swept bare even of the smallest bushes, as if the guide, Madore, had felt it his duty to protect it from the encroachment of the forest. The wind, racing over this empty space, drove the dry snow before it in thin sheets like gauzy skeins of blown cobweb. This drifting had filled any earlier footprints, so that the place had a deserted look broken only by a feather of smoke from the main chimney.

"It looks pretty grim from here," the girl confessed, "but inside it's quite comfortable—furnace and everything. Coming this way we sort of sneak up on it from behind because it faces the river."

She led the way through a storeroom, which served as a vestibule, and into the kitchen. There they found Jeff and Barbara stirring a custard with an unnecessary amount of collaboration.

Sherry winked at Rogan.

"It must be love."

Jeff looked up and grinned. "Hello, you two. Come in and watch me being housebroken."

He was a large young man with 'ex-tackle' written all over him. His face had once presented a collar-ad type of male beauty, but a kindly Princeton halfback had stepped on it. Jeff had wisely refused to have his nose set, so it now resembled an island of William Bendix entirely surrounded by Robert Taylor. He waved a hand in introduction.

"Miss Daventry, this is Rogan Kincaid. Take a good look so you can avoid him in the future. He's a professional heartbreaker."

Barbara licked the custard spoon meditatively, blue eyes on Rogan.

"He might be fun, though."

"Try it," Sherry dared her, "and come spring they'll be dragging the lake for a yellow-headed corpse."

The Dane put his front paws on Barbara's shoulders and regarded her solemnly. She frowned at him.

"Thor, you have a mean and hungry look, like Julius Caesar or somebody."

She vanished into the storeroom and returned bearing a huge bone, which she tossed on the floor. Thor growled politely and set to work with relish.

"There goes tonight's soup," Barbara remarked wistfully. "And now that the subject of tonight has been brought up unobtrusively, Sherry, do you mind if I inject a touch of humor into the séance? Nothing coarse. Just a few quiet shrieks, and perhaps a pool of blood in the center of the table so the fun won't be over when the lights come up."

Jeff groaned. "Barbara Daventry, the poltergeist of the north country."

She jerked a thumb at him. "Jeff's an old fuddy-duddy and won't play. Personally I think games in the dark with more than two people go best with youthful jollity."

Jeff groaned again. "Sherry, you'll have to talk this wild woman out of her ideas. I've tried to remind her she's your stepmother's guest, but the girl has no social conscience."

"Pooh," said Barbara, "just because Jeff's mother was scared by a prohibitionist or something isn't any reason the rest of us should pass up a chance for innocent merriment. Can you gibber, Mr. Kincaid? Or take off your head? Surely you have some talent that will put everyone at ease and help the evening pass smoothly. Sherry lamb, I have your part all worked out. You're to make bloodcurdling squeaks on the accordion."

"Is that a crack?"

"Of course not, darling. You play divinely, but you *could* make squeaks if you *wanted* to, couldn't you?"

"But I don't want to," Sherry assured her. "Irene's bad enough when she's her sweet, silly self. With hysterics she'd be more than I could bear." She stood. "Whew! These ski clothes are hot in here."

"Then why don't you take them off, my pet?" Barbara advised. "It's a shame to hide such lovely legs."

Sherry said, "I think so myself," and vanished.

Barbara twinkled at Rogan. "You can't blame her at that." She turned back to Jeff. "You ought to be glad to help me get a little fun out of this séance. You've read up on these things. Maybe we could even kid your uncle out of believing in spooks. You know you don't like the idea of his getting business advice from the spirit world."

"I've told you a dozen times," said Jeff patiently, "there's no way to cure a believer. Uncle Luke's a great guy, but once a man gets to be a sucker for spooks you can't laugh him out of it and you can't talk him out of it. Even if his favorite hant turns out to be five yards of phosphorescent gauze, he swears it's an 'apport' brought by unfriendly spirits to discredit the medium. Look at Conan Doyle. He used to explain Houdini's tricks by saying Houdini was a medium and didn't know it. Houdini spent the last ten years of his life telling the world that the things he did were tricks and nothing but tricks, but he couldn't pound any sense into Doyle."

"Oooh," exclaimed Barbara, "you've given me another lovely idea. We can make Thor a set of terrible teeth out of grapefruit rind and he can be the Hound of the Baskervilles."

Rogan stood. "The Hound of the Baskervilles seems to have finished his bone. So I'd better break the news that Latham sent us to tell Jeff to come home and get dinner."

"I can see there's no use appealing to your chivalry," Barbara observed wisely, "but sometimes a bribe works wonders in such cases." She pointed. "Go through there into the dining room. Sherry's door is on the left. Knock before you enter, 'cause according to my computations she's just about reached the pink-silk-pantie stage."

"And," Jeff added, "if you see something queer wandering around, don't let it scare you. It's a friend of Mr. Ogden's."

"That man can haunt a house without any help."

Barbara gave a mock shiver. "If a ghostly hand touches me at the séance tonight I won't know whether it's Mr. Vok or Jack the Ripper. What's more, I won't care."

Kincaid drifted into the dining room. From behind the door on the left came Sherry's voice, raised in a song that made up in piquancy for what it lacked in decorum.

Mais oui,
But yes!
Of course,
Monsieur.

He decided that the knock Miss Daventry had recommended would be a mere formality. Nevertheless, it is well to be punctilious in these matters. He knocked.

The song stopped. A moment later Sherry opened the door just enough to display one eye and half the opulence of the yellow sweater.

"You disappoint me," Rogan informed her. "The little girl next door said you'd have reached the pink-silk-pantie stage."

Sherry, realizing he was alone, pulled the door wider and stepped into the opening.

"I have."

He nodded approval. "Evidently you began at the bottom and worked up. I confess the sweater lends an unexpectedly provocative note."

She flirted her hips at him. "I'm glad you like the effect. Only you'd better go now because somebody might walk through the dining room, and that would be just too bad."

Rogan sighed. "And I had hoped for a private viewing."

Sherry winked. "That might be arranged." She kissed him. "But later. Off with you."

Mr. Kincaid was smiling as he walked through the broad archway into a living room that ran the full width and height of the house. Whatever it might be like in the full light of day, the place was gloomy now. Dusk seeping through small windows illuminated only the lower half, so that the hand-hewn roof timbers slanted up into darkness.

The gambler made a practice of examining any place in which he found himself, with the eye of a general surveying a possible field of battle. It was one of the reasons he was still alive. A stair climbed the wall that separated the living room from Sherry's bedroom. In the wall opposite there were two doors. He opened them. One led to the vestibule, the other to a closet—its floor littered with boots. Deep window seats flanked the doors. A great fireplace of smooth stones rose against the wall to the right. The ancient musket and powder horn which decorated it were hung so high they were nearly lost among the soot-stained shadows.

The log walls, dusty with neglect, were covered with a motley array of Indian relics, faded snapshots, and the paraphernalia of northern sports.

Behind him he heard Sherry singing,

Mais oui,
But yes!
Of course,
Monsieur.

He strolled over and looked at the photographs. Obviously they represented Sherry's father and his friends, but the dim light made it impossible to see more.

The girl's husky contralto had given way to accordion music. It was strange that he had not noticed the instrument in her bedroom. True, his eyes had been occupied, but they had not missed much of the room's furnishings. An accordion is not an easy thing to overlook.

Besides, this accordion was behaving very oddly. It played a snatch of Sherry's tune and then interpolated a few notes of another melody—a melody as eerie as the little song had been insouciant. There was no connection between the two. The effect was like opening first one booth and then another in a record shop.

Before he had time to guess at the reason for this, Sherry's door banged open and she came running in.

"Rogan!" She stopped at sight of him and her hands twisted in the folds of her skirt. "Weren't you playing?"

"I thought you were. Shhh!" He held up his hand. "It's stopped."

There was a cupboard under the stair landing. Sherry turned to this and pulled open the door. A swift step brought Kincaid to her side and they peered in. She pointed to an awkwardly-shaped black case and whispered:

"Open it."

He dragged it from the cupboard and pressed the catches. The lid fell open to reveal the chromium and plastic of the accordion.

"Nobody could have played it while it was locked in the case." In the dim room her upturned face was white as a moon flower, and her whole body trembled. "That was Father's tune."

Shuffling footsteps sounded on the landing above. The girl drew out of Rogan's arms with a little cry. He needed no word from her to tell him that the man who peered down out of the gloom was Svetozar Vok.

Seen from below he almost bore out Sherry's extravagant description. His height, his gaunt figure, and his black, ill-fitting clothes gave him a startling resemblance to a great bird of prey.

"Miss Ogden." The voice was low and vibrant, marred only by the harsh Czech consonants. As Vok came swiftly down the steps they moved to meet him. He stopped in front of the girl with a ceremonious and oddly theatrical bow.

"I hope I am not intruding. I have heard music and . . ." His eyes found the accordion in its half-opened case.

"Miss Ogden was showing me the instrument," Rogan explained smoothly.

"I was struck by the curious tune you were playing," Vok told her. "I came out of my room and found this. I think it must have been stuck in the door-crack of the room of your stepmother, but it seems to have slipped out and fallen to the floor where I found it. It is"—he groped for a word—"alarming."

The Czech held out a white card with words written on it in jet-black ink. Rogan read over Sherry's shoulder.

I am in agony. You must go on without me.

III

The Road to En-dor

Then said Saul unto his servants, Seek me a woman that hath
a familiar spirit, that I may go to her and enquire of her. And
his servants said to him, Behold, there is a woman that hath a
familiar spirit at En-dor.

—*I Samuel XXVIII, 7*

SHERRY'S RESPONSE to the words surprised Rogan even more
than it did Vok. She laughed, and despite the underlying note of
hysteria, it was the laughter of relief.

"I'm sorry," she apologized. "We should have warned you
about my stepmother's little habit of writing notes like this. She
does it so much we get used to her exaggerations, and forget they
may startle our guests. This is just her way of persuading me she
has a headache and hopes I won't ask her to help with dinner."

The Czech seemed puzzled. He took the note and bent over it
so the dying twilight could fall on the words.

"I do not understand. This is not what I saw." He flipped the
card over and his frown disappeared. "Yes, this is it. It must have
fallen face down."

He returned it to Sherry. Then he bowed slightly, and without another word made his way silently up the stair. Rogan and the girl looked at the back of the card and saw scrawled in pencil:

The Night is for Retribution

She turned and stared up at him. Her eyes were wide with consternation, and her lips moved almost without sound.

"Father!"

When the party from the lodge, with Thor in attendance, reached Cabrioun that evening, Frank Ogden opened the front door for them. He was a spare individual, a little above middle height, with a heavy-featured, colorless face and thin lips. It was easy to guess that Sherry had no liking for this man. Everything about him spoke of a narrow Puritanism that had married wealth and coveted more without knowing how to enjoy it. Even his rimless nose-glasses had a primness that the girl must have found galling. Nevertheless, he greeted them warmly, made some remark about the fact that Professor Ambler had shot a record buck that day, and complimented Latham on his guest's marksmanship.

Sherry had changed into a close-fitting dress of her favorite yellow, and had just finished setting up a large folding table in the center of the room.

Barbara sat on the sofa and made eyes at Vok for practice.

After stating that his wife would join them shortly, Ogden went around collecting coats.

"I was interested in your talk with Madore today, Professor."

"Goodness," exclaimed Barbara, "what did you ever find to talk to him about?"

"Souls," said Ambler.

"Souls?"

Latham grunted. "Shouldn't have thought Madore had one."

"That wasn't the point." Ambler smiled benignly at Barbara's blond youthfulness and sat beside her on the sofa. He was a wiry wisp of a man. His merry blue eyes laughed out of a magenta complexion under a cockatoo's plume of white hair as soft as thistledown. Even the bushy feathers that marked his eyebrows swept upward to emphasize his good humor.

"You see," he explained, "I'm an anthropologist. So while I was out with Mr. Ogden's guide I made use of my time to hunt other things besides deer. Luke's plans for the séance tonight had set my mind running on the beliefs of various peoples in regard to existence after death. The French peasant looks on the dead as enemies, and most Indians would agree. Madore has inherited the ideas of both stocks."

Rogan laughed. "Under those circumstances, it's a wonder you were able to get him to talk at all."

"Oh, Madore likes to pretend he isn't afraid of anything," said Ogden. "I didn't tell him we were holding a séance tonight, though, or his primitive superstitions might have taken some of the bluff out of him."

"It is not only the primitives who are superstitious." Vok had been silent so long that it came as a shock when he spoke. In the warm lamplight he appeared even less human than he had at dusk. His cadaverous face with its tightly drawn skin, yellow as old parchment, was topped by an upstanding brush of short gray hair. Great black brows swept in a continuous double curve over keen, wide-set eyes. The long nose, which seemed to have been crushed against the face by embalmer's wrappings, gave point to Sherry's picture of him as a mummy—a mummy with a satanic twist provided by the sharp smudge of black whisker under the lower lip.

"Besides," he continued, "the superstitions of the primitive are at least logical. It is the earthbound spirits which frighten him: the restless dead, compelled to haunt the scenes of life because they have not altogether done with living—because they have left some task unfinished, some vengeance incomplete. Those who are truly dead have better things to do than to bother with those of us they have left behind."

"Of course you are joking." Ogden frowned. "But it seems to me that blasphemy is even worse as a joke than when it is spoken seriously."

"Of course I am joking, but I do not blaspheme. I discuss primitive beliefs—and not only primitive. Does not the Church teach that there is a limbo—a place where those who are not completely dead may finish their account with life?"

"My church has no such teaching," Ogden retorted stiffly.

Vok spread his hands. "Is not the Bible in substantial agreement? Does it not imply that there is, beneath our feet, a surging world of spirits—each striving desperately to break through the barrier which separates them from us?"

Latham snorted. "Never read anything like that in the Bible."

"It is there by implication only," Vok answered, "but it is there. How else can you account for the bitter denunciation of witchcraft? *Thou shall not suffer a witch to live.* Remember, the Bible witches were not simple old women who charmed warts and rendered dry the cows. They were necromancers, people who trafficked with the dead, like the witch of En-dor. If the dead were friendly, or even harmless, there would be no sin in necromancy. But if we are fighting an endless war against the dead, as the Dutch fight an endless war against the sea, then necromancy is the supreme crime—treason against the living."

"That," Ogden pronounced flatly, "is ridiculous!"

"My friend, the entire matter is ridiculous, but that is not a reason for us to be illogical."

Ambler leaned forward. "I should like to ask Mr. Vok whether his definition of a witch would include a modern medium. She also calls up the dead."

"It would," said Vok, "if the medium were genuine."

Ogden bridled. Latham put a stubby hand on his arm.

"Take it easy, Frank. He's just trying to get a rise out of you."

"If you are seeking a parallel for modern mediumship," Ambler continued to Vok, "it seems to me you will find it less in witchcraft than in the idea of possession."

"You mean," asked Barbara, "like the Gabardine man in the Bible with the pigs?"

"Something like that," the professor said, smiling.

"Aren't we getting mixed?" Sherry put in. "I thought the people in the Bible were possessed by devils."

"I'm afraid," replied Ambler, "that the idea of demonic possession has no better foundation than a mistranslation. The word in Greek is δαίμονες and Josephus tells us specifically that in New Testament times it meant 'the spirits of wicked men which enter the living.'"

Miss Daventry cupped her chin in her hands and stared up at the professor with suspicious innocence.

"Do you mean a nasty old ghost could just get inside one of us and take charge?"

"I think that's what the Bible meant. But don't laugh at possession. It's a very real thing. I've seen cases myself. Explaining them, of course, is a different matter."

"Are not possession and mediumship the same thing?" inquired Vok.

"I shouldn't think so," Ambler responded. "Theoretically a medium can call up the spirits of the dead without letting them take control of her."

Vok laughed. "My old nurse, who comes from Stary Hrozenkov, would have called such spirits *'duchy',* which is a Czech word for poor futile wraiths, powerless to do more than squeak and gibber. The Hrozenkárstí peasants say that it is only when a dead soul has forced the barrier at some weak spot that it enters this world and becomes dangerous."

Latham shook his head. "I've seen too many spirits not to believe in 'em. Can't swallow this possession idea, though."

"But you do," Ambler assured him, "whole. You believe in trance mediums, don't you? If the spirits of the dead take charge of a medium's vocal organs, and speak through her mouth, that is possession."

Ogden said, "But my wife . . ."

Irene Ogden chose that moment to move out upon the stair landing. She was a large woman clad in a house robe of purple velvet. Her face still showed traces of a beauty which must have been flamboyant in her youth, but she had fought age with the wrong weapons. The implausible black of her hair made her look five years older than she was.

As she swept down the stairs, her eyes caught Peyton Ambler's—and turned away a fraction too suddenly. It was a small thing to go on, but Rogan would have bet heavily that the introduction her husband supplied a moment later was unnecessary.

"Oh, Professor Ambler," said Barbara, with just a shade too much awe in her voice, "Mrs. Ogden is a wonderful medium.

She has a spirit guide who is a Hochelaga Indian. I'll bet he knows a lot more what the Indians think about souls than Madore does. Do you speak the Indian language?"

"I know something of Indian languages, but no one knows much about Hochelaga, which is no longer spoken." Ambler's eyes twinkled. "Perhaps Mrs. Ogden's control would be willing to give me lessons. If I could work out a grammar of Hochelaga, I could create quite an anthropological furor."

Mrs. Ogden replied stiffly that Indians were notoriously unreliable and she couldn't promise. However, she hoped Stadacona would come that evening.

"Well, I hope he won't," Barbara pouted. "My goodness, it would spoil everything if we have to sit around listening to some dead Indian lecture on verb endings."

Ogden smiled thinly. "I am afraid we would hardly have time, anyway. As you all know, Irene is holding this séance tonight for a special purpose. I hope you will concentrate on that." He turned to his wife. "Shall we begin, dear?"

"Oh, Frank . . ." Her hands fluttered. "Do you really think we should? I mean . . ."

"We've been over that fifty times." Ogden was firm. "It's settled now. That's why we came up here, and why we decided to hold the sitting tonight."

The woman gave in, though Rogan was certain her reluctance was genuine. She had brought with her a black shawl, and a large knitting bag made of the same purple velvet as the house coat. She draped the shawl on the back of the sofa and sat with the bag on the table in front of her.

"It will be better," she began, "if *all* of us ask questions of our friends who have passed over. They seem to find it easier to communicate when a number of them can come in succession and feel sure they'll be recognized."

Her voice was low and flexible, with a hint of accent—French, with a difference. The gambler decided she was Canadian.

"I get better results when people write their questions." She fumbled in her bag and produced a stack of white envelopes. "Mental questions are usually vague, and sitters often change their minds about what they want to ask. That almost always makes an unsatisfactory séance."

She rose and began to distribute the envelopes. Rogan opened his and drew out a correspondence card some four inches high by five broad. Ambler, sitting opposite Kincaid, had evidently thought his question out in advance, for he took a pencil from his pocket and wrote rapidly. The gambler decided that a knowledge of the question would make it easier to follow the answer. He read upside down:

> Dear Walter,
>   Gene and I have often wondered what happened to the invention of which you spoke just before your death. Possibly . . .

The professor looked up and saw Rogan's eyes on him, Kincaid smiled politely.

"May I borrow that pencil when you get through?"

Mrs. Ogden swept up to him. "Haven't you anything to write with, Mr. Kincaid? Here, use this."

She drew a large, black fountain pen from her bag and offered it. He wrote:

>   I would like to know whether old Grandmother Kincaid finds heaven up to her expectations.
>
>   R.K.

That seemed innocent enough, but—as has been recorded elsewhere*—the gambler had started life as Michael Dundas Braxton, and Grandmother Kincaid had never existed.

"If you've all finished," Mrs. Ogden said, "turn your questions over, so that I cannot possibly see them, and then slide them into their envelopes face down."

Rogan noticed that she pointedly refrained from looking at the cards until they were hidden by the envelopes.

Jeff licked the flap of his and scrawled his name across it, so that it could not be opened and resealed without leaving traces. The idea impressed Kincaid favorably, particularly as it might enable him to keep track of his question. He signed his name in an even bolder hand than Jeff's.

At her stepmother's request, Sherry gathered the questions. She had to let Rogan's wait, as he was still waving it to dry the ink.

Mrs. Ogden came over to retrieve her pen. By that time the envelope had dried and she took it in her left hand. She dropped the pen into her bag and passed her right hand over the face of the envelope, which she touched to her forehead.

Rogan decided the gesture was for effect. Certainly she had gained no information from the envelope. She had not even looked at the signature on the back, which had been in his view the whole time.

Sherry returned, and the medium took the other questions from her, added Rogan's, and started to put them all in her bag. Before they were hidden from sight she took them out again, saying:

"No. It will be easier for us to concentrate on our questions if we can see the envelopes. Will you stand them on the mantel, Sherry darling?"

---

* *The Hangman's Handyman.*

The fireplace was a huge affair of native stone that ran up to disappear among the shadows near the roof. The mantel shelf, however, was very narrow—so narrow that Sherry could not have laid the envelopes flat had she wished, but was compelled to stand them on edge. In that position Rogan's signature on the top envelope was clearly visible.

Ogden who had been betraying signs of a growing nervousness, asked, "Are we ready to begin?"

His wife bit her lip.

"Oh, Frank . . . do you think we'd better?"

"Of course I do. You don't want us to log Onawa without his permission, do you?"

"Oh, no!" She cringed.

"Then pull yourself together and get on with it."

"All . . . all right. Sherry dear, we'll need your accordion so you can play for the hymns."

When they were all placed, Rogan found himself sitting beside the medium on the sofa, with Sherry in the chair on his right. There turned out to be no chair for Jeff, but as Barbara had curled in the overstuffed chair at the foot of the table, he seemed pleased to sit on its arm.

"Now," Mrs. Ogden directed, "we must put our finger tips on the table and concentrate on our questions, while Sherry plays."

The girl inflated the accordion and began *Lead, Kindly Light.* When the song ended without incident the medium seemed relieved.

"Perhaps there won't be any manifestations tonight."

"Nonsense," her husband snapped. "This is our best chance to get through to him. Try again."

Rogan noticed that neither Ogden referred to Grimaud Désanat by name.

Sherry played another hymn without result.

"You see, Frank," Mrs. Ogden said, "it's useless."

He flared at her. "You're not making an effort. You don't really care whether we get his permission or not, but it means a lot to Luke and me. If you can't get him this way we'll have to try a dark séance."

"No, Frank. I wouldn't dare. I—"

The sentence was interrupted by a peremptory rap that seemed to come from the very center of the table.

IV

The Dark Circle

There are also a number of professional mediums who can be possessed at will.

—REV. G. OWEN, *Chinese Recorder,* 1887.
Quoted by VON DER GOLTZ
in Zaubereiund Hexenkunste in China

Iʀᴇɴᴇ Oɢᴅᴇɴ's frightened eyes sought the faces around her. Then, as if against her will, she asked:

"Is it . . . Grimaud?"

"Rap, rap." The sounds were low-pitched and had about them a solemnity that impressed Rogan in spite of himself.

The medium looked relieved. "Are you using two raps for 'no' and three for 'yes'?"

"Rap, rap, rap."

She drew a deep breath and explained to the others.

"That's easy to remember, because there are the same number of raps as there are letters in the words."

The knowledge that her ghostly visitor was not her first husband seemed to have relieved the tension under which she labored. She turned back to the table.

"Are you Stadacona?"

"Rap, rap."

"Have you a message for anyone here?"

Three raps.

"Please give the initials."

The medium began to run through the alphabet. When she reached 'R' she was stopped by a sharp rap. She began again. This time the rap came at 'K.'

"Oh,' Barbara exclaimed. "It's for Rogan."

The table gave three quick raps. Then it went on to spell out:

"E-X-I-S-T-E-N-C-E   H-E-R-E   I-S   B-E-Y-O-N-D E-X-P-E-C-T-A-T-I-O-N-S."

Mr. Kincaid found himself puzzled. He had hardly supposed that the medium would fall headlong into the simple trap he had set, but this went far beyond mere shrewdness. Mrs. Ogden's response was obviously based on a knowledge of his question, but how could that knowledge have been obtained? He had taken particular pains to see that no one looked over his shoulder while he wrote. The envelope had been in the medium's hands for a minute at most. During that time it had never left his sight, and its sweeping signature was still visible where his envelope stood in front of the others on the mantel.

His speculations were interrupted by a rattle of knocks higher-pitched than the others. Thor, who had paid no attention to the earlier raps, sprang to his feet and stood staring at the table as if he expected it to attack him. Jeff put out a hand to quiet the dog. The table went on rapping in short bursts like submachine-gun fire. Thor dropped to the floor and lay there, growling softly.

"What's the matter, Thor?" asked Barbara. "Is it a message from someone you don't like?"

"It wasn't a message from anyone," Ogden grumbled, "not if

we're supposed to count letters. If we are, I make it C-G-G-C-A-B-E."

"Maybe he's practicing," suggested Barbara.

The raps went on: six-six-one-one-three—

"He *is* strangely limited to the first part of the alphabet," Ambler agreed. "'G' seems as far as he can get."

"Possibly," said Vok, "it represents a melody, and the letters stand for notes. Miss Ogden might play it for us."

Sherry fingered the keyboard of her accordion. The result was nearly tuneless. The letters supplied only the changes of pitch, so that every tone was the same length and without stress. To the girl's ears, however, they meant something. Rogan heard her catch her breath, and a moment later he recognized her father's song. Then her fingers trailed off into chords without meaning.

For the rest of the circle, the rhythmless tune seemed to have no significance. It did not, as Barbara put it, sound like Irving Berlin's best. Ogden flatly pronounced the raps gibberish.

"We're only wasting time this way," he said. "We aren't going to accomplish anything without a dark séance, and the sooner we admit it to ourselves the sooner we'll get this over with."

Kincaid, watching the medium, saw something that made his pulse jump. Irene Ogden turned pale! It was not due to any trick of light or change of expression. The woman was simply, starkly, afraid.

"No, Frank," she begged. "I wouldn't dare."

"Why not? That's what you came here for, isn't it?"

"Yes, but . . . well . . . I can't put it into words, but . . . it's different up here. It's not like it was in town."

"I hope you're right. You didn't get any results in town."

She put out a hand toward him.

"Please, Frank, let's keep on with the raps a little longer. I'll manage in time. I know I will."

"We haven't got time! This is the anniversary, and it's after nine now. We can't tell how long it will take. It doesn't matter to you, perhaps. Your whole capital isn't tied up in this timber. Luke and I aren't so fortunately situated. We've got to log Onawa or go under."

"Frank, you can have anything that's mine."

"Thanks. I prefer my own—with no strings attached. Besides, Luke's in this too, you know."

"But," she persisted, "a dark séance wouldn't be fair to the others, P-Professor Ambler, and Mr. Vok, and Barbara."

"Oh," said Barbara, "I vote we turn out the lights. What's the good of a séance if you don't get scared?"

Irene Ogden winced, but she gave in. It is difficult to oppose Miss Daventry with dignity.

"We have to form a circle first," the medium explained. "Everything depends on a continuous flow of odylic force. That means we must make perfect contact with each other. Let me take your wrist in my right hand, Mr. Kincaid. Sherry dear, put your accordion on the sofa and give Mr. Kincaid your wrist. That's the way. Now, take Professor Ambler's wrist, and so on around the table. Remember, everyone holds the wrist of the person on his right. And"—fear swept over her again so that Rogan felt her tremble—"whatever happens, don't let go!"

Jeff rose. "I'll get the lights." He blew out the oil lamp on the desk and then strolled to the bracket near the fireplace, which was the only other light in the room.

"It's cold here." Mrs. Ogden shivered. "I wish Madore hadn't let the fire in this room die out." She took her shawl from the sofa and settled it about her shoulders.

"Ready?" Jeff asked.

The medium threw a pleading glance at her husband, but he ignored her.

"Certainly, put it out," he told Jeff. "We've wasted too much time as it is."

Jeff turned down the wick. The flame in the glass chimney flickered and died. Appropriately the wind chose that moment to moan in the chimney. Miss Daventry squealed. Someone whispered, "Shhh!" and Rogan felt Irene Ogden's hand on his wrist again.

"We don't need it pitch-dark like this," she complained. "Frank, you must speak to that guide about the fire. We've only been up here three days and he's let it go out twice." She brought her attention back to the circle. "Now we must all put our left hands on the table and spread our fingers to make the contact as perfect as possible. I think we'd better have another hymn, too, although Sherry can't play for us as she mustn't break the circle."

She began *Rock of Ages,* and the others joined. Sung in darkness, the old tune had an uncanny power. It seemed less an invocation of the shades of the dead than a spell sung as a bulwark against the forces of the pit. Rogan found himself wondering what would happen if the singing stopped. Then, before the last note died away, he felt the table quiver under his hands like a living thing. Sherry's wrist was almost jerked from his grasp, and the girl whispered:

"I . . . I . . . felt someone breathe on my cheek!"

Almost at the same instant, phantom fingers touched Kincaid's face. A moment later a glow of light appeared, shaped like a star. It moved in slow spirals and then came to rest the height of a man's head from the floor. During all this the table remained alive. It was no longer an inanimate thing, but a force to be reckoned with.

The medium began to speak in a wooden voice that Rogan had difficulty in recognizing as her own.

"I have a message for someone from an old friend. I get the letter 'P,' then 'E.' 'P-E-Y—'"

"Peyton." Ambler's voice came from under the star of light. "That must be for me."

"Yes, that's right," she confirmed. "Your friend comes to me as a man in middle life. His hair is graying and he carries himself with a slight stoop." The table gave a little convulsive movement, and she hurried on. "He has been in the spirit for some years now."

Rogan wondered if the medium's method of attack bore out his idea that she had known the little professor before. She seemed to have made a guess as to the identity of the man to whom Ambler's question was addressed, and to be testing it by giving her statements a rising inflection. In that way, any mistake she made might be interpreted as a question.

"I get the impression," she went on, "that your friend left the body for some reason connected with the elements, heat—or cold."

This time the inquiring lift at the end of the sentence drew a response from Ambler.

"Co—"

"North!" she declared. "That's it. I am seeing more clearly now. Your friend's influence comes to me from the north! There is a great deal of snow, and the wind howls night and day."

Some of Mr. Kincaid's uneasiness slipped away. He felt he had discovered her method. The half syllable of Ambler's answer had confirmed her guess—had given her the one piece of definite information she needed. She had cut him short as if she had not heard him. Later, most of the circle would forget he had spoken at all.

The table grew more restive.

Irene Ogden's speech took on a note of urgency. "I get the letter 'W' and perhaps a 'G' or a 'Q.' The writing is blurred but the message is clear. He refers to something of which he spoke just before he left the body."

The last sentence laid Rogan's theory in ruins. It contained a literal quotation from Ambler's question. There was not even the chance that she had hit on the phrase by accident. She would have used 'he spoke of,' instead of the awkward purism 'of which he spoke.' That meant Mrs. Ogden knew the very words Ambler had written.

Rogan could find no explanation. She had not read the professor's question while he was writing it. During the half minute it had been in her possession it had been enclosed in an opaque envelope and buried in a pack which contained seven others. Under these conditions even X-ray vision could not have deciphered it. Was it possible that Latham was right—that this apparently silly woman possessed some power beyond human understanding?

The whole atmosphere of the room cried out that she did. The table was throbbing now—swaying from side to side like a bull working up its fury to attack. Mrs. Ogden's speech grew more rapid, as if she hurried to finish before something happened.

"I see your friend surrounded by apparatus of some kind. He is a scientist, or perhaps an engineer. He tells me you are interested in a plan of his which—"

The words ended in a startled gasp, and the medium's rings bit into Rogan's wrist. The end of the table struck upward so that he had to fall back to avoid it. Then the far end left the floor and the whole table plunged sidewise and overturned. The light over Ambler's head gave a frightened leap and darted into a corner of the room.

From the confusion and shouting in the dark, Rogan gathered that Ogden and the professor had been thrown from their chairs. Latham, busily helping his friends to their feet, called to Jeff to light a lamp.

"Don't do it!" Ogden's command was startling in the darkness. "No one's been hurt, and at last we seem to be getting somewhere."

"No, Frank, please," his wife faltered. "I can't go on . . . not after this. I'm afraid."

"Pooh," said Barbara, "ghosts can't hurt you—just make tingles go up and down your spine. Rough ghosts are a lot more tingly than sissy ones."

"The girl's right," Ogden insisted. "There's no danger."

"But, Frank, we don't know. We don't *know.*"

"Nonsense. We're not doing this for fun. We may have to put up with a few more of these *poltergeist* tricks, but that's all. You might even find a way to discourage those if you tried."

"You know I can't control the spirits. All I do is act as a channel when they want to communicate."

"Might try changing our positions," Latham suggested. "Sometimes get different influences that way."

"Wouldn't that destroy the favorable conditions?" inquired Ogden.

"Never did before. Anyway, we're after Grimaud. Haven't got him yet. Shifting might help."

"That's good enough for me," Barbara piped up. "Let's all change places and try again."

In spite of a general atmosphere of unwillingness, no one raised any further objection. Rogan helped right the table and made for the far end. There was a bustle as the chairs were straightened. He put out his hand and touched something soft which a little squeal identified as Barbara.

"I didn't move, 'cause I had my shoes off and I didn't want to get trampled," she confided. "I've lost Jeff, though, so if a ghost gets fresh you'll have to make faces at it and scare it away."

Rogan smiled in the darkness. His own nerves were taut as fiddle strings, but this amazing child was cool. Even her pulse, when his fingers found her wrist, told of nothing more than a pleasurable excitement. He wondered if under these conditions her instincts were surer than his own—if this whole affair were simply an elaborate mummery on the medium's part to excuse herself from carrying out her dead husband's instructions and at the same time to convince Latham and her living husband more firmly than ever of her powers.

It was a comforting thought, but everything he had observed of Irene Ogden denied it. The woman was afraid. He would have risked his life on that certainty.

Above all, he had the steadily growing conviction that they were faced with something larger and more monstrous than any of them guessed. He had only his subconscious to trust for that belief and, he told himself, after its ridiculous behavior in the woods his subconscious was no longer dependable. Still, there was a difference. Outdoors he had been like a child alarmed by terrors it knows do not exist. Here every trained nerve in his body warned him that the danger was real.

The scrape of a chair on his left recalled him to himself. A man's hand touched his arm and groped its way along until it gripped his wrist. When the stir subsided, Ogden's voice identified him as the owner of the hand.

"We'd better make a circle as before," he directed. "And remember not to let go, whatever happens."

A curious inflection on the last words told Rogan that Ogden was less sure of himself than he had pretended. Kincaid was given no time to speculate further, for the phenomena recommenced almost at once. The table quivered with new life. Sherry gave a little cry as if a spectral hand had touched her face. Her stepmother's breath grew audible and came in shorter and shorter gasps.

"I feel . . . as . . . if . . . I . . . were . . ."

Thor leaped to his feet with a growl and pressed against Rogan's leg.

"It . . . is . . . not . . ." Suddenly the medium screamed. "Oh, Frank . . . please . . . somebody . . . stop . . . Grim—"

Her voice changed in the middle of a word, like a radio that has been tuned to a new station. The new voice was that of a man, blurred and all but inaudible. Rogan could make out only that the language was French—spoken with a curious accent. The tone was so utterly unlike that of the medium that Kincaid found himself wondering if she were the speaker.

Irene Ogden's voice broke in.

"No, no, not this way! It . . . is . . . too . . . cold . . ."

"*Tais-toi!*"

An icy wind, that seemed to blow from where the medium sat, swirled around Rogan. Thor pressed closer and the gambler could feel the dog's great body quiver. There was a confused noise, as if of a struggle from the medium's end of the table, and the man's voice shouted:

"*Femme, laisse-moi partir! Je ne désire pas te posséder.*"

Irene Ogden shrieked—shrieked as if something were being torn out of her. Her cry was drowned by a shrill note of accordion music, then another and another. The single notes became short runs which turned into a snatch of melody, and Rogan recognized the Provençal folk song.

As the tune died away, Kincaid felt Ogden's hand on his wrist give a convulsive jerk.

"Something's . . ." Ogden gasped, "something's materializing in mid-air. One of its feet touched my shoulder."

Ten feet over their heads a new light appeared, grew larger, and flickered for a moment. Then it split into three.

Rogan made out the face and hands of a man.

V

Grimaud Désanat

[Her] own spirit had left her body and a new one had taken possession, making her frame a mere instrument or as it were a speaking-trumpet.

—From the account of DR. REID CLANNY

THE FACE that glared down out of the dark was haggard with exposure and suffering. The forehead was hidden by matted hair. A beard shadowed the hollow cheeks and left only the pallid lips visible. The hands twitched. Nothing of the figure could be seen, but Rogan somehow knew that Désanat in life had been a small man. The voice spoke again.

"Cacho-pecat! Parce que je t'ai permis de perpétrer tes escroqueries impies et sans frein tu as décidé d'en commettre une en mon nom. Scélérate!"

The words were in the slurred accents of Provence, but each phrase lashed like a rawhide whip. Kincaid found himself struggling against belief in the spectral reality of this thing. It was totally unlike the sheeted spooks of the séance room. There was an almost overpowering quality of death about it, while at the same time it seemed instilled with a new and loathsome kind of life.

48

That it should exist at all was blasphemy. That it should move was an abomination. The thin lips writhed and spat oaths which even the gambler, familiar with the worst dens of Marseilles, had never heard. He knew now why men for a hundred centuries had looked on the spirits of the dead as evil.

Rogan's wanderings had brought him into contact with the dregs of mankind. Even they, being human, had retained some faint spark of humanity. This thing had none. It was as if death had drained the good from Désanat and left only malevolence.

The hands matched the evil of the face. The phantom chafed them as if to rid them of a cold that could chill even the blood-less. They seemed to melt and run together, yet when they were separated a moment later they were as strongly shaped as if bone and sinew moved inside them. The left hand lacked a finger.

"Ma chère femme," Désanat's voice went on in a tone that charged even the slurred French of the Midi with venom. "My dear wife—or should I rather say 'my dear widow'—for years you have chosen to utilize the most sacred ties of the human heart to swindle the living. I let you. What are the living to me?" The sneering voice dropped lower. "Besides, there is a punish-ment for that, a punishment which will be—ample. Tonight is different. Tonight you sought to cheat your husband and your friend, to cheat them by pretending I had put restrictions on my timber, to put a lie into my dead mouth. For that no punishment is adequate."

"What's he saying?" Ogden whispered. "In God's name, won't somebody tell me what he's saying?"

No one answered him. None had attention to spare from the enemy above their heads. For enemy it certainly was, not of the medium alone but of all humanity. Even more alarming than the thing's hatred was the impression it conveyed of a powerful intelligence. Whether Désanat were alive or dead, he was a foe to be reckoned with.

The maimed hand clawed at the straggling beard.

"Tell them that you have lied. Tell them that I placed no restrictions on my forest. That if I had, I would not have trusted you to carry them out. Tell them!"

"I . . . lied." Terror dropped Irene Ogden's voice to a whisper. "You made . . . no . . . restrictions."

The phantom gave an obscene giggle. "Now repeat it in English so they can all understand." When she had complied, he laughed again. "You did not expect me, did you? Not really. Yet you gave me the means to come, my dear. You gave me the means."

"Imbecile!" Désanat's voice rose to a shriek. "You dabble in mysteries you are not able to comprehend, like a child playing on the rim of a volcano. *Imbecile,* like the child, to think that which lies dormant cannot engulf you."

Again the bloodless hands were chafed together, and again the creature giggled.

"Pray, Irene! Pray to the God whose mysteries you have profaned. Pray to the dead you have insulted by your mummery. Pray to me, my widow. Pray that I will have pity on you and slay you now. Pray in vain!"

He turned away, and his mutilated hand rested on the rail of the stair landing. Then he swung back to add:

"I have a better plan, a plan that will make the Master Himself laugh in the depths of Hell. You, too, will learn about it in due time. Meanwhile, remember that since I have taken possession of you I am free to possess others. Thus I may wreak my vengeance, not on the spirit only, but on the body as well."

The specter turned again and seemed to drift through the railing as though it were not there.

Rogan knew afterward that what he did then was motivated by fear rather than by courage—fear that the giggling enormity might vanish before he could prove its falseness to himself, with underneath the deeper fear that it might prove only too real.

He wrenched his left wrist from Ogden's grasp and rose. A stealthy sound from the far side of the table warned him that someone else was bound on the same hunt. They were already too late. As Rogan slipped past Barbara, the phantom floated into the throat of the hall.

Kincaid bounded up the stairs, but when he reached their top and peered down the passage, the phantom was already at its far end. An instant later he seemed to be blotted from view.

A voice beside Rogan whispered, "We've got him now," and the gambler felt Miss Daventry's cheek against his shoulder as she peered around him.

"What do you mean?"

"Well," she said, "you can't do that sort of thing with mirrors, so Q.E.D. or what not, it must have been somebody dressed up."

"What makes you so sure it wasn't a ghost?"

"Oooh, you wouldn't scare me, would you? Anyhow he can't get away 'cause there aren't any back stairs. Just make certain he doesn't double back and slip past us."

"He won't," Rogan assured her grimly. He heard a match struck, and light glowed from a doorway on the left of the narrow hall at the far end of which Jeff stood before a closed door. There was another closed door on the right. Except for Jeff the corridor was empty.

Jeff blinked at Barbara. "It wasn't you, then?"

"Don't be a dummy-doodle. If I could make spooks like that I'd go in the business. I thought it was you."

The door on the left swung wider and Vok emerged, carrying a lamp.

"I went into my room to get this," the Czech explained. Then, "No one is there, anyway."

"He couldn't have gotten into your room," said Jeff. "I followed him further along the hall than that. The only place he can be is in there." His gesture indicated a door that blocked the far end of the corridor.

Ambler arrived then with Thor at his side.

"I don't know exactly what we're hunting," the professor observed, "but it struck me that the dog might be a good idea."

"Come on, Thor." Barbara caught him by the collar and started to lead him into the corridor. The great dog walked a few steps and stopped. Surprised, she pulled, but to no avail.

"Damn it, Thor, what's the matter with you?" Jeff demanded. He caught at the collar and jerked. The Dane drew back whimpering. Then he sat on the floor and howled.

That was too much even for the nerveless Barbara.

"Mercy, Jeff, maybe this isn't so funny, after all."

Rogan slipped past them to the door at the end of the hall. He listened. When no sound came, he pressed the latch and flung the door wide in one swift movement.

The room was empty.

The others came crowding after him. Vok's lamp revealed a good-sized bathroom.

"Goodness!" said the girl. "You couldn't hide a herring in here."

"He must have gone out a window." Jeff strode to the nearest one and raised it. Three inches of untouched snow lay on the sill.

Rogan threw up the other window. It, too, held a band of snow. He put his head out and struck a match. The rising wind whipped out the flame, but not before he had time to see that the flat roof was innocent of footprints.

As he withdrew his head he heard Vok ask:

"The other door, it leads to a closet?"

"I think that goes to the Ogdens' room." Barbara tried the latch. "It's bolted."

"On which side?" Vok tested it himself, twisting the thumb grip of the hidden bolt back and forth. "Both sides, apparently," he reported.

"You know"—Jeff scratched his head—"this is beginning to look queer as Hell."

"Perhaps," Ambler suggested, "we were wrong in supposing it to be a man. It might have been an illusion of some sort."

"I know it was a man." Jeff was positive. "Damn it, I was near enough to tackle him! I would have, too, only I wasn't quite certain where his legs were."

No one had any reply to that. They drifted back to the hall and found the other men grouped at its mouth with Sherry and Thor. Ogden was saying:

"I knew in my bones he never told Irene not to log Onawa. That's why I insisted on getting in touch. She might lie to us, but she'd never dare lie to him." His eyes fell on Jeff and he snapped, "Haven't you any better sense than to raise all this commotion at a séance?"

"I'm sorry, sir, but I wanted to know what this was. I never saw anything like it in my life, and I had to make sure."

"Well, now you've made sure, I hope you've learned enough not to interfere like this again."

"Beg pardon," Vok interposed, "but we have not made sure—yet. We have looked in my room and in the bath, but we have not looked in your room."

Ogden stiffened. "I fail to see the necessity for that."

"It is best to be thorough, is it not?"

Ogden snorted, but he flung the door open and stood aside while the others filed through, led by Thor, who seemed to have regained his self-assurance.

The room bore out Sherry's statement that the house had not been visited since her father's death. The walls were covered with hunting trophies and Indian relics that could hardly be thought of as representing Ogden's taste or his wife's. Scattered among the relics were numerous faded snapshots. Rogan noticed that one figure appeared in several of them, and concluded this must be Désanat.

Except for his size, the man in the photographs bore little resemblance to the specter. He was small and dapper, with handsome, well-cut features. In most of the pictures his face was clean-shaven but for a mustache. However, a few taken in camp clothes showed ragged beards in various stages of growth. Rogan decided that the little lumberman had not considered a razor necessary in the woods. In all the camp photographs he wore a mackinaw and moccasins, so that only a close look could distinguish him from his guides. The left hand appeared in several of the pictures. Its index finger was missing.

Jeff lifted the windows and examined the snow on the sills. Vok dropped on his stomach to peer under the bed. Rogan wandered to the door of the bath and found it bolted on both sides, as the Czech had said. Another door in the same wall opened into a closet, which a two-minute search convinced him contained nothing but clothing. As he stepped out of the closet he noticed that Ambler was missing, and drifted through the hall in search of him.

The professor was in Vok's room. He had a lighted flash on the floor beside him and was just shutting a large trunk of European workmanship as the gambler entered.

"It occurred to me," Ambler observed, "that someone besides Vok should check Vok's things. However, there's nothing in the room and I'll swear nothing crawled out of the windows."

"What's in the trunk?"

"Some of the most amazing things you ever saw, but no ghost."

The others were moving back to the hall by that time. Rogan and Ambler joined them.

"I hope the skeptics are satisfied." Ogden was still bitter. "Perhaps I should not really blame you, but you must remember that any disturbance of this sort is bad for a medium. I don't like having Irene subjected to it."

Latham caught his breath at that, and his round face lengthened as he turned to the others.

"Where is Irene?"

VI

Expose?

It is common to many of these accounts that the demons describe themselves as the outcast spirits of the unhappy dead.
   —J. KERNER, *Nachricht von dem Vorkommen des Besessenseins*

VOK DARTED downstairs into the dark void of the living room. The others crowded after him. His lamp revealed the medium's limp figure slumped on the sofa with her head and the upper part of her body enveloped in her black shawl.

Ogden snatched off the shawl. Sherry caught at her stepmother's wrist. A moment later the girl gave a sigh of relief.

"It's all right. She's only fainted. Help me lay her down, you men."

Ogden assisted in arranging his wife comfortably on the sofa and watched for a moment while Sherry rubbed her wrists. Then he pounced on Jeff.

"You should have known better than to create a disturbance of this sort. Surely you've attended enough séances to know how dangerous it is for the medium."

"Oooh!" A gleam of pure mischief appeared in Barbara's eyes. Jeff saw it and started toward her, but he was too late. She was already staring up at Ogden with her best little-girl expression. "Do you mean the séance and all was *real?*"

Ogden snapped at her. "Of course it was."

"Goodness. If I'd known that I'd have been scared to death!" The blue eyes grew even wider. "You mean it was *all* real—those lights we saw, and everything?"

Ogden assured her, vehemently, that he did.

"Then"—Miss Daventry leveled a pink finger—"what's that?"

'That' was a star-shaped object lying on one of the window seats. Ambler picked it up and examined it. Ogden snatched it from him and snorted angrily.

"This is only a scrap of pasteboard!"

"But it's got five points like that star we saw," Barbara answered reasonably. "And besides, look at the paint."

"You mean this greenish-white stuff?"

"Uh-huh. Phosphorus."

Jeff strode to the mantel and took down the envelopes. He spread them fanwise, turned them over, and tossed them on the table.

"Take a gander at these while you're at it."

Ogden scowled. "What's wrong with them?"

"They're dummies."

"Nonsense! Look at Kincaid's signature on his."

"What I'm looking for," said Jeff, "is my signature on mine."

He caught up the medium's knitting bag and dumped it on the table. It contained no knitting, but it did hold a number of curious objects—including more phosphorescent shapes, and seven sealed envelopes.

Jeff ran through them.

"Here's mine with my name on it."

Ogden's jaw dropped, but Barbara clapped her hands.

"Now we're going places. How did she switch envelopes?"

"That was easy." Jeff was enjoying himself. He pointed to a metal clip fastened inside the mouth of the bag. "You remember, Mrs. Ogden began to put the envelopes in this bag and then pretended to change her mind? What she really did was to drop the questions into the bag and pick the dummies off the clip at the same time."

"As I recall it," Ambler objected, "the envelopes didn't go all the way into the bag."

"Rogan's didn't. She used that as a screen and switched the others behind it."

"The clip does look queer," the professor conceded, "and I can't think of any other way to account for the fact that your card was certainly in Mrs. Ogden's bag. However, the envelopes are still sealed, so she couldn't have read our questions. Nevertheless, she knew what I'd written in mine. How can you explain that?"

Jeff frowned. "There you've got me."

Vok glanced up from the medium's shawl, which he had been examining. "Perhaps I can supply the answer." He picked a small flashlight from the table.

"This was in her bag. If it had been held behind an envelope the writing could have been read."

"If she'd lit that thing in the dark," said Latham, "we'd all have seen it."

"Ah," Vok replied, "that's where the shawl comes in. It is lined with a rubberized fabric to be light-proof, which is not a customary feature of ladies' shawls."

"You mean," asked Ambler, "that she threw it over her head like an old-fashioned photographer?"

"Precisely. And then held the torch behind the questions."

"If the shawl is lightproof," the professor commented, "it is probably airproof as well. That might explain why she did not recover sooner from her faint."

Ogden sprang to his feet.

"I don't believe she fainted at all. It's just a trick to get sympathy after something went wrong with her séance." He spun around and stared down at his wife. "All right, Irene. You've tricked me all these years, but no more. You're not fooling anyone by lying there, so you may as well sit up."

"No, really, Frank, she's fainted." Sherry turned to him from her place beside her stepmother. "See how pale she is, and her hands are like ice."

"Rubbish! She's faking. She's faked ever since I married her. Throw a bucket of cold water over her. That'll bring her to, quick enough."

"Sherry's right, Frank," Latham growled. "As for Irene making a fool of you, you're taking care of that job yourself right now. She'll wake up in a minute. Why don't you wait and see what she has to say?"

"She's awake now. She just hasn't nerve enough to face me after what she's done."

"Hell and tarnation, man! You don't know she's done *anything*. You saw a scrap of cardboard. Vok has some fancy theories. What do they prove? Irene answered Rogan's question. That wasn't in her bag. Took clairvoyance to read that, anyway!"

Ogden glanced doubtfully at his wife, who was beginning to stir, and then up at the gaunt Czech.

"Luke's right. She didn't have a chance to play tricks with Kincaid's question."

"Not the same sort of tricks."

Latham exploded. "Irene held Rogan's envelope for less than half a minute. All of us watched her. Couldn't have read what was inside it. Impossible!"

"Nothing is impossible."

Vok took the gambler's sealed question from the table and made passes over it as the medium had done. Then he raised it to his forehead and said:

"The exact wording is: *I would like to know whether old Grand-mother Kincaid finds heaven up to her expectations. R. K.*"

Ogden seemed stunned. "You can't really know that. You're playing some trick."

"Of course. The same trick your wife played. See, the envelope is transparent."

Vok extended the question and Ogden grabbed it. The others crowded around him. Rogan's writing was plainly visible through the paper.

Jeff snapped his fingers. "Odorless alcohol! I should have thought of that."

"Alcohol that doesn't smell?" Latham was incredulous. "There's no such thing."

"Oh, yes, there is," Vok assured him. "There's some on this." He opened his right hand and displayed a small pad of cotton. "It was in the knitting bag and had a tin lid. Once the alcohol was rubbed on the envelope it dried in a few seconds and left no traces."

"The alcohol," Jeff added, "also explains why she lent Rogan her fountain pen. It's a special type that takes India ink. She needed to have the writing jet black so it would be easy to read even by lamplight."

"You're proving too much now," his uncle objected. "Irene used that pen for everything."

"Of course." Vok was bland. "So when she employs it in a

séance no one notices that it is unusual for a lady to have on herself a pen of a kind made especially for artists."

Ogden turned on Latham. "I'm convinced if you aren't. She's been making fools of us with her lies for years. You can let her go on if you like. I'm through!"

His wife could hardly have selected a worse moment to open her eyes. Ogden sneered at her.

"So you've decided to come to, have you?"

She seemed not to hear him, but stared blankly at the ring of faces. Then memory came and she asked weakly, "Has he gone?"

Her husband glared. "Has who gone?"

"Grimaud."

"Don't keep that up," he snarled. "Not with your rotten bag of tricks scattered over the table—dummy questions, forms smeared with phosphorus. Do you suppose I don't know what you were up to? You couldn't stand the idea of my having money of my own any longer, could you? Couldn't stand the way my royalties were beginning to make me independent of you. So you thought you'd shut off the source by refusing to let us cut timber off Onawa. That would close Luke's mills, and you knew it might be years before I could persuade anyone else to take up my process. You knew it would bankrupt Luke, too, but you didn't care about that, did you? And, of course, you wouldn't come right out and say, 'Onawa's mine. You can't log it.' Oh, no, you tried to blame it on a dead man!"

"Hold your horses, Frank," Latham broke in. "Give Irene a chance to tell her side."

"And stuff us with more lies?"

"Oh, stop it, Frank," Sherry snapped at him. "Be decent for once in your life. Can't you see you're driving the poor thing nearly crazy? The séance wasn't her idea."

"It didn't have to be. She'd made her point when she kept us off Onawa. The séance fitted her plan, though. It was so easy. She'd been raising spooks all her life. Why not Grimaud's?"

"She wouldn't have done that," said Sherry. "She was afraid of him."

"That is perhaps true," Vok acknowledged, "but it proves nothing. Many mediums are their own dupes. It is easy to believe. Even the old wives' tales I told this evening left some of you half convinced. But do not forget that when a good actress pretends fear, at the end she is really afraid. That was part of the atmosphere. So were the messages to Professor Ambler and Mr. Kincaid. They were to establish the power of the medium beyond question and lead up to the climax of Désanat's appearance. Showmanship is the most important part of any imposture."

Latham faced the Czech belligerently.

"Been talking a lot about impostures, haven't you, Mr. Vok? Tricks, too. How'd you learn so much about 'em?"

It was Ogden who answered. "I'll tell you how he learned." He caught Latham by the shoulder and swung him around. "Mr. Vok is a celebrated conjurer, with a European reputation for exposing fraudulent mediums. In the last year or so, Sherry and some of her friends have begun to doubt Irene's powers. I believed, God help me, that the best way to prove my wife was a genuine medium was to have an expert at one of her séances. So when I met Mr. Vok in Quebec a few days ago I considered it a heaven-sent opportunity and brought him back with me. In my innocence I felt sure he could not help but be convinced that the manifestations she produced were authentic. That was to settle the skeptics."

He laughed shortly. "Instead it settled me. I know now what a fool I was for trusting my own wife."

"Mr. Vok may be the authority you say," Ambler put in, "but it seems to me you are both missing the essential point." He turned to the Czech. "As I understand it, you claim the revenant of Mrs. Ogden's first husband was a trick of hers to support her statement that she had promised not to log the Onawa tract. How do you reconcile your theory with the fact that the ghost did nothing of the kind? On the contrary, he even went so far as to force Mrs. Ogden to deny her story."

"I do not reconcile those points—yet. You must give me time. These problems cannot be solved at once. For instance . . ."

Vok ran his fingers through the apparatus on the table and selected a cylinder some four inches in length, made of black fiber.

"To begin with," he said, "the effects of a medium are not produced only by one trick, but by a combination of many tricks, of which each contributes its part. The odor-free alcohol, the dummy envelopes, the lightproof shawl, were all elements which together made it possible for Mrs. Ogden to read our questions without opening them."

He held up the black-fiber cylinder.

"This is another item in her list of effects. The catalogues of the commercial houses that supply séance equipment list it as a 'reaching rod.' It is made of a long strip of thin, stiff material rolled like a bandage." He caught a tab in the middle of one end and pulled it out. "A well-made one like this will extend over two meters. It is very strong and light. The medium uses it for various effects. She can with it create a phantom breeze at the far side of the circle by blowing through the hollow center of the rod. Forms like the star can be attached to one end and moved through the air." Here Vok picked a stuffed glove from the table and slipped it over the end of the rod. "Fitted like this it can be used to imitate the touch of ghostly fingers."

Ogden took the fiber rod and studied it. Then his face darkened as a new thought struck him.

"This must have been what she used to work the ghost trick. Remember, it started when I thought Grimaud was materializing in mid-air, because a rawhide moccasin touched my shoulder?"

Vok's black brows rose in inquiry. "What is a moccasin?"

"Sort of an Indian boot. Grimaud always wore them in the woods." Ogden indicated the pictures on the walls.

"You are right about the trick," Vok agreed. "What touched you must have been this Indian shoe on the rod. The foot and body of Désanat were the product of your imagination."

"That's true, isn't it?" demanded Ogden, glaring at his wife. "And of course you played the ghost we saw yourself."

"No." She cringed against the back of the sofa. "I was going to, but I didn't."

"Oh, 'you were going to, but you didn't.' Do you expect anyone to believe that? If it wasn't you, who was it?"

"I . . . I . . . told you." Terror dropped her voice to a whisper. "It was Grimaud."

"It's no use, Irene." He laughed at her. "Your trick's missed fire."

"Hell's bunkers, man," Latham growled angrily. "It's you that's going off half cocked."

Ogden stared at him in surprise. "You mean you aren't convinced yet?"

"As a matter of fact, neither am I," Ambler announced. "Certainly Mrs. Ogden could not have impersonated Désanat. You forget that neither of her hands was free. I can vouch for one of them myself because she was holding my left wrist."

"Perhaps you were too interested in what was happening to realize she had let go."

"No. I remember particularly the moment when you spoke of the moccasin touching your shoulder. I had *your* left wrist in my right hand. You gave a little jump and your voice sounded frightened."

"I had a right to be," Ogden said defensively. "It was exactly the sort of thing he must have been wearing when . . . I tell you I was never so startled in my life."

Rogan grinned. "You were startled, all right. You froze onto my wrist and nearly broke it."

"My point is," Ambler persisted, "that I can vouch for Mrs. Ogden's presence at the moment when Ogden cried out. Immediately after I felt his arm jerk, she gave a gasp and clutched my wrist so tightly that her rings dug into my flesh."

"Are you certain of that?" Vok asked.

"Absolutely."

"And you, Mr. Kincaid, you are convinced that Mr. Ogden's right hand was gripping you at the same time?"

"I'd give heavy odds on it."

"Good. Now we have the material with which we can demonstrate the unreliability of testimony at a séance. I shall request the professor and Mr. Kincaid that they take the places they occupied before, and shall seat myself on the chair of Mr. Ogden between them. It is not necessary to put out the lights, but will you both close your eyes. Professor Ambler, be so kind as to take my left wrist into your right hand. Thank you. Now, Mr. Kincaid, please put *your* left wrist into *my* right hand."

Rogan extended his wrist, but instead of taking it in his right hand the conjurer grasped it with his left, so that his right was still free. He peered at their closed eyes.

"Are you sure you each have control of one of my hands?"

When they replied in the affirmative, Vok brushed their faces lightly with the fingers of his free hand.

"Yet I can still touch you. Open your eyes and look how I do it."

Ambler blinked and then smiled sheepishly. "So that's the way it was done."

"You need not be ashamed, I beg. It is a trick which has fooled many fine magicians." Vok released Rogan's wrist and looked around the circle. "You see how it was simple for Mrs. Ogden to free herself and touch her husband with this Indian shoe, to make him believe someone floats through the air above his head?"

"I'd be more easily convinced," Ambler told him, "if you'd keep to the point. You've already admitted the ghost could not have been a creation of Mrs. Ogden's, because it sided against her."

"I have admitted nothing," Vok retorted. "We do not know what Mrs. Ogden's real motive was—only what her husband thinks it may have been. I assure you that in matters of this sort, motives may be as deceptive as methods."

"Talk sense, man," Latham grumbled. "Forget the motives. Irene couldn't have been the ghost. Peyton Ambler said she had him by the wrist."

"When she used the shoe trick, yes. But that caused no little excitement, which gave her the opportunity to free both hands and slip up the stairs to the landing. From there she could carry out the appearing of the ghost without difficulty. The make-up was complicated, of course, but she had ample time to assume that beforehand under cover of her lightproof shawl. When she removed that, the apparition automatically 'materialized.' When she wrapped herself in it again the spook 'vanished.'"

"Hell," said Jeff scornfully. "Mrs. Ogden never was on the landing. While the ghost was hanging over us she was still on the sofa between Mr. Ambler and me. I grant you she wouldn't have had any trouble getting one hand free, but she couldn't have freed *both* hands."

"That's true," Ambler agreed. "And as long as Jeff and I held one of her hands on the table, Mrs. Ogden would have found it awkward to stand on a landing five feet higher than our heads."

"Yes," chimed in Latham, "and if Irene did a trick with a moccasin—where's the moccasin?"

VII

Search for the Shadow

Vok faced Jeff. "You are certain you held Mrs. Ogden's wrist while the apparition was over our heads?"

"Absolutely. I can remember the way her arm moved when she twisted around to look up."

"So do I," Ambler confirmed. "Your other explanations seem to fit the facts, but you are definitely wrong about this."

The Czech paused for a moment while his fingers stroked the tiny triangle of black beard beneath his lower lip.

"You are right," he announced. "The obvious answer is so often the correct one in these matters that I have fallen into the habit of accepting it automatically. The present situation, however, appears to possess unusual features. But do not exchange one error for another. Do not believe in ghosts because my too-hasty

68

guess turns out to be wrong. Remember that I am a stranger here. The ways of American mediums are fresh to me, although the rest of you may have many times seen similar phenomena."

"Not me!" replied Latham. "I've seen plenty of materializations, but nothing like that."

"Uncle Luke's right," Jeff agreed. "That was the damnedest thing I ever ran across. Don't get me wrong. I don't believe it was a spook, but it wasn't Mrs. Ogden, either. What's more, whoever it was didn't stand on the stair landing. He hung in the air above our heads. Besides, there's something else . . . something none of the rest of you saw. He didn't just walk down the corridor. He floated almost a foot off the floor!"

Silence fell in the room, so that all the night noises in the woods outside became audible—even the soughing of the wind through the dry branches of the trees fifty yards away could be heard plainly. The windows shook in their frames. Ambler spoke.

"There is another point we must consider. The same reasoning that proved Mrs. Ogden could not have slipped away from the circle applies to the rest of us as well. Mr. Vok may have been right in believing someone could have freed himself during the excitement which followed Mr. Ogden's announcement that something was taking form in mid-air. Later, however, when the apparition became visible I think each of us must have given at least a moment to wondering if the circle were still complete, and checked as far as he could by noticing the people to right and left of himself. For instance, I distinctly remember touching Mr. Ogden's knee with mine, as well as holding his wrist. I imagine everyone else had a similar experience. The table wasn't really large enough for nine people and we were packed fairly close together."

"You shame me," Vok sighed, "but again I must concede you

are right. Certainly you have described my own experience." His glance swept the others. "Did the rest of you share it? If you did not, now is the time to say." There was a general murmur of agreement. The Czech looked from one member of the group to another until he was sure each of them had indicated his individual conviction. Then he spoke again.

"As long as I—how do you put it?—eat crow, perhaps I should add another reason that occurs to me for thinking the circle was not broken. I lit a lamp in my room within a minute of the masquerader's disappearance. Mrs. Ogden was covered by her shawl, but everyone else was visible to at least two other people. So complicated a disguise could not have been removed completely in so short a time."

"But I don't understand," said Barbara. "If it wasn't one of us, there isn't anybody else it could have been."

"It wasn't any phosphorescent dummy, either," Jeff asserted. "You could be certain of that by the way it moved."

Suddenly Ambler sat bolt upright. "Maybe it really was Désanat! I don't mean his ghost. I mean the man himself."

Rogan saw Sherry wince and interposed. "That can't be right, either. Désanat is definitely dead. Latham identified the body."

"No doubt about it," Latham declared. "Besides, fellow named Querns got lost at the same time. They sent his remains back to his wife in Rhode Island. She recognized 'em."

"Yes." Ambler stroked his chin thoughtfully. "That would settle the matter. I don't see how both of you could have been wrong. Unfortunately, together we appear to have covered every possibility."

Vok smiled his undertaker's smile. "And if all the possibilities are exhausted, Professor, we must therefore credit the impossibilities. Is it not so?"

"I don't say that."

"But I do!" Latham asserted. "You admit it wasn't Irene, or one of the rest of us, or a dummy. Grimaud's dead. That covers everything—except his spirit."

Vok smiled again and shook his head.

"Why doesn't it?" Latham insisted hotly. "Man, we're in a howling wilderness up here. Isn't another living being within five miles."

"You do not know that is true. In fact, you know it is not true. What about the guide? He was free to come and go as he pleased. Besides, he speaks French, like our ghost."

"Madore's French isn't much better than his English," protested Sherry.

"It would not have had to be." Vok answered. "Our ghost did not carry on a conversation. His words were practically a monologue. They could have been memorized."

"Maybe." Jeff was doubtful. "I can't picture a half-breed taking any chances with spirits."

"The fact that the country around here is empty," Ambler remarked, "means it would have been easy for someone to come here unobserved. That might explain how our phantom was able to appear, but it is no help in solving the problem of his disappearance."

"That's going to take some explaining, too," declared Jeff. "The disappearance itself was easy enough. All he had to do was to go into the bathroom and shut the door. Only he couldn't have gotten out, and there wasn't any place to hide."

"Maybe he slipped into one of the other rooms," Ogden suggested.

Ambler shook his head. "The hall was a cul-de-sac. The fact that there were three doors in it made no difference, as the rooms behind them were thoroughly searched. Certainly our man could not have doubled back, because Mr. Kincaid was plugging the mouth of the hall like a cork in a bottle."

"Please, Mr. Magician," Barbara begged, "explain that one."

Vok raised his shoulders. "It should not be difficult. Escape must have been made through a secret door."

"American houses don't have secret doors," Latham told him.

"The houses of practicing mediums of all countries have secret doors. Do not forget that Mrs. Ogden spent a great deal of time at Cabrioun during her first marriage."

"If there is such a door here," Ogden asked, "do you think you could find it?"

"No doubt. It is largely a matter of knowing where to look."

"Come on, then. I can't rest until this thing is cleared up."

He led the way up the stairs and down the hall. Irene Ogden watched her husband and Vok disappear and then dabbed at her eyes.

"Frank will never forgive me for this. He's made up his mind to divorce me. I know he has."

Sherry said, "Good riddance."

"Sherry! You mustn't talk that way about Frank. He's all I've got."

"Cheer up. You'll find some way to work around him in the morning. You always do."

"Not this time. You don't understand. He'll leave me. I know he will."

"What you need," the girl told her, "is a drink."

As she rose to her feet, Ogden came out onto the landing.

"Vok," he reported, "hasn't found the trap yet. He thinks it may be in the ceiling of one of the closets. That seems to be a common place for them."

"There's an attic over that part of the house," Jeff suggested. "If we looked up there we might learn something."

"That's what Mr. Vok thought." Ogden started down the steps. "There's a ladder in the cellar. Will you give me a hand with it?" He disappeared through the dining room archway with Jeff at his heels.

Irene Ogden began to weep again.

"He didn't even speak to me!"

"Never mind," Sherry soothed, "you can always write him a little note."

"He wouldn't read it if I did."

Nevertheless, she put her pen in her knitting bag and began aimlessly to collect her other stage properties.

"There's brandy in my trunk. I'll get it." Sherry lit a lamp and passed it to Rogan. "You wouldn't like to come with me, would you? Just in case . . ."

Her bedroom seemed to have been swept by a pink snowstorm.

"Welcome to my bower. Only it seems Barbara has been bowering in it last." Sherry caught up an armful of frothy silk and tossed it into the bathroom. Then she opened her trunk. "The brandy's in here somewhere. It was . . . Father's. He left gallons of it. Frank won't touch anything alcoholic, so it didn't go very fast. Luke likes it, though. I really brought it up for him."

She found the bottle and rose. "I hate being hard-boiled with Irene, but if you show her any sympathy when she starts feeling sorry for herself she dissolves in tears and cries all night long."

Suddenly the girl was in Rogan's arms, sobbing, her face pressed against his shoulder.

"I'm . . . a . . . fine one . . . to . . . talk . . . about Irene, aren't I?" She caught her breath then and began to speak more calmly.

"It's just that I don't know even what to hope for. I'm sure it was Father. I never saw him with a beard except in snapshots, but there's no doubt at all about his voice. Besides, did you notice his left hand? Father lost that finger when he was a boy. For a minute tonight I tried to believe the hands I saw weren't real—that they were like Irene's stuffed glove. But they weren't. You could tell by the way they moved. It couldn't have been just somebody with a finger folded down, like they do sometimes in the movies. You could see the palm of the hand."

Kincaid held her close and felt her whole body strain against his.

"Oh, Rogan, what does it all mean?"

He tilted her head back and smiled down at her.

"I've saved myself a good deal of worry at one time and another by putting off my thinking until I've gathered my facts. So far all we've had is theories. Until we find something definite, we won't have anything to think with. Don't race your mental motor. It's bad for it."

"I can't help myself. I've been afraid of Father all my life. After he died I used to dream he'd come back. When I woke I couldn't persuade myself it wasn't true. I wanted to ask other people just so I could hear them say he was really dead. But I didn't dare, for fear they'd think I was crazy. Sometimes I went for days half expecting to see him walk into the room. Once, when I was eighteen, I came all the way up here, by myself, just to look at his grave."

Rogan put his finger under her chin, lifted her face, and kissed her.

"Your stepmother needs that drink. So do one or two of the others. Professor Ambler didn't work up that complexion on midnight oil."

Sherry tucked the bottle under her arm and they went to the

storeroom for glasses. The searchers had been before them. Every hiding place, big and little, had been turned out. Even the spare bedding had been unpacked, and sheets and blankets lay in an untidy heap on the table.

While the girl filled a tray, Rogan looked out the back door. The wind had blown the sugary snow into their tracks of the afternoon and no one had been in or out since.

As they returned through the dining room, they met Jeff struggling with a ten-foot rustic ladder. He had already knocked over a chair and was thinking up new swear words, so Rogan offered his help.

"We've been over the house with a fine-toothed comb," Jeff informed them. "The attic is only an air space. It isn't used for storage and the dust's twenty years deep. If a beetle walks across it you can see the track."

Sherry went into the living room. The two men carried the heavy ladder to the kitchen and slid it through a trap which Jeff opened in the floor.

"I want another look in the cellar." Jeff began climbing down the ladder with Rogan after him. "We went over the second floor again and everything on the first floor except Sherry's room. There wasn't a sign of Désanat *or* his ghost. The only moccasins we found were a pair Ogden wears with his snowshoes. They were in the coat closet and couldn't have been used, because every time you open the door the hinges screech like a rusty cat."

The cellar was a mere pit with a wood-burning furnace, its pipes like monstrous arms reaching out in all directions. Cobwebs festooned the ceiling and showed that if any hidden opening existed, no one had passed through it that night. A flight of steps in one wall ended in overhead doors which evidently led outside and were used by the guide, Madore, when tending the furnace. A row of tiny icicles had formed between them, proof they had not been opened for several hours.

Wood was piled near the furnace. Jeff shone his flashlight between the logs to make sure nothing was hidden there. When he had examined the last chink he straightened up.

"What are we playing hide-and-seek like this for, anyway? We know damn well nothing vanished out of the second-story hall and wound up down here."

Rogan smiled wryly. "Because we'd rather believe that than think something vanished out of the hall and didn't wind up anywhere."

Jeff said, "Hell!" very distinctly.

"And," the gambler continued, "in case you've been giving a little worry to the idea that Barbara, the blond banshee, did this for a joke, forget it. We held hands all the time Désanat was hovering over us."

Jeff looked at him and grinned. "I'll bet Babs didn't turn a hair."

"She didn't. All I detected was a distinct feeling of regret that she hadn't brought her trusty bean blower."

The younger man sobered abruptly. "I wish to God she wasn't mixed up in this business. The crazy kid hasn't sense enough to be scared."

"Meaning you think there's something to be scared about?"

"Hell, man, of course there is. Not any ghost, either."

"What, then?"

"How should I know? But there's something up, something putrid. I can feel it in my bones."

Mr. Kincaid was feeling it in his bones, too—and not liking it.

They climbed the ladder. As they passed through the living

room, Sherry's door opened and Ogden emerged followed by Vok and Barbara.

"We've turned over everything," she reported, "till the place looks like the morning after the Yale prom. All we found was three hair-ribbons I thought I lost on the train."

Ogden turned to the conjurer, desperation in every line of his face.

"What can we do now? You say the thing we saw couldn't be either a dummy or an illusion. You're convinced it wasn't my wife, or any of the rest of us. Now we've proved it wasn't an outsider. We've searched the house from top to bottom. We've looked in places where a rat couldn't hide. We not only haven't found a man, we haven't even found a moccasin. If what we saw wasn't Désanat, in God's name what was it?"

"Your argument goes only halfway, my friend," Vok responded. "That it was either a man or a ghost, I agree. If a man, it was not one of *us*. Again I agree. But when you say, 'An outsider must be in the house,' then I do not agree at all. On the contrary, I suggest that the most logical place to find an outsider is—outside."

Ogden gnawed his thin lips. "We can't search the whole forest."

"It would not be necessary. A treeless clearing some fifty yards wide surrounds us. This outsider of ours must have crossed that, as he is no longer in the house. He could not have taken one step in the snow without leaving a track. It is as simple as that. One circuit of the house and we can prove that our 'ghost' is very much alive."

"Why don't you go out and look, then?"

"Not without you. You are the one who needs conviction. Two hours ago you regarded spiritualism as proved beyond dispute.

Then I had a little luck and was able to open your eyes. Now, because I cannot explain everything, you are once more a slave to credulity."

"If you find the tracks that will settle things, won't it?"

"As far as I am concerned they are already settled. The tracks are there. But I have met too many spiritualists to think one can be disillusioned by anything he does not see with his own eyes. You would say I was mistaken, or that I lied, or anything else that might keep you from being robbed of your childish belief."

Ogden exploded. "After what's happened, do you think I *want* to believe in ghosts?"

"Yes."

"You're dead wrong." Ogden stared apprehensively at the black panes of the window. "Couldn't we wait for daylight?"

"You are proving how right I am," Vok taunted him. "The snow is like flour. The wind will have blown the tracks away by morning. Then you will swear they had no existence."

Ogden stared into the tall Czech's eyes for a moment. Then he swung on his heel.

"Come on. I'll go with you."

VIII
Windigo

His astral body expends itself in painful efforts to obtain new material organs and so live again.
— ELIPHAS LÉVI, *Dogme de la Haute Magie*

IN THE living room they found Mrs. Ogden still on the sofa with the others around her. All the lamps had been lit, but they seemed only to make the shadows that clung to the rafters darker by contrast.

Vok climbed the stairs to his room. Ogden struggled into his mackinaw and sat to pull on the hunting boots he had taken from the coat closet. Rogan noticed that they were from different pairs and saw in this further evidence of the man's worry, for otherwise he was dressed with a prim foppery that was as much in keeping with his character as it was out of place in the woods. He finished tying the laces just as Vok came down the steps clad in a voluminous black cape which made him look more sinister than ever.

Ogden caught up a flashlight. In the doorway he turned and spoke to Latham.

"Do you mind if we take the dog?"

"No, of course not."

Ogden called Thor. The Dane hesitated, then rose and walked forward stiff-legged, as if he did not relish the idea. When the door closed behind them Latham asked:

"Where are they going?"

Rogan told him.

"I should have stopped them," Irene Ogden whimpered, "but he wouldn't have listened to me. Frank's in danger. I know he is."

"You mean Mr. Vok's right about there being a man out there?" Jeff demanded.

"No. It's Grimaud. Ever since I married Frank I've been afraid for him. I know you won't believe me after what I did tonight. I do get genuine phenomena sometimes, but no one can get them always, and Frank is so impatient."

She had started talking now and could not stop. Her whole pitiful story came out. It was hard to imagine anyone loving the frigid Ogden, but this woman did. She did not put it into words but it stood naked in her eyes. When she had married him she had been beautiful—had believed her beauty was the magnet. Now she knew it was her money and only her money that had drawn him.

"I couldn't let him go. I have enough for us both—only, it . . . would have made things easier if what he had came from me." She stood. "I'm sorry, Luke. I didn't want to hurt you. I'd have made it up to you some way. Truly I would. Don't hold what I tried to do against me. You can log Onawa now."

The men rose with her. Latham, embarrassed by her frankness, mumbled some conventional response, but she passed up the stairs with no further word.

As the door closed behind Mrs. Ogden, Sherry said, "Poor thing, she ought not to be alone," and ran after her.

Ambler remained standing as the others dropped back into their seats. "Well," he announced, "as far as I'm concerned that settles it. Our ghost wasn't some trick of Mrs. Ogden's."

Latham grunted. "Never thought it was."

"By God I did," declared Jeff. "But Mr. Ambler's right. This isn't one of her tricks. She was as scared as anybody."

"You have real proof of that," Rogan pointed out. "Her faint was certainly genuine. Otherwise she'd never have let you and Vok examine her bag."

"That's true," Ambler agreed, "but to me the strongest argument is that the ghost was definitely opposed to Irene. He not only failed to play the part she had laid out. He did the exact opposite, and publicly humiliated her in the bargain, by making her confess herself a liar."

Jeff snapped his fingers. "You know, there's an idea behind that. Mrs. Ogden didn't have a motive for making the spook act like that, but somebody must have. That somebody must have faked the ghost himself."

"Luke had a motive," Ambler observed with a sly smile. "Mrs. Ogden was trying to wreck his business."

Latham looked sharply at his friend, saw the expression on his face, and contented himself with another grunt.

"Oooh, I know." Barbara's eyes were as big and as blue as morning glories. "What about *Mr.* Ogden? He didn't want his wife to get away with her stunt. It would be just like him to take a nasty way of fixing it so she couldn't."

Suddenly Latham brought his hand down on the table with a bang.

"Thunder and blazes! What's the use of going on like this? What we saw was Grimaud Désanat!"

Jeff stared. "You said he was dead."

"He *is* dead. But that was Grimaud."

"Come now, Luke," Ambler protested. "You couldn't have recognized that. It was just a face."

"Not to me. Recognized the man, too. Know Grimaud better than I know you. Worked and camped with him for twenty years. Everything about it was just like him—voice, way he talked, kind of things he said, everything. There are better ways of knowing a man than his face, even."

"Perhaps," Ambler admitted, "except where there is deliberate fraud. Good acting can be more real than life."

Rogan had been seated facing the sofa, his eyes on Latham. Now an almost imperceptible sound caused him to look up. A man had entered from the dining room, a man who walked so softly on moccasined feet that none of the others heard him. His high cheekbones, and the greasy curls that showed under his red hunting cap spoke of mixed blood. Rogan realized that this must be the half-breed guide, Madore Troudeau. He carried an armload of wood for the fire, but something in the conversation had caught his ear and he paused to listen.

Ambler was saying, "If human beliefs count for anything, most spirits are hostile. There are a thousand men who dread the denizens of the other world for every one who welcomes them."

"Maybe they're right," Latham conceded gloomily. "Used to think that when people passed to the other side they left their meanness behind with their bodies. Even the worst ones. Now I don't know. Shakespeare said the evil men do lives after them. He wasn't wrong often. Grimaud Désanat was my friend, but he was all evil tonight. Made you feel like you were standing on the slippery edge of Hell." He sighed. "I guess you were right about the possession business, too. It's only logical when you come to think of it."

Rogan, watching Madore for the effect of Latham's words, saw the guide stiffen. It was as if something he had been expecting had come out into the open at last. Then a crafty expression tightened the corners of his eyes. The gambler had seen that look on the faces of a hundred antagonists, the look of a man who foresees an attack and who believes he has a weapon ready to his hand. A sneer curled Madore's thick lips, and he dropped the wood to the floor with a laugh.

The men leaped to their feet. Jeff caught himself half out of his chair as he recognized the guide, and swore savagely. The half-breed laughed again.

"Huh, you swear 'cos you 'fraid M'sieu Désanat come back."

Latham snapped at him. "How do you know he's back?"

"You say so. But I know all de tam M'sieu Désanat is windigo. *Tout le monde* say M'sieu is dead. Me laugh at dem, say windigo don't stay dead 'less you tear heem on pieces. Now hees come. But don't you be 'fraid. Madore won't let heem get you."

He was swaggering again. His hot eyes drifted over the group till they reached the blond Barbara. Then they traveled with slow insolence from dainty ankles to pale hair. Rogan saw Jeff's great shoulders bulge under his hunting shirt.

Barbara's blue eyes opened wide and she looked straight at Madore.

"What's a windigo?"

Miss Daventry's direct questions had disconcerted more experienced men than Madore, but he laughed again.

"Don't you be 'fraid, leetle lady. Me tak' care of you."

His glance swept Barbara again. Latham stepped protectingly in front of her. Ambler caught Jeff's huge fist and pressed it against his side.

"There are lots worse things in the woods than windigos." The little professor spoke with exaggerated amiability.

"You t'ink? Dat's 'cos you no see one. I seen windigo. Is phantome de wors' kind feller can meet on de wood. *Loup garou an' feux follets* dey is plaintee bad too, but windigo is more bad still. Wen he's call feller dat feller mus' go. Windigo jus' touch heem wance, den dat feller is windigo too. Hees soul she go away. Hees body she is windigo. Dat feller run t'roo wood. Tak' great jomp, feefty . . . honder feet wan step. Fly mos' lak bird."

Ambler laughed. "It's no use trying to frighten Miss Daventry, Madore. It won't work."

The half-breed flung his arms wide. "W'y for she be fright'? I tol' her me tak' care of her. Wit' me, anywan she's safe." He thrust his hand inside his collar and drew out a tarnished disk on a buckskin thong. "Is medal of Saint Benoit. Wen feller got dat, no kin' of devil w'at walk on de wood can get inside heem. But I don' stop dere, non! Wen windigo come, me keel. Dere's plaintee way keel windigo for man dat ain't 'fraid. Injun say tear heem on pieces. *Ma gran'-mere,* she is *française,* say is more better to drive hazel stick t'roo breas'. Wen she is girl on Rat Reever, French peop' ketch windigo. Drive stake t'roo heart. Hees never come back. Bes' way of all is shoot wit' silver bullet."

The assurance, the very practicality, of the man's belief was infectious. It crept over the faces of the others: belief in a dark bird-thing, made gigantic by imagination, that traveled through the woods in great flying leaps—belief in a disease for which torn bodies and driven stakes were rational remedies.

Madore looked from face to face around the circle. Suddenly Ogden's absence struck him and he asked, "W'ere boss?"

No one felt like answering that. A moment later they were spared the necessity. There was a cry of pure terror from outside.

The scream rose in a horrid crescendo as it drew nearer. They heard feet, clumsy with fear, sound on the porch, and the outer door creaked as it opened. Madore leaped toward the inner door. Before he could throw his weight against it, it was flung wide, and Ogden staggered through to collapse in Latham's arms.

The man was in a frenzy of fear, and babbled at the others to close the door. When Madore had forced it shut against the wind and shot the bolt, Rogan seized Ogden by the shoulders and swung him around.

"What's happened to Vok?"

For a moment Ogden stared at the gambler blankly. Then realization swept over him and his eyes widened in new horror.

"Oh, my God!" he said. "Oh, my God!"

Rogan flung the man on the sofa and turned to Jeff.

"Get our coats."

"Don't go out!" Ogden shrieked at him. "Do you hear me? Don't open the door!" His face was the color of wet newspaper and his teeth chattered so he could barely form the words.

"What's happened out there?" Rogan demanded. "You've got to tell us, man!"

"It . . ." Ogden shuddered. "Something flew at me out of the air."

"You mean a bird?"

"No, no! It was bigger than that—bigger than any bird that ever lived."

Jeff returned with the coats. He gave Rogan his and handed another to Latham.

"You'd better come too, Uncle Luke. Vok's out there somewhere, probably scared out of his wits. A man who doesn't know these woods will get lost sure."

Latham struggled into his mackinaw.

"If he does, he'll never last the night out in this weather."

Jeff caught up the two flashlights and tossed one to his uncle. "Come on, then."

He put his hand on the latch. Ogden screamed, "Don't open that door!"

Barbara ran across the room and caught Jeff by the arm.

"You mustn't go out there, Jeff."

"He'll die if we don't, and every minute we waste is making him harder to find."

"But suppose whatever . . . happened to him happens to you?"

"To hell with that. Nothing's happened to Vok—yet. He and Mr. Ogden saw an owl or something and panicked. Let go. There isn't any time to lose. That river ice is treacherous. If Vok wanders onto it, God help him!"

He shook the girl off and raised the latch. Wind blew the door in his face. Jeff grabbed for it and then froze in his tracks as a gust of wild laughter came from outside.

He slammed the door shut involuntarily and leaned against it.

"What was that?" Barbara whispered.

It was Madore who answered.

"Windigo!"

Muffled steps dragged on the porch. Something fumbled at the outer door—something that made a queer mewing sound in its throat that was certainly not human.

Strengthened by terror, Ogden rose from the couch to lurch across the room and throw his weight on the latch as it began to lift. There was a moment of silence broken only by the heavy breathing of whatever was outside. Then the door was shaken and a voice called:

"Let me in."

Jeff said, "It's Vok."

"No, it isn't," Ogden yammered. "It sounded queer. It may be a trick."

"We'll soon find out," Rogan told him. He forced the almost delirious man out of the way and pulled open the door.

Vok stood there with Thor pressed against his leg. The vulturine figure, towering over the huge dog at its side, seemed scarcely less forbidding than the phantom they had more than half expected. The Dane with the lamplight in his amber eyes and the red tongue lolling from his mouth, looked like a fiend from the pit. Actually he was weak with terror. He dropped to the floor and crawled to Latham's feet.

Vok paused for a moment in the doorway to look around the circle of faces and ask slowly, "What is wrong?" Then his eyes fell on Ogden and he burst into renewed laughter.

"Forgive me," he begged at last, "but I cannot help it. Outside I laugh at myself. Inside I laugh at you. Two grown men made afraid by an owl."

"Owl!" Ogden flared. "You're crazy!"

"You have other big birds. Perhaps eagle? I was too much frightened to look plainly."

Rogan, watching the Czech closely, realized with a stab of uneasiness that his amusement was a pose.

"I think," said Ambler, "you'd better tell us exactly what happened."

"Gladly." Vok flung off his cape with a gesture that was pure theater and seated himself on the sofa. The others sat or stood where they were, except Barbara, who pulled Jeff down on one of the window seats and huddled against him.

"You know we went out to look for footprints," Vok began.

"Did you find any?" inquired the professor.

"No," Ogden put in, "we didn't. We walked all around the house and examined every inch of the snow."

"That was odd, certainly," Vok conceded, frowning. "There must be some solution. Perhaps the track had been smoothed out."

"Can't smooth out a footprint," Latham informed him. "Just make a bigger mark."

"That's what I said," Ogden snapped, "but he keeps insisting on explanations when there aren't any. When we made sure there was no track near here, he wanted to look at the boathouse. What was the point in that? There are a hundred feet of smooth snow between the two buildings. A cat couldn't walk on it without leaving a track you could see five yards away."

"In an affair of this sort"—Vok turned his hands palm upward and opened his fingers in a gesture which he contrived to make vaguely insulting—"in an affair of this sort we must consider all the possibilities."

"And all the impossibilities," Ogden sneered. "Anyway, we looked in the boathouse. There was a skiff and two old canoes, but nothing else. Madore had cleared out the paddles and things for the winter. There wasn't a hiding place big enough to cover a rat. It was just after we started back that I saw . . ." Ogden closed his eyes as if he were trying to shut out memory rather than recall it. He drew a deep breath and went on. "As we came out of the boathouse, the wind drove at our faces. The dog was somewhere behind us. I heard him whimper. Then I saw it! It was about twenty feet in back of me and over ten feet off the ground. Vok must have caught sight of it at the same time, for he shouted something and started to run. The dog shot past me and nearly knocked me down. I dropped my flash and made for the lights of the house."

Madore shuffled his feet.

"Is bad see windigo."

"What's that?" Ogden asked sharply.

"Sometam hees call you! Den you go," the guide replied.

Ogden turned to Ambler. "What's he talking about?"

"Windigo is the Indian name for a kind of evil spirit. Madore believes Désanat has turned into one. Madore also believes windigos are"—Ambler sought for a word—"infectious."

"It was evil enough." Ogden shivered. "The thing seemed to be playing with me. I was running as hard as I could, but I looked back once. It was floating along lazily, and I knew it could catch me any time it wanted to. Then, just before I reached the house, it soared up as if it was about to pounce." He winced at the memory. "I think that was when I started to scream."

Vok leaned forward and put his hand on his host's arm.

"Of screaming you need not be ashamed, my friend. Or of running, either. The dog ran, did he not? I have had great experience in these things, yet I ran also, and faster than either of you. I think to myself: Miss Ogden has told me this morning you have bird here called great horned owl—a meter and a half, perhaps, across wings. Then I know it is that we have seen."

"Whatever it was, it wasn't any bird."

Ogden seemed to shrink physically as if the picture of the thing were before his eyes and he were still afraid of it.

"It was the wrong shape . . . and . . . it had hands!"

IX

The Magic Weapon

The open-minded reader will, I trust, find herein abundant evidence that demonism is a fact. My records contain three hundred and four cases observed in my own field.

—REV. HUGH W. WHITE, D.D.
Demonism Verified and Analyzed (1922)

Sherry came down the stairs. "Irene's gone to bed. She's calmer now." The girl saw Ogden and hesitated. "You didn't . . . find anything."

"You have expressed our failure perfectly," Vok assured her ruefully.

She bit her lip and turned to Ogden. "You look all in, Frank. Why don't you let me borrow some of Irene's veronal for you?"

Ogden glanced up sharply. "You know how I hate any form of drugs. I don't want to take them unless it's absolutely necessary."

"At least try my sleep-producer—a hot bath in the dark and then slip into bed before you wake yourself up."

"A slug of rum is good, too." Jeff splashed brandy into a glass and shoved it into Ogden's hand. He turned to the Czech. "How about you, Mr. Vok?"

"Thank you, but I warn you I accept it under false pretenses.

It is never difficult to me to sleep. In 1916 I was captured by the Russians because I slept through a battle."

Sherry heard a choking sound behind her, and whirled to see Ogden take his empty glass from his lips.

"Good heavens, Frank! I never thought I'd see you take a drink. What's gotten into you?"

Ogden looked up, startled, and then stared down at his glass. Slowly the color which the fiery liquid had forced into his face drained away. A muscle twitched in his cheek.

"There's nothing wrong with me. It's just that . . . I don't feel very well."

Ambler gave Sherry no time to digest this seemingly contradictory statement. He coughed and said, "We've had enough excitement for one evening, but it's over now and time we were all in bed. I confess I'm tired." He caught the guide's eyes on Barbara and added, "Madore, if Mr. Ogden will let you come back to the lodge with us, there's something about which I'd like your advice."

Madore laughed. "M'sieu Ogden he no stop me if me wan' to go. Not'ing stop Madore."

Ogden showed no sign of resenting the man's arrogance. Instead he turned to Ambler.

"You're not going back to the lodge tonight?"

The guide laughed again. "M'sieu Ogden hees scare. Madore not scare'. I show you."

He strode to the door. As his hand touched the latch, Ogden started up in protest, then cowered back on the sofa, knuckles pressed against his teeth in an agony of apprehension.

The party from the lodge bade the others good night and followed Madore. As they passed through the vestibule, some of the half-breed's bravado oozed out of him. He clutched his medal in his fist and muttered a prayer under his breath. Then he opened the outer door a mere slit and turned his flashlight in all directions before venturing further.

Latham followed on the guide's heels. Jeff caught Ambler's arm and growled in his ear.

"What's the idea of leaving the girls like this?"

"Think a minute. If we had stayed, they would have wanted to know why. We couldn't have given a logical reason, so they would have jumped to the conclusion that we were holding something back. Miss Daventry doesn't seem to have a nerve in her body, but it wouldn't take much to throw Miss Ogden into a panic. Besides, if we'd stayed, Madore would have stayed, too."

"If he had, I'd have taken him apart," Jeff declared grimly. "Did you see the way he looked at Babs?"

"I did. I wasn't pleased by his attitude toward his employer, either. I don't think we were more than five minutes from a fight, which wouldn't have improved Miss Ogden's nerves—or ours."

"The professor's right," Rogan put in. "This way we get Madore away from Cabrioun. If he speaks out of turn we can dissect him."

Jeff gave in. "O.K., but he's mine first."

With that the talk died. The wind had risen and filled their tracks with drifting snow almost as fast as they were made. Rogan, glancing down, had an uncomfortable realization of how easy it would be to get lost. Even his own back trail could not have been followed far.

Thor padded soundlessly. Except for an occasional clink of his license against his collar he might have been a shadow. Then, as they left the cleared space and passed under the trees, he disappeared entirely. It was inky black. Even the bare branches were enough to shut out the little light that came from the sky. Madore seemed to find his way by instinct, for he used his flash sparingly. Jeff used his more often, shining it over his shoulder. He was at some pains to explain that he did this only because he "wanted to get a look at the thing Mr. Ogden saw, and find out what it really was."

Rogan paid little attention to his companions. His own dislike of the wild had returned and was intensified by the darkness. He tried to shake off the feeling and concentrate on seeking a rational explanation of the apparition. There seemed no way to formulate any theory in terms of a living agency. The thing had been carried too far to have been a mere hoax on Barbara's part. Rogan's original suspicion that someone might have created the ghost to get around Mrs. Ogden's refusal to have Onawa logged would no longer hold water. That point had been settled and still the phenomena went on. He could think of no third possibility.

He struggled fruitlessly with the problem until the dark bulk of the lodge loomed through the trees. They stamped in, but even when Jeff had closed the double doors behind him and bolted them, there was no relaxation of tension. The lodge had its own electrical system, and the bright glow of its lights was welcome after the gloom of Cabrioun. Under normal conditions the living room was a pleasant place. Its low ceiling and its rambling L-shape gave it a coziness that was entirely lacking in the high house Désanat had built for his bride. But tonight its homely magic had no effect. Rogan's wariness refused to leave him. He caught himself thinking: "Nothing has happened here—yet."

The professor waited until they had removed their coats before he spoke.

"Luke, I saw an old case of dueling pistols up here. May I borrow them?"

"They're Jeff's."

"Sure you can borrow them," said Jeff. "Why?"

"I noticed that the outfit included molding equipment and a powder flask." Ambler opened the mahogany case which Jeff brought from the gun room. "Yes, everything is here. I'm going to ask Madore to mold a silver bullet for me."

"You mak' for keel windigo?"

"I'd like to be prepared to try."

"We mak' hot fire on kitchen. I show you."

Madore turned and swaggered down a narrow passage opposite the main door. Jeff looked at Ambler.

"What's the idea?"

"Partly anthropological curiosity—I've never seen a magic bullet made. Partly a desire to keep our friend busy until I'm ready to deal with him." He took the mold and melting ladle from the case and started after the guide.

"Wait a minute." Jeff ran after them. "I'm coming with you."

Latham and his remaining guest strolled into the other wing. Rogan dropped on one end of the sofa and fell to examining the magnificent workmanship of the pistols.

"Jeff brought that pair up here last summer," explained Latham. "Tried 'em out. You hear stories about the old-timers splitting cards with 'em. By golly, they could have, too. I can do it myself, twice in five shots." He fell silent.

Rogan asked, "I've been wondering what you think of tonight's happenings."

"Most of it's an old story to me. Breaking up séances seems to come natural to magicians. One way it's a good thing. Mediums are a lot like the early radios. Sometimes they get messages. Sometimes they don't. People feel like a pack of fools when they sit in the dark a couple of hours and nothing happens. Naturally the medium wants to please 'em. If she can't get real manifestations she fakes. Human nature. Mediums do so many things that are really wonderful, the sitters reach a point where they swallow everything. I guess the magicians help keep the mediums in line."

"Then you don't think the fact that Vok caught Mrs. Ogden cold-decking us on the questions proves the spook we saw later was synthetic?"

"Wish I could think so. Grimaud's up to some sort of meanness. He can be the nastiest skunk in creation when he tries. No, Irene's cheating doesn't prove anything. Some men steal. Doesn't show everybody's a thief. Doesn't even show the thief's dishonest all the time. Come right down to it, the fact some mediums cheat is positive proof of another world. Before a medium can fake a phenomenon that phenomenon must have happened. Can't imitate anything that doesn't exist."

"If that's true, how would you tell a sham specter from a real one?"

Latham squatted on the hearth and absently scratched Thor's ears.

"Grimaud's real, all right. Tell you I know the man. He's dangerous."

"You don't think he's done with us, then?"

Latham eyed his guest shrewdly. "No. Neither do you. What do you suppose he went after Frank Ogden for?"

"That's one of the big puzzles."

"Not to me. Frank drank that brandy, didn't he? Something he'd never done before in his life. Drank it all in one gulp, too."

Rogan raised one eyebrow. "Are you suggesting that Ogden is under Désanat's control?"

Latham nodded. "I'd heard about those from the other side coming back and getting control of people over here. Never gave it much thought. When Peyton spoke about it tonight I thought he was making game of Vok. But it's reasonable once you think of it. If a spirit's really going to do anything, it needs a body."

"But Ogden wasn't possessed. I admit he wasn't quite himself."

"That's it," said Latham. "He wasn't quite himself. Don't guess spirits can control everybody. Frank isn't what we call a sensitive. Grimaud couldn't do much with him. But he did his best."

"If Ogden wasn't a good subject, why should Désanat pick on him?"

"Picking on Frank is the easiest way to hurt Irene." Latham straightened, threw a log on the fire, and turned. "Do you think we'd better send Madore back to his cabin or keep him here?"

"Keep him here," Rogan advised, "where we can watch him."

"He'll bear watching. I'll put him in the back room upstairs. Want to come with me while I rustle some blankets, or don't you mind being alone?"

"I'll be all right. These dueling pistols fascinate me."

When Jeff returned from the kitchen he found Kincaid studying the damascening on the barrel of one of the old weapons. Rogan looked up.

"Hello. Did you make your silver bullet?"

"It's not mine. We got it cast, though—out of a bent spoon I found in the storeroom. Mr. Ambler's waiting for it to cool." Jeff jerked his head toward the kitchen. "Do you think he could have anything to do with this business?"

"Ambler?"

Jeff nodded somberly. "There are a couple of queer things. To begin with, he hasn't any business to be up here."

"You mean he wasn't invited?"

"He was invited all right, but he shouldn't have come. The

University doesn't have a real Thanksgiving holiday—just the day itself. He's taking the whole week off. Must have left Charlottesville Sunday night."

"Professors play hooky, too—in deer season."

"Not old Ambler. He's a conscientious codger. He came to class for three weeks once with his leg in a cast. Besides, there's something else. That 'message' Mrs. Ogden dug up for him was supposed to be from some scientific bozo whose initials were W. G. or W. Q. Well, the guy who got lost with Sherry's father was a chemist and his name was Walter Querns."

"Suppose it's the same man. What does that prove?"

Jeff hunched his great shoulders. "Nothing, except that Mr. Ambler's never said anything about knowing Querns, or the Ogdens either, for that matter. I took a couple of courses under him in college and introduced him to Uncle Luke. They got clubby, went hunting together a couple of times, and I believe Mr. Ambler bought a little stock in our company."

"He may have heard about Querns from your uncle."

"Maybe," Jeff conceded, "but why would that give the old boy enough interest in Querns to ask questions about him at a séance?"

He broke off as Ambler returned. The little professor dropped in a saddlebag chair near one end of the sofa. Rogan picked up a pistol and offered it.

"Now that the ord'nance department has finished, will you charge the piece, sir?"

"The load isn't quite ready," Ambler informed him, smiling. "Madore's putting the magic into it now. He wouldn't let me watch him."

Jeff bristled. "Wouldn't let you . . . ? I'll—"

"Cool off, my boy. You might make him let me stay, but I

wouldn't see anything. That's the trouble with anthropological studies. The things that matter are done in secret. A man's private prayers would tell you more of his real beliefs than the services at the church he goes to."

"Speaking of beliefs," remarked Rogan, "what's this windigo business?"

"I'm not quite certain. I'd always thought the word applied to some vague, evil power—a sort of personification of all the terrors of the wild. Now Madore has given me a new viewpoint on the subject. He describes a windigo as if it were both a possessing spirit and the person possessed. That thought never occurred to me before, because possession is not supposed to be an Amerindian concept. Since Madore's pointed it out, however, I realize that our ideas on the subject were mistaken. For instance, certain forms of possession by animal spirits were thought to be fairly common among the Chippewas. Madore's suggestion goes far toward explaining the whole windigo belief."

"Do you think there's any real basis for it?"

"That's hard to say. Men go mad sometimes in the isolation of the big northern snow-deserts."

Jeff scratched his head. "You think Madore may have heard some yarn that Désanat turned crazy when he got lost, and went windigo?"

"Something like that. Perhaps after the look Madore got at Ogden's face tonight he thinks Ogden is a windigo in embryo. I won't say I'd find that hard to believe myself. I never saw a man so touched with terror."

The guide strode into the room with studied insolence, juggling the silver bullet in the palm of his hand.

This, he proclaimed, was something very special, guaranteed to kill permanently any windigo at which it was aimed. He tossed the metal sphere to Rogan, who displayed it on his palm so the professor and Jeff could examine it. The ball was perhaps half an inch in diameter. Madore had scratched on it a cross and the letters J-M-J for Jesus, Mary, and Joseph. There were other scratches, too. Mr. Kincaid decided that the half-breed had mixed Christian and Indian talismans with complete impartiality. The guide held out his hand.

"I put heem on pistol, yes?"

"You'd better let Mr. Jeff do it," Ambler said pleasantly. "There's a trick to these muzzle-loaders."

Madore's face grew surly, but the expressions of Jeff and Rogan did not encourage rebellion. Even so, an argument over the size of the charge brought them to the verge of a quarrel. When the loading was finished and Jeff offered the gun to Ambler, Madore snatched it and strode to the window.

"Now, by Gar," he shouted, brandishing the weapon, "me ready for windigo!"

As if in answer, a shot rang out. For a moment Rogan thought the guide's enthusiasm had carried him away. Then he realized the explosion was not loud enough for that, and the surprise on Madore's face gave him the answer.

The shot came from the woods.

X

The Struggling Shadows

As [my father] entered I seized a fowling-piece, which I had secreted under my bed, and fired it at him. Fortunately, the charge went over his head into the ceiling.

—From the statement of a possessed person made to the REV. JOHN L. NEVIUS, D.D., who adds, "Of course [his] statements . . . of what he did when he was in a state of unconsciousness depend on the testimony of those about him. *(Demon Possession)*

WHILE THEY stood rigid, running feet pounded on the steps outside. Madore swung round with a startled oath and leveled his pistol at the door. Rogan knocked his arm up.

Latham clattered down the stairs, his round face tense with alarm.

"Someone's shooting in the woods!"

Outside, fingers clawed at the latch and a voice panted, "Luke, Luke, it's Frank! Let me in."

Faced with a present danger, and deprived of a chance to use his weapon, Madore's confidence drained out of him.

"Dat not Boss' voice," he whispered.

Jeff said, "Who cares?" He shot back the bolt and Ogden

stumbled into the room. Rogan slammed the door and turned to see that the man carried an ancient flintlock.

"What happened?" demanded Latham. "Who shot at you?"

"Nobody . . . I fired."

"That blunderbuss?"

"What were you shooting at?" Jeff asked.

"Nothing. Let me get my breath a minute." Ogden staggered to the sofa and dropped on it. "I'll be . . . all right . . . when I get my breath."

He laid the musket on the floor and pulled off his heavy gloves. Something about his left hand troubled him. He stared down at it, moving the index finger as if surprised to find it still there.

"You need a drink."

As Ambler poured it, Jeff seized Ogden's arm.

"Has anything happened to Barbara?"

"No, no. The girls are all right." Ogden snatched the drink and downed it. "Nothing's happened to anyone." He looked down at the empty glass and began to shiver. "Unless it's happened to me."

Latham said, "Better tell us."

"Yes . . . I guess I had. After the others had gone to their rooms I . . . wasn't so sure I had been in the right, so I came to the conclusion I should apologize to Irene."

Ogden told how he had gone upstairs, but finding his wife's door locked decided not to wake her. He had returned to the living room and taken another drink. Then he had stretched out on one of the window seats. His sleep had been troubled by ter-rifying dreams, of which he could remember nothing except that it had been bitter cold and that something seemed to be wrong with his left hand. He had awakened, shivering with cold and fright, to find Vok bending over him holding a match.

"What was Mr. Vok doing downstairs?" Jeff inquired.

"I asked," Ogden replied, "but even after I lit a lamp and saw from the man's face that something was wrong, he kept putting me off. It was five minutes before I dragged the facts out of him."

Vok, Ogden continued, had been aroused by footsteps in the hall outside his room and heard someone try the lock on Irene's door. He had assumed it was Ogden attempting again to make peace with his wife, but a minute later his own door opened. Vok had struck a match and was astounded to see his host standing in the opening with a gun in his hands. He aimed at Vok's heart, and before the Czech could cry out, Ogden had pulled the trigger. The hammer snapped, but there was no explosion. However, Ogden had seemed satisfied, for he turned and left the room. It had taken Vok several seconds to collect his wits. Then he decided that Ogden was sleepwalking, and had gone in search of him for fear he should do himself an injury. Vok had found his host fast asleep on the window seat, and was bending over him to make sure he was well when Ogden awoke.

"That," Jeff pronounced, "is the damnedest story I ever heard. What's Vok up to, anyway?"

"I thought he was lying, too, at first," replied Ogden. "You see, Vok claimed I'd carried an old-time flintlock—not a hunting rifle. The only flintlock at Cabrioun was a relic of . . . Désanat's that hung on the chimney breast. It hadn't been touched since he died, and was still there while Vok was talking. It was so high up, and so covered with rust and dirt, I had to hold the lamp over my head to see it."

"I've noticed that gun," said Jeff. "You couldn't get it down without a ladder. The mantel shelf is too narrow to stand on."

"I pointed that out to Vok, and told him I couldn't have reached the gun without flying. He insisted that if it was the only musket in the place it was the one I must have used. Of course, I argued that if the gun had been touched there'd be finger marks on it in the dust. He had to admit that, so we got the ladder out of the cellar and looked. The marks were there, and a fresh chip had been knocked out of the flint!"

Ogden shivered and chafed his hands together, holding them out to the blaze.

A movement drew Rogan's attention to Madore, who had been displaying signs of a growing uneasiness. Now his eyes narrowed and he lashed out at Ogden.

"Wen windigo chase' you, is ketch you!"

Ogden jerked erect. "That's a lie!"

"Wat mak' you fly, den?" the guide retorted.

"I didn't."

Jeff exploded. "To hell with this little-brother-of-the-Manitou business. The prints must still be on the gun. Let's test them."

"We did." Ogden stood and moved to the fire. "Apparently Vok has had some experience with fingerprinting in connection with his exposes. He got some cold cream to grease my finger tips and pressed them on one of Irene's cards. Then he scraped a little fine dust from the lead of a pencil and blew it over the prints. They were beautifully clear. I got my gloves and took the gun down. We compared the prints on it with the ones I had made. There was no doubt the two matched."

"Did you take Vok's word for that?" asked Latham.

"Do you think I'm a fool? I examined them myself. The patterns were exactly alike."

"Couldn't be sure. You're not an expert."

"He wouldn't have to be," Jeff declared. "I wanted to be a detective when I was a kid, and took a correspondence course in fingerprinting. It's easier than you'd think. With a complete set of prints almost anyone could make a comparison."

Ogden nodded. "I never touched the gun without gloves. I didn't let Vok touch it at all. As for the prints, you can compare them yourself if you like. Here they are."

He drew an envelope from his pocket and offered it. Jeff pulled out the card and stared at it. Then, without a word he lifted the old gun and went over to the desk, where he began to arrange a light to his liking.

"There's an old reading glass in that desk somewhere," Latham told him.

"Even if you're right about the prints," Ambler said to Ogden, "I can't see it proves anything. Vok might have taken the gun down himself, and pressed your hands to it while you slept."

"I thought of that, but it won't answer. He couldn't have reached the gun without using the ladder. No one could have moved that clumsy thing in the dark by himself without making a racket that would have roused the house. Besides, there are half-a-dozen prints of both hands on the musket, all just where a person would naturally handle it. He couldn't have pressed my fingers to the gun without waking me. Certainly no sane man would have taken the chance of being caught in such a position without any possible explanation."

"Even if Vok could have done it," Rogan said, "can you think of any reason he should?"

"No," Ogden admitted, "I can't. I've been all over that, too. The fellow was destitute when I picked him up in Quebec three days ago. I've done him nothing but kindness since. As a matter of fact, he's in a pretty nasty position in case I want to make trouble for him. Officially he hasn't any right to be in this country at all. I didn't want any bother with the immigration people, so coming back from Quebec I crossed the border by the lane of a deserted farmhouse this side of St. Pierre."

Suddenly realizing that he had been chafing his hands together, he tore them apart almost by violence and put them behind his back before he continued.

"I even went to the length of supposing it might be some sort of crazy European vendetta, but neither Irene nor I have ever been abroad, and as far as I know, neither of us ever met a Czech before."

"That wasn't exactly my point," said Rogan. "There's no doubt Vok takes his business of exposing mediums seriously. Why should he go about creating mysteries of his own?"

"That's certainly true," Ogden agreed. "Even this business hasn't convinced him. He walked halfway here with me, trying to persuade me to be what he called 'reasonable' and go back to Cabrioun."

"Did Vok have any explanation of this gun episode?" asked Ambler.

"Oh, yes," Ogden replied scornfully. "He says I had a subconscious desire in my sleep to revenge myself on Irene for tricking me with fake séances. He claims that when I couldn't get into her room, my anger turned against him because he'd exposed Irene and made my position public."

Latham grunted. "If Vok couldn't have gotten the gun down, I don't see how you could have either—not walking in your sleep. That ladder's heavy. If you'd pulled it out of the cellar you'd have waked everybody else in the house and yourself too."

"Did Vok find any way around that?" Rogan inquired.

"No, and that's what . . ." Ogden broke off to stare uneasily at his left hand. He thrust it angrily into his pocket and began pacing before the fire. "Vok's theory is bad enough, but it's the appalling alternative . . ."

"That's nonsense!" Ambler said sharply.

"You don't believe it's nonsense. You spoke of . . . possession . . . tonight."

"I doubt if I made myself clear, but even if there is such a thing, that doesn't mean it's happened to you. A man can believe in smallpox without having it."

Jeff left the desk and came back to the group. Ogden scowled at him.

"The prints check, don't they?"

Jeff nodded. Ogden looked at Ambler.

"You see."

"I grant you it's queer," the professor conceded. "However, suppose Désanat did manage to gain control of your mind in some fashion. He certainly couldn't have endowed you with the power of flight. That flintlock was twelve feet off the floor."

"And there was no way to reach it. But Vok's idea is almost as bad." Ogden turned to Latham. "That's why I came over, Luke—to ask you to give me a room, one that can be locked from the outside."

"Good God, man!" Jeff burst out. "You don't mean you want us to lock you in?"

"What else can I want? I can't take a chance. Do you think I could ever go to sleep again if I thought I might kill someone before I woke up?"

"Hell! You haven't come any nearer killing anyone than I have. That old muzzle-loader is only a curio."

"Jeff's right, Mr. Ogden," said Ambler. "You certainly have no reason to believe yourself possessed. You simply walked in your sleep. Sleepwalking is probably like hypnotism. That's why you picked the musket instead of your deer rifle. A hypnotized person may stab someone with a rubber dagger but never with a real one—not unless in his waking state he really means to kill."

"Sleepwalking!" Ogden repeated. "Oh, my God! Have you forgotten the shot just now? I snapped the gun again—in the woods. That time it went off. If it hadn't missed fire before, I'd have been a murderer!"

Latham and the professor went upstairs with Ogden. As they disappeared, Madore glanced at Rogan and Jeff.

"Bapteme! I tol' you!" He caught up the powder flask and poured the black grains into a screw of paper. "Me need dis for primin', by Gar."

"Before you go shooting your silver bullet into something," Rogan advised him, "you'd better be sure who that something is."

"If my own broder he be windigo, I shoot. Windigo is more better dead."

The guide glanced nervously up the stair, and Rogan saw that Ogden's talk had robbed him of much of his bravado. Jeff went to the closet and returned struggling into his coat. Rogan looked inquiry.

"Cabrioun?"

Jeff nodded. "We ought never to have left in the first place. Now I certainly am not letting the girls stay alone with a queer duck like Vok, whether he's up to something or not."

"I'll go with you."

When Rogan emerged from the closet with his coat, Latham and the professor had returned. Latham held up a key.

"Frank can't leave his room unless he flies out the window."

"Maybe he can," said Rogan.

"Hell!" Jeff snorted. "You don't believe that!"

"I wish I were sure I didn't. That gun business was a little too queer for comfort."

"Damn it! He could have reached the gun with the ladder. It's a lot more likely he did that in his sleep without waking anybody than to think he flew up and picked the musket off the chimney breast."

"Granted, but how did he get the ladder *back?* Vok couldn't have waited in his room for long after Ogden left. If you gave me my choice between flying and getting that heavy ladder through the dining room and down a trap door in the dark in less than five minutes without making an unholy racket, I'd try flying. It's easier."

"If you're going to Cabrioun," Ambler observed, "I think I'll go too. I want a look at that mantelpiece, to see if the situation is really as impossible as it sounds."

When they started for the door Madore moved with them. He mumbled something about going along to protect them, but it was a hollow pretense. It was obvious that in spite of his medal and the silver bullet he was afraid to stay in the same house with Ogden. Jeff glowered at him.

"Come if you like, but you're not going to Cabrioun. We'll leave you at your cabin."

The guide opened his mouth to protest, but he heard Rogan's step behind him and gave in.

It had grown bitter cold. "Snow some more 'fore day come," Madore grunted, and pulled the collar of his mackinaw about his ears.

The wind had almost effaced their earlier tracks, so that to the gambler's city-bred eyes, the single line of Ogden's footprints was the only landmark. Even he could read in them the terror-born urgency that had driven the haunted man toward the lodge.

Rogan never forgot that walk. Misshapen trees and bushes lurked just out of range of their flashlights. The woods seemed never twice the same. Now the wind had dropped so that he could no longer feel it against his face, and the whispering in the branches overhead was the only sign of its presence. In spite of the comparative calm, the cold stabbed through his clothing.

After they had covered a hundred yards, Ogden's trail bore from the right, but Madore kept straight ahead.

"His cabin's this way," Jeff whispered, "and I want to see him to it."

A minute later Ambler's flash picked up a snow-covered log hut. Madore left them. As they trudged on, they heard bolts being shot and furniture dragged across the floor.

Another fifty feet brought them to the top of a slight rise from which they could see the house. Jeff whistled.

"Hello! I thought Mr. Ogden said his wife had gone to bed. Her lamp's still on."

"I wouldn't blame anyone," said Ambler, "for not turning their light out tonight."

A dark shape crossed the blind. Rogan put out his hand.

"There's something wrong. Whoever's in that room is moving too fast!"

He began to run. As they emerged from the trees they got a clear view of the window shade. Two shadows were struggling on it. One had the other by the throat, and as the three men watched they saw a hand, armed with some axlike weapon, rise and fall.

XI

The Red Tomahawk

The transformation of personality is absolutely marvelous. . . . It is exactly as if a stronger man drove the owner from his house and looked out of the window.
—J. KERNER, *Geschichten Besessener neuerer Zeit*

JEFF SPRANG forward. "My God, it's Vok! He's killing Mrs. Ogden!"

The snow that covered the fifty yards to the house made treacherous footing. Ambler fell once. Rogan pulled him to his feet and plunged on. They scrambled up the steps to the front porch, flung open the door, and charged into the living room. As they paused for an instant to get their bearings, a voice in the darkness ahead whispered:

"Who's there?"

Jeff's flashlight picked out Barbara in the opening that led from the dining room.

"Thank the Lord you're safe!"

"I couldn't find a match," she said. "There's something terrible going on upstairs."

"We know," Jeff assured her and hurried on, with the others after him.

A line of light showed under Irene Ogden's door. Jeff seized the handle and pressed the latch, but the door was locked. He hurled his weight against it and was answered by a volley of oaths from within—French oaths, with a Provençal accent behind them.

Jeff's jaw dropped. "My God! It's not Mr. Vok. It's Désanat."

"Never mind who it is," Rogan said. "We've got to smash in the door. Where's an ax?"

"I'll find one." Jeff turned and started for the stairs. The sound of a breaking mirror from inside the room followed him down the steps.

Rogan tried the door of the bath, but it was bolted. As he turned back, Vok came out of his room, pulling his cloak over his night clothes.

"Oh, Mr. Vok," Barbara gasped, "can't you do something? It's Mr. Désanat. He's killing Mrs. Ogden. We can't get in to help her."

"I can!" Vok turned to his own door and took the key. "Has someone a match, please? Thank you. These locks are only toys. Now, Professor, if you will hold your light so it shines in the keyhole."

"Hurry, man!" Ambler urged.

Vok knelt, and with deft fingers used the match to turn the inside key so that it was in line with the hole.

"I should have waked sooner. Why must I sleep like a dead man. If harm has come to the poor lady, I shall never forgive my—"

The key inside fell from the lock. With a cry of triumph the Czech thrust in his own key and turned it. He flung open the door and hurled himself into the room with Rogan behind him.

"*Zlotrilce!*" shouted Vok, and sprang for the inner door of the bathroom, which was still moving. Before he reached it, there was a crash of glass, and cold wind blew in their faces. Rogan had time for only one glance at the havoc in the room. Irene Ogden lay on the disordered bed, her limbs fearfully awry, her face covered with a mask of blood. Then the gambler tore his eyes away and followed Vok into the bathroom. It was empty, but the broken pane in the window opposite the door left no doubt as to the path of escape.

The tub stood between them and the window. Vok stepped over its rim and started to put his head through the gaping hole. Kincaid held him back.

"Maybe he's waiting for you."

He raised the other window, and directed the beam of his torch through the opening. There was no figure on the flat roof outside, but a line of footprints ran to the rail that marked its far edge.

"At least our spook left tracks this time," Rogan announced.

Vok gave a long sigh of relief and sat on the edge of the tub. For a moment Kincaid was surprised. He had pictured the Czech as a man without nerves. Then he realized that his own tension had relaxed, and understood how near he had been to believing they were on the heels of a murderous phantom.

He heard Vok's breath hiss through clenched teeth, and swung around to see the man holding his hand in the wedge of light from the open doorway.

"Blood!"

Rogan pointed the beam of his torch downward. A trail of viscid red ran across the floor. A great gout of blood had fallen on the rim of the tub, and the Czech's touch had reduced it to a sticky smear.

"And look!" Vok took the flashlight and focused it on the bottom of the tub. Rogan saw an Indian tomahawk which had evidently formed one of the decorations of the bedroom. The clotted head hold its own story. "He must have brained her with that, and the blood on the floor dripped off it as he ran."

Vok leaned forward to pick up the weapon. Rogan stopped him.

"Better leave it where the fellow dropped it."

They returned to the bedroom. It seemed to have been wrecked through sheer love of destruction. Most of the furniture had been overturned. One of the chairs was smashed, and the mirror of the dressing table lay in a jagged glitter on the floor. Even the curios had been torn from the walls and hurled about the room.

Rogan looked down at Irene Ogden's corpse, incredibly distorted, like a murdered woman done in wax. Her face was barely recognizable. There was a raw wound on her right cheek and another on the temple. Blood had run down and formed puddles in the eye sockets.

"Are you sure . . . ?"

"She's stopped breathing, and"—Ambler displayed red-smeared finger tips—"her heart isn't beating."

"Poor lady." Vok righted a chair and moved it to a place where the foot of the bed hid the body. Then he took Barbara's arm and made her sit. "Mr. Kincaid has from this learned one thing. He has laid our ghost. Our ghost which talks French is no longer without substance. No, he breaks out a window to escape, and leaves footprints in the snow of the roof."

Rogan did not wait to hear more. He slipped down the stairs and groped his way to the door of Sherry's room. As no light appeared under it, he pulled it open. Before he could strike a match he heard her voice whisper:

"Who's that?"

"Rogan."

"Thank God. I didn't know . . . I was afraid it . . . Don't make a light. Someone else might come, and I haven't any clothes on."

"Are you all right?"

"Yes. What's happened? I've been so frightened. Is it Irene? She's dead, isn't she? You've got to tell me. Anything's better than not knowing."

"Yes, she's dead."

"She didn't scream. She would have screamed if she'd been alive. That's an epitaph for you, isn't it? 'She would have screamed if she'd been alive.'"

Suddenly the girl was in his arms, sobbing.

"I was taking a bath," she told him, "a hot one in the dark because I couldn't sleep. Then I heard a terrible commotion overhead. My nerves aren't too good and I simply panicked. For a minute I just lay there and tried not to think. Then I pulled myself together and crawled out of the tub. I couldn't find any matches. It was dreadful being in the dark, naked, wondering what was happening upstairs. Finally I found a towel and came in here." She held up her face and pressed her cheek against Rogan's. "I'm glad it was you who found me."

A minute later she was sobbing again.

"Oh, Rogan, what am I going to do? It was Father who killed her, wasn't it? She always knew he would. Even after he died she was afraid."

"You're wrong." He kissed the girl's tear-wet face. "We don't know who it was, but it wasn't your father. The man got away, but he left tracks in the snow on the roof."

"It doesn't do any good to try to keep things from me. It was Father. I knew yesterday I was right when I thought the voice I heard was his. And when I realized Irene was dead I knew he'd killed her. No one else would have cared enough." Sherry choked back a sob. "That's an epitaph, too. Poor Irene."

"They may need you upstairs," said Rogan. "You'd better get dressed."

She held him close. "You're going after Father, aren't you? Don't . . . do anything to him you don't have to, and . . . don't let him do anything to you."

"I won't."

He kissed her and was gone. As he closed the door he saw Jeff coming from the living room.

"Where have you . . . ?" Jeff asked. "Oh. Is Sherry O.K. ? Vok told me you said there were footprints. We'd better get after the guy right away. Mr. Ambler'll stay with the girls. Vok's coming after us as soon as he's dressed."

"This way, then." Rogan started through the kitchen. "He went out over the back end of the roof."

"That's a fifteen-foot drop. We won't have much trouble finding the place. There'll be a big mark where he lit. Maybe he's still there."

Rogan opened the back door and they peered out.

"I thought you said he jumped down here?" Jeff swung his flashlight from side to side.

"I could have sworn he did, but he doesn't seem to have left any tracks. I didn't see him go over the rail. I could be wrong about the place he landed. I know he isn't on the roof, so he must have come down somewhere. We shouldn't have any trouble finding the spot if we walk around the house."

"Wait till I get a light." Jeff rummaged in the storeroom, tripped over two canoe paddles and a boat hook, and finally emerged with a can of kerosene and a battered lantern. It required all of his profanity to coax more than a feeble glow from the lantern, but at last it burned brightly and they set out. "You take the left side," Jeff directed, "and I'll take the right. Shout if you find anything."

It was an eerie experience, plowing through that unbroken expanse of snow, looking for signs of a man who must have been there but who seemed to have left no track.

Rogan's dislike of the wild returned with new force, but this time the reason for it broke over him. The relief was so great that he stopped to let the idea grow clear in his mind.

Yes, that was it. He felt unsafe in this country, as a cavalryman might feel unsafe in a jungle—because it was a bad place for his school of fighting. The dread of surprise lies under every lone adventurer's heart, and the woods were one huge ambush. The snow was a white carpet on which an assailant could creep within striking distance on silent feet. Trees had limbs on which an enemy might lie in wait to attack with all the force of gravity behind the first blow. The wind was an ever-varying, and—in these surroundings—unfamiliar sound which might drown a needed warning. True, the gambler had been subconsciously alarmed by these things when he had not known there was an enemy within a hundred miles. Now, one waited just outside the range of the flashlight, with the blood of a murdered woman still warm on his hands. Nevertheless, much of Kincaid's confidence returned. The next minute might find him battling against this world or the next, but at least he was at peace in his own mind.

Besides, he reminded himself, the snow has advantages. It shows marks. If there are tracks on the roof there must be more on the ground. I haven't found them because they're on Jeff's side. If people would wait until the evidence was all in, there'd be fewer ghost stories.

Near the front of the house his light picked up the main path from the lodge as it curved to meet the steps at the side of the porch. The path swung too far out for anyone to have reached it from the kitchen roof, so it offered no solution for the problem of the vanishing murderer. Nevertheless, Rogan stooped to examine it. Then leaving nothing to chance, he walked back along the path to the point where it came nearest the rear of the house, some fifty feet away. Before the wind dropped, it had blurred the earlier prints with drifted snow. Fresh marks would have been easy to recognize. There were none. He carried his search a few yards further and then retraced his steps to the porch.

As he approached it, he saw Jeff waiting for him.

"Why didn't you shout?" Jeff demanded.

"Because I didn't find anything. Don't tell me you didn't either."

"Not a trace. Maybe the path—"

"That occurred to me, too. I examined it for fifty yards. What about the tracks we made when we came?"

"They're still ours. No one else has walked in 'em." Jeff led the way to the other side of the porch, and pointed out the individual prints. "The flat prints with almost no heels were made by my ski boots, so they must be yours. The other big set is mine and the little ones are Mr. Ambler's. I followed them all the way back to the crest of the hill where we first saw the shadows. Every print is as sharp as a new dime. If anyone else had stepped in 'em you'd have known it after one look. Besides, nobody could have reached our trail from the back of the house.

Vok appeared at the front door, muffled in his great cloak.

"I heard your voices. Did the assassin come this way? I thought—"

"Yeah," said Jeff. "So did we."

"I'm going back on the roof," Rogan declared, "and have another look at the prints there. Jeff, why don't you keep on around the house and check the ground I covered? Vok can go the other way, to make sure you didn't overlook anything. By the time you meet in back I'll have some kind of information for you."

He entered the house and ran upstairs. Voices drifted from the dead woman's doorway. Rogan slipped into the Czech's bedroom. The windows were all closed, but he was too familiar with the European dread of night air to be surprised. He raised the one that overlooked the roof and stepped over the low sill. The roof was really a sun deck with a railing, but at this time of year it looked as cold and lonely as a deserted summerhouse.

Four feet in front of him a line of prints, roughly parallel to the wall, led to the broken window of the bath. Apparently the murderer had entered that way and closed the sash after him, so that he had been compelled to dive through it in making his escape. The shattered glass had pockmarked the snow. Kincaid stepped carefully over the track that pointed to the window, and followed the second line of prints. This led directly to the rear of the roof. The snow on the railing showed a bloody hand-mark, as if the murderer had grasped it and vaulted over.

Kincaid bent over the rail without touching it. There were lights below and Jeff's voice floated up, asking if Rogan had found anything.

"There's a track all right," the gambler answered. "Here's where he went over."

"Hell," said Jeff. "We've covered the ground around here for forty or fifty feet. No man alive could jump that far."

Icy fingers crept up Rogan's spine.

"No man alive."

XII

The Oracle of the Alphabet

The Tarot is the key of letters.

—ELIPHAS LÉVI,
Correspondence with Baron Spédalieri, No. 7

The Tarot is a veritable Oracle and replies to all possible questions.

—ELIPHAS LÉVI,
Rituel de la Haute Magie

KINCAID REALIZED with a sense of shock that he was only now, for the first time, seriously considering the phenomena connected with Désanat's appearances as problems to be solved. Before, his own reactions to the wild had so colored his thinking that everything else was judged by their light. He decided to check each scrap of evidence with extreme care.

The mark on the rail was badly blurred, as if the murderer's hand had slipped. In fact, it was impossible to tell whether one hand or two had been used, or whether gloves had been worn. Nevertheless, the mark was certainly the spot from which the man had taken off.

There seemed to be no place he could have landed except

the snow-covered ground below. The clearing around the house stretched for fifty yards in every direction. No leap could have spanned that distance. Even fantastic ideas, such as stretching a tight-rope to the nearest tree, were out of the question. The rail, topped by a ridge of snow, offered no path of escape, and the three windows which opened off the porch were twenty feet away from the bloody hand-mark.

Rogan stooped to examine the footprints. The wind had fallen before the murder, and the snow had ceased to drift, so they were as sharp as if made in plaster. There was nothing fantastic about the prints. They had been made by heavy hunting boots with hobnails in their soles. The solidity of those boots, their very weight, made the situation madder by contrast. That anyone should have vanished into thin air was impossible. That he should have done it while wearing anything so everyday, so eloquent of commonsense, as hobnailed boots was not merely impossible, it was unthinkable.

There was, however, one element of strangeness about the prints. The arrangement of the hobnails had something peculiar about it. As Rogan studied them the impression grew, but cudgel his brains as he would, he could not find the basis for the idea. At last he reminded himself that he was no tracker and gave it up.

He went over to examine the incoming trail. This started several feet from the side of the roof, but the snow on the rail was unmarked. No one, however gymnastic, could have climbed over that rail without touching the snow. It was barely conceivable that the man might have come from the roof of the second story, but when Rogan let the light of his torch play there, the snow-covered shingles put even that possibility out of the running. Irene Ogden's slayer seemed to have arrived from the same nowhere into which he had later disappeared.

Kincaid abandoned the problem. He stepped back into Vok's room and closed the window. The trunk which had so surprised Ambler caught his eye and he decided to have a look at its contents. He lifted the lid and removed the tray, which contained clothing—chiefly carefully darned linen. The body of the trunk was filled with a collection of miscellaneous conjuring equipment. This included examples of mediums' apparatus, such as would have been useful in Vok's exposés—a reaching rod, much like Mrs. Ogden's, a dozen school slates for spirit messages, and a collection of tambourines and bells which no self-respecting spook would have been able to resist. There was nothing that could possibly be connected with Désanat.

In the bottom of the trunk Kincaid came across a scrapbook. He opened it to find pictures of a man of distinguished appearance in the court dress favored by European conjurers. It took him several seconds to realize that their subject was the ill-clad scarecrow downstairs. Accompanying these photographs were clippings telling of various honors—a command performance in London, a record of five consecutive weeks in Toulon, made official guest of the city of Aries—all of which went to prove that the Czech had been a great man in his time and had fallen on evil days. Earlier pictures showed him in tights, accompanied by a succession of shapely and smiling female partners. Before that he seemed to have been a child actor in the more turgid variety of melodrama.

Rogan closed the book and swiftly repacked the trunk, being careful to leave everything as he found it. He had barely finished when footsteps sounded on the stairs. Barbara entered the room, with Ambler trailing behind her.

"We're on a straw-snatching expedition." Miss Daventry was enveloped in a fluffy robe which was apparently made of blue rabbit's fur. She sat on the edge of Vok's bed and let her infini-tesimal feet dangle, with her mules swinging from her toes. Her hair was done up in short plaits with little bows on their ends. She looked all of ten years old.

"Jeff says," she informed the gambler, "that nobody could possibly have gotten away from the house without leaving *some* sort of marks on the snow, and of course there weren't any, so we're looking in every room. We've turned downstairs inside out, and chased the spiders out of every cobweb in the cellar. Then I remembered we hadn't searched here."

"I've gone all over it," Rogan declared, "and there isn't a sign."

"I didn't expect to actually find anything," she confessed cheerfully, "and, anyway, I don't really think it was Mr. Désanat, do you? I mean there's such a thing as snatching at a straw and swallowing a camel."

"She has Mr. Ogden cast for the role of first murderer," Ambler explained. "I told her the poor man had been locked in his bedroom at the lodge, but"—his eyes twinkled—"log walls do not a prison make nor iron locks a cage, in the bright lexicon of youth."

"Well, my goodness!" Barbara dropped her mules to the floor and tucked her feet under her. "It's got to be *somebody,* and everyone else is *nice.*"

Rogan grinned. "I thought you said Vok looked like Jack the Ripper?"

"He does, but I like him. He has alarming eyebrows." She wiggled her own slim brows in unsuccessful mimicry.

"The connection escapes me," said Ambler. "However, I'll admit even a professional conjurer can hardly be on both sides of a door at once."

"I don't think we need to worry about Vok," Rogan agreed.

"He could hardly have profited by the murder. Besides, he's out of bounds south of the line. Mrs. Ogden's death will bring him in contact with the police, which is something he'd want to avoid at all costs."

"So, my dear," Ambler finished, "I'm afraid we're left with Désanat as our best suspect."

Barbara shook her blond head. "Not mine. My motto is: 'Of two husbands, choose the latter.' I mean, there isn't any way to be logical about this, is there? Not with ghosts popping in and out. So we might just as well trust our intuition, and mine says Mr. Ogden did it."

She slipped into her mules and stood. "I guess we'd better be getting downstairs, or Jeff will think I've vanished too. Maybe."

Every available lamp had been lighted in the living room, but the folding table with the chairs still grouped around it remained as an eloquent reminder of the recent séance and its aftermath. Vok and Sherry huddled in front of the fireplace, in which Jeff had started a blaze.

As Rogan came downstairs the Czech was saying:

"But I do feel responsible. I was the only man in the house. I should have stayed on guard and not gone to sleep like a stupid peasant."

"It wasn't your fault," Jeff consoled him. "Don't take it so hard."

"I have seen too many dead women!" Vok stood for a moment with his eyes focused somewhere beyond the walls of the room. Then he spoke again. "I was brought here to solve a puzzle and I should have solved it. If I had, the poor lady would be now alive."

"This is more of a puzzle than you bargained for when you agreed to come," said Ambler.

Sherry broke in. "Why do you keep pretending there is any puzzle at all? You know Father did it."

Vok looked at her in amazement. "Surely, Miss Ogden, you do not think—"

"Frank isn't my father. He's just the man my stepmother married. Besides, Frank never killed anyone. He hasn't the guts."

"But then . . . ?"

"My real father is Grimaud Désanat. You saw him tonight."

The magician's expression softened. "You distress yourself without cause. Your father is dead. He cannot return."

"You said Irene was a fake," Sherry reminded him. "But she believed he could come back. She was afraid of him."

"Many mediums believe in their own frauds," Vok replied, "just as mothers believe in the innocence of their sons after they have been caught by the police redhanded."

Sherry shook her head. "Thanks, Mr. Vok, but it's no good. You may be right about spiritualism, but that doesn't clear Father. Whether he's alive or dead, he killed Irene, and every one of us knows it."

"Vok's right, Sherry," said Rogan. "Even on your own theory, if your father came he wore moccasins. The man who murdered your stepmother wore hunting boots—with hobnails."

"I'd better get a look at those tracks," said Jeff, "before something happens to them."

He sprang lightly up the stairs and disappeared down the hall.

"Mr. Vok," Ambler began, "I agree with you that it is a trick. I suppose we all must in those moments when our senses aren't giving the lie to our instincts. However, I confess your failure to find a solution has troubled me. On the stage, of course, things are different, but here—well, there seem so few possibilities."

The Czech smiled. "That does not show it is not a trick—only that it is a good trick. Besides, you are not to regard me as infallible. Consider that I am a stranger, unacquainted with your ways. Perhaps the key to our enigma is something peculiar to this country—something of which I have never heard. Once I learn that, believe me, the rest will automatically follow."

Ambler looked at him in surprise. "You speak as if there were a formula for solving problems of this kind."

"But there is."

"I should like to learn it."

The Czech spread his hands. "I can put it in one sentence: *Look for the unnecessary.*"

"Your explanation," Ambler replied, "is as obscure as our riddle itself."

Vok smiled his mortician's smile. "Such things are hard to explain but easy to demonstrate. Look." He strode across the room and took a pack of bridge cards from the desk. "It is as much against the principles of my profession to reveal a legitimate conjuring trick as it is a duty to expose the frauds of mediums, so I shall confine myself to displaying one of my own discoveries in the field of prognostication."

He began to shuffle the cards as he talked.

"I say 'my own,' but actually the basic principle was taught me by a Transylvanian nobleman who had devoted his entire life to the study of the ancient and mysterious tarot cards. He contended, with reason, that most systems of fortunetelling depend too much on interpretation to be reliable. As he often remarked, of what use was the knowledge that a fair woman would influence your life if you could not be sure whether it would be a blond siren or your white-haired grandmother? Through his study of the Tarots my friend had discovered a system of divination that produced answers which were not Delphic but as simple and clear as print. My contribution lay in demonstrating that his discovery would work equally well with ordinary playing cards, and that its application would even be simplified."

The idea of having fortunes told fascinated Miss Daventry.

"You mean," she asked, "you're going to tell us something that you can't wriggle out of afterward?"

"Precisely, and which cannot be misunderstood. This method rests on a mysterious sympathy between the alphabet and a deck of cards. Few people have ever observed that a pack of cards contains two alphabets—twenty-six red cards and twenty-six black ones."

Vok placed the deck in front of Ambler.

"Pray cut. In using these card alphabets, we have only to remember that hearts precede diamonds and that spades precede clubs. Thus the ace of hearts will represent 'A,' the deuce of hearts 'B,' and so on. Again we start with the ace of diamonds, which signifies 'N,' and continue until we come to our card 'Z,' which is the king of diamonds. Similarly in the black alphabet, the ace of spades is 'A,' and we go through the black suits until we reach the king of clubs, who symbolizes our second 'Z.'"

The magician turned to Barbara with a little bow.

"Now, Miss Daventry, if you will graciously lift the cards and deal them out one at a time just as you would at bridge. Only please to make five piles instead of four. And remember: *Fate is in your hands!*"

Silence descended on the room during the deal. The gaunt magician's manner had impressed Barbara, and she dealt each card with an awesome concentration, as if its fall guided the iron tread of destiny.

"Fifty-two," she finished and laid down the last card.

"Thank you. Now turn over the packets and begin to read."

"You mean the cards will spell something?"

"I do."

Her fingers quivering with excitement, Barbara squared each pile of cards and turned it face up.

2C 7H 4S 5H AC

"Two of clubs. That's the second thirteen." Her lips moved. "'O.'"

Rogan, counting more swiftly, raced ahead of her and read the whole word:

OGDEN

"Now," Vok instructed her, "remove those five cards and look at the ones underneath."

Hurriedly Barbara uncovered the second row.

4H 5S AH 7D 8S

Again Rogan computed the corresponding letters, but this time he did not announce the word:

DEATH

XIII

The Witness of the Blood

In most cases the spirit takes possession of [the] man's body
contrary to his will, and he is helpless in the matter.
—REV. JOHN L. NEVIUS, D.D.
Demon Possession

THE CONJURER put the tips of his fingers together. "Quite apart
from the fact that my oracle prophesies after the event, I realize
that none of you will mistake this somewhat infantile bit of legerdemain for genuine divination. But granted that it is a simple
trick, how is that trick done? Remember, our rule is: *Look for the
unnecessary.*"

"Well," Barbara suggested, "you could have left out all that
about your friend from Pennsylvania and the what-do-you-call-
'em cards."

"Oh, no. Think a moment. *If* my demonstration had been
genuine, the preliminary explanation would have been both real
and important. We must ask ourselves what was done during
the course of the trick that would *not* have been needed if the
demonstration had been genuine?"

"I can think of one thing," said Ambler, "though I confess I
can't see how it affected the trick one way or another."

"Ah, that is the way a magician disguises his secrets. Something is done, and because the spectator cannot see any reason for it he thinks it incidental. Not so. Of a trick every part is important. The fact that the onlooker cannot discern the reason usually means that if the reason were found, it would disclose the mystery."

"Well," said Ambler, "the point I noticed is not likely to penetrate your secret. However, as there were only two words to be read, dealing the remaining forty-two cards was unnecessary."

"But of course!" Vok cried. "That is the key. Did I not tell you it would be? Think a moment. What would have resulted if only the necessary cards had been dealt?"

"I'd have put down five," Barbara told him, "and then five more on top of them."

"Precisely. And from where did you get those ten cards?"

"From the top of the pack."

"To be sure. My whole trick, then, consisted in bringing ten cards together in a certain order, and arranging matters so Professor Ambler would cut to the first of those ten cards. That is what the dishonest gambler does when he stacks the deck. Any competent sleight-of-hand performer can accomplish it. If ten cards only had been dealt, the trick would be obvious. However, when the whole pack is used, the idea that but ten cards are significant is disguised, and as the thought of stacking the entire deck would explain nothing, the mystery is safe."

"That's neat!" Barbara exclaimed. "And you mean there's something like that back of every trick?"

"I do. The 'unnecessary' step is the key to them all," Vok assured her. "Take tonight's séance. Why did the medium pass her hand over Mr. Kincaid's envelope? To help the spirits read it? No. Simply to rub on the envelope the alcohol."

"And," Ambler supplemented, "it was also unnecessary for the séance to take place in darkness—unnecessary for the spirits, but the only condition under which the medium could use her apparatus without being detected."

"Precisely. So when we discover what step was for the ghost unnecessary, we shall be on the trail of the murderer."

"We're already on the trail of the murderer." Jeff came out of the hall and down the steps. "Only the trail ran out on us."

"Perhaps," Vok hazarded, "the fact that he left a trail at all this time, when he was able to disappear completely before, is the unnecessary step. I shall think about it. In the meanwhile I have a necessary duty to perform. Putting it off makes it no easier. Mr. Ogden left me in charge of this house. The least I can do is to inform him how I failed in my trust." He turned to Jeff. "Will you go with me? I have never been to your lodge. I am not sure I could find the way alone."

Jeff assented. He picked up his coat and Vok's cloak, and they left through the dining room. As the rear door closed behind them, Ambler moved to the window and stared out at the night. Barbara spoke:

"Mr. Vok didn't need Jeff to show him the way. He could have followed the trail you made coming over."

Ambler turned back to the room. "Yes, my dear, but I think our Mr. Vok is more impressed by tonight's events than he cares to admit, even to himself." The professor glanced over his shoulder at the window and then added, "As Mr. Kincaid is here, do you mind if I leave you for a few minutes? I should like to have a look around outside for myself."

Sherry's eyes widened. "You mean you're going alone?"

"Unless you'd rather I stayed here." Ambler smiled apologetically at Rogan. "I know it's absurd to suppose either you or Jeff could miss anything so obvious as a line of footprints. However, the whole business is so incredible I'd like to see everything with my own eyes."

"And you're actually going to hunt for tracks?" demanded Barbara.

Ambler nodded, with a grave smile on his face, pleasantly aware that most men would have lacked the courage to venture alone into that night, and mildly conscious of the fact that it was ridiculous for him to enjoy appearing before this blond child in a favorable light.

"Because," Barbara finished, "if you're going out, I'm going too."

The little professor's face fell, but fortunately only Rogan noticed it, for Sherry was staring at her friend in astonishment.

"Babs! You're not?"

"Of course I am. I want to see where the footprints aren't, just as much as he does."

"But you're not dressed."

"I can put on a coat and galoshes, can't I?"

She dove into the bedroom and reappeared a minute later with the legs of her pajamas tucked into high galoshes and her slim body wrapped in a mink coat with a collar so huge that only her eyes and the tip of her nose were visible. Ambler had recovered from his discomfiture and now seemed as happy about setting out on this expedition as a schoolboy on a picnic.

Sherry watched them vanish through the front door.

"Babs certainly has what it takes. Young ones, old ones, they all fall for it."

Rogan said, "I don't."

She looked up at him with a sudden smile.

"You're sweet." Then: "I . . . I . . . don't feel like being by myself. Will you come to my room with me while I dress?"

"Rogan, you don't believe Father did it, do you?"

He shook his head, and she asked:

"Who do you think it was? Professor Ambler?"

"Why pick on Ambler?"

"Well, what we saw tonight couldn't have been a puppet or anything like that. If it wasn't . . . Father, it must have been one of us. If Father had been a big man almost anyone could have impersonated him—even Luke, I guess, with some sort of thick-soled shoes to make him look taller. But Father was tiny—not much over five feet. The only people anywhere near his height are Barbara and the professor."

"It's difficult to estimate height under conditions as they were tonight," Rogan reminded her. "You're probably judging more by what you remember about your father than by what we actually saw. You might have been three or four inches out in your guess."

"Even that would only let in Luke and Madore. The other men are much too tall. Madore hasn't the brains for this murder, and the idea of Luke killing anyone is fantastic. Professor Ambler fits everything. He's small . . . like Father. He has plenty of brains to work up a scheme like this. He knows a lot about . . . queer things . . . so he could have made it seem authentic."

"If Ambler was the man, why didn't your stepmother cry out when a stranger entered her room?"

"Maybe she couldn't. Maybe she was unconscious."

"You mean she was asleep?"

"I guess you'd call it that. I think she tried to commit suicide again."

"Again! Has she tried before?"

"Twice, but not very hard." Sherry bit her lip. "That's a mean thing to say about her, isn't it, now she's dead? Poor Irene, she always wanted people to take her seriously. I did my best, honestly I did, but you just couldn't."

She fumbled under her pillow for a handkerchief and began to cry quietly.

"What makes you think your stepmother had another go at suicide tonight?" asked Rogan.

Sherry took her robe from a chair and produced a white correspondence card from the pocket.

"This. I found it under the edge of her bed. It must have fallen there when the dressing table got knocked over."

The note was written in Irene Ogden's flamboyant backhand.

> I'm so wretched, Frank darling. I haven't forgotten what you said the last time I made you angry and I know you'll never forgive me again. I suppose I can't blame you, but I do love you so. I couldn't stand a divorce. This is the only way out. It will be better for you. Please don't think too hard of me.
>
> Your
> Irene

"I put it in my pocket without saying anything," Sherry explained. "I was fond of her in a way, truly I was, and I didn't want anyone else to see what she'd written. It was like leaving her naked for strangers to stare at. I didn't think it had anything to do with what's happened. She hadn't killed herself, and I wasn't even certain it was a suicide note. You couldn't be—not when it was from Irene. She's written wilder things than that when she forgot to order mint sauce for the lamb."

"She was crying when she wrote this," Rogan said. "You can see little round blurs where the teardrops blotted the ink."

"She would have cried over the mint sauce, too." The girl began to sob again. "I'm being a beast tonight. I don't seem able to stop."

"When she tried suicide before, what did she use?"

"Veronal, or something like that. People do die of an overdose sometimes, but it isn't terribly dangerous. Irene just stayed asleep longer than usual. It never got her any sympathy from Frank, only made him mad, but the poor dear never learned."

Rogan tapped the note. "You believe this means she might have taken an extra dose of veronal tonight, and that anyone could have gone into her room without waking her?"

Sherry nodded. She dried her eyes and began to dress.

"If you think Ambler killed your stepmother," Rogan went on, "*you* must have some idea about the motive."

"I have. I think they were lovers—not now, but a long time ago. All that white hair makes the professor look ancient, but he's really only about fifty. According to Jeff, the professor is almost a legend around Charlottesville. They say that back in 1920 every petticoat in Virginia fluttered at the sound of his name. Irene used to be a bit of a girl in *her* youth, too."

"Just because they both shared the same taste doesn't mean they indulged it together."

"She was afraid of him," Sherry insisted. "We got here Monday. Frank went on to Quebec. There wasn't any man in the house, so Luke came over. At dinner that night he told us he was having a friend up for the shooting—one of Jeff's professors at the University, a man named Ambler. I happened to be looking at Irene at the time. She went white as her napkin. I admit it didn't take much to make Irene turn pale, and even the stoutest-hearted matron is entitled to a qualm or two when an ex-bedfellow shows up."

A sound caught the girl's ear and she stiffened.

"I heard a man's voice!"

"It's Ambler coming back with Barbara."

"I'm afraid of everything tonight," Sherry lamented. "You'd better go. They'll probably be here in a minute."

"I," Rogan complained, "always seem to be leaving at the pink-silk-pantie stage."

With her door closed behind him, he listened for voices, but heard nothing. He strolled into the kitchen and peered out one of the rear windows. There was no one in sight. Puzzled, he went through the house silently, so as not to alarm Sherry. There was no one in front, nor could he see any sign of life from either end of the porch.

He tried to recall the voice he had heard, but without result. He had assumed it was Ambler's. Now he knew it might have been any man's voice. Besides, where were Ambler and Barbara? They could hardly have gone so far that their flashlights would not have been visible.

Rogan re-entered the house and paused to glance around the living room. The only objects which he had not already examined were the rumpled blankets on the window seat where Ogden had slept, and the sack coat he had worn earlier in the evening. Without moving it, Rogan ran swiftly through the pockets. His search produced a mechanical pencil, a business card from the representative of a brokerage house, and three envelopes addressed to Ogden. The first bore the name of a lumber company with offices in Quebec and contained a brief note making an appointment for the previous Monday. The second held an invitation to attend services at a spiritualist church in Toronto. The third envelope was empty. Rogan stared into it for a moment. Then he noticed that the paper was damp and that ink from the letter it had once contained had come off on the inside face of the envelope. He could even make out parts of one line: 'emit' or 'omit,' then a space broken by blurred scrawls, then a surprisingly legible V then another space followed by what might be either 'net' or 'nat.'

He tried working these into a sentence, but there proved to be too many possibilities. 'Please *remit* in full. We quoted *net* price,' would fit nicely, but so would a number of other things such as 'You omitted the information *that Désanat* had tied up the property.'

Rogan turned the envelope over and looked at its face. It was of the squarish type used by business houses for formal announcements and bore the imprint of a firm of chemical engineers in Quebec. He pondered over this until he noticed that the postmark was dated the previous June. Annoyed at himself for wasting time, he returned the envelopes to Ogden's pocket and mounted the stairs.

The lamp in the dead woman's room was still burning. Rogan halted in the doorway to contemplate the chaos before him. It seemed impossible to conceive of any human motive for such wholesale destruction. Broken glass from Irene Ogden's formidable supply of beauty lotions littered the floor. A heavy inkwell had been hurled at the mirror of the chiffonier and the long-dried ink was spilled like black sand on the white towel that served as a throw.

He had to force himself to notice these details, for, try as he might, his eyes kept coming back to the ghastly figure on the bed. Shakespeare's phrase 'blood-bolter'd' rose in his mind and with it a new thought.

No living being could have inflicted those wounds and escaped unstained.

XIV

The Road to Nowhere

In many cases of possession the first symptoms occur during sleep.

—REV. JOHN L. NEVIUS, D.D.
Demon Possession

IF THEY were dealing with a living murderer at all, he had either changed his clothes—or had not worn any!

Mr. Kincaid did not find the idea to his liking. Yet once it had suggested itself there was escape from it. Nothing that did not fly could have crossed the belt of unbroken snow that surrounded Cabrioun. The house itself had been thoroughly searched. Put together, those facts meant beyond any possible question that only six living beings could have killed Irene Ogden: Rogan himself, Jeff, Ambler, Vok, Barbara—and Sherry. All of them, except Sherry, had been together in the hall while the murder was being committed. None of them, except Sherry, had any chance to change clothes or bathe after the door had been broken open. Rogan even had a distinct recollection of each pair of hands, held in a strong light and obviously free from blood: Barbara's, tiny and pink, lifted as if to ward off attack when the circle of Jeff's torch had found her on their arrival; Ambler's hands, white, small-boned, aristocratic, caught for an instant in the beam of Rogan's flash and silhouetted against the blackness of the hall outside Irene Ogden's door; Vok's deft fingers, bathed in light as he probed with his match at the keyhole; Jeff's great hands lighting the lantern in the storeroom.

Sherry had been naked at the moment of the murder. She had bathed at a most unlikely hour. The explanation she had given of that in advance proved nothing. She might have taken advantage of an established custom in building her murder plan. When Rogan had entered her room in the dark, almost her first words had warned him against striking a light. That was natural enough, but it might mean she had not had time to examine her body in a mirror and make sure no stains had been overlooked.

Yes, there was no dodging the fact. No one could have come to Cabrioun or gone out of it without leaving a track, and of the six people in the house Sherry alone could have cleansed herself of blood.

New facts kept linking on with an alarming plausibility. The phantom had spoken French—so did Sherry. She could almost certainly manage a Provençal accent well enough to fool any one of the party. Experience with many séances might have supplied the technical knowledge she needed to simulate her father's specter. The 'voice' on the lake could have been a bold-faced lie to provide atmosphere. Furthermore, it would probably be easy to find a motive. Even if no one had cared enough about Irene Ogden to kill her, her money provided a strong incentive. The Ogdens had adopted Sherry, so she would probably inherit a large share of her stepmother's estate.

One point remained in her favor. Vok had examined the house for a hidden door, and Rogan did not believe the conjurer had missed one. Lacking such a door, there was no way for Sherry to escape from her stepmother's bedroom and reach the floor below without passing through the upstairs hall. She could not have done that without being seen.

That brought him back to the track on the roof. The hobnailed prints which led from the broken window to the far rail must have been made by the fleeing murderer. Any theory that did not take them into account was worse than useless.

Thoughtfully he circled through Vok's bedroom, stepped out onto the porch, and followed the trail to the far edge of the roof. It was not until he reached the rail and leaned over, casting the beam of his flashlight downward, that he discovered anything new. One of the kitchen windows was directly under the bloody hand-mark on the rail.

The rail itself was small enough to permit a firm grip. It was just possible that Sherry could have vaulted it and then, without releasing her hold, let herself drop to the full extent of her arms. From that position she might have reached the window sill and climbed into the kitchen without ever touching the ground outside.

Kincaid retraced his steps through Vok's room, down the stairs, and out the rear door. The beam of his flashlight found the window sill and played along it. The snow lay fresh as when it had first fallen.

The idea was impossible on another score as well. The railing was some nine feet above the sill. Sherry's toes would not have reached below the middle of the window.

The middle of the window . . .

Rogan returned to the kitchen and lowered the top sash. Yes, that would do it. With the sash all the way down, its upper rail and the upper rail of the bottom sash were on the same level. Together they formed a support which could be reached from the roof and was clear of any giveaway coating of snow.

He resolved to test this. There were two windows in the rear of the kitchen. The other would do for his experiment, and he need not confuse the prints on the roof and railing upstairs. Closing the top sash of the window under the hand-mark, Kincaid then lowered its counterpart on the window he meant to use for his test. He returned to the roof and, making sure he was in exactly the right spot, grasped the rail with both hands and jumped.

The jerk nearly broke his grip and the projecting eaves scraped his side painfully, but his toes hung a little below the bottom of the opening in the window. Without effort he secured a foothold on the sashes. Then he wriggled through the window, dropped lightly to the floor of the kitchen, and raised the upper sash to its place. He had made his way from the roof to the first floor without leaving any trace of his passage.

Mr. Kincaid was not given to dodging the results of his thinking, but the choice of suspects could hardly have been less palatable. Sherry—or her father. No one else could have killed Irene Ogden. Before he could plan a course of action, the door opened and Ambler entered. Rogan stood.

"Where's Barbara?"

"We met Jeff and Mr. Vok. She went with them."

When in doubt, attack! was an axiom with the gambler. He acted on it automatically.

"I'm glad to have a chance to talk. I've been collecting hints about you. Put together they add up to something."

Ambler looked up, speculation in his eyes. "Something significant?" he asked slowly.

"I haven't gotten that far. Right now I'm wondering how intimate you and Mrs. Ogden were fourteen years ago."

Ambler kept his torch on the other's face for a moment before he replied. "Come into the living room. We can't talk here."

Neither man spoke again until Rogan had pulled the easy chair to the fire and lighted his pipe. Ambler had thrown off his coat and stood with his hands thrust in his jacket pockets and a frown on his red face.

"Now," he demanded, "suppose you tell me what you're driving at."

"I was in Quebec," Rogan complied, "headed for New York. Jeff offered me a ride and I took it. I didn't count on being mixed up in a murder, particularly one with supernatural trimmings. I don't intend to let the police keep me here for three or four months while they run around in circles. The only way out is for me to clear the matter up myself. I'm going to tear things open before I get caught inside."

He took his pipe from his mouth and held it with the bit thrust out like a sword.

"You're the place I start tearing. You took a week's vacation you weren't entitled to, to come up here, and you didn't do that because you like to hunt. You knew Mrs. Ogden before—well. There wouldn't be anything to that if you'd admitted it, but you didn't. There might be several reasons for keeping your acquaintance secret, but only one could be called likely. Also you knew the man Querns who got killed when Sherry's father did." He leaned back. "Is that enough to start with, or do you want more?"

"Quite enough, thank you." Ambler's hands came out of his pockets. He thrust a cigarette between his lips and lit it. "I can see how this situation must appear to you. I didn't want to talk until I'd tested my suspicions, but you leave me no choice. Luke wrote me about his logging difficulties because I'm a friend, and because I happen to have two hundred shares of stock in his company. That's not much, perhaps, but it represents the bulk of my savings. I don't want to spend my last days as a pauper on a government old-age pension."

Ambler turned and poked the fire before he went on.

"Naturally I gave Luke's problem a great deal of thought. The whole setup was so unusual I smelled a nigger in the woodpile. It happens that Ogden owns the patent under which Luke's mills operate. How did he get it? It covers a complicated chemical process. That wasn't the sort of thing anyone could stumble over. It had to be worked out by a man with training and experience. Now, Ogden used to be a patent lawyer before his marriage and presumably knew something of chemistry, but that didn't satisfy me—particularly because I happened to know that Querns had been an industrial chemist."

Rogan leaned forward again. "This begins to be interesting."

"That's how I felt. I asked a friend in Washington to look up the date of the patent. He found that the application had gone in six months after Querns' death."

"Your theory is that the invention was made by Querns, and that Ogden stole it?"

"It was hardly a theory, barely a suspicion. Still, as you say, it was interesting. Like you, I wanted to get inside and start tearing. For that I had to be on the ground."

"What was the point of the question you asked at the séance tonight?"

"I hoped for a lead. The séance could hardly be a plan to swindle Luke unless Mrs. Ogden were in on it. As things turned out, her answer to my question was interrupted and I learned nothing. In fact, so far I've been unable to confirm my suspicions in a single particular. Now they seem unimportant because . . ." He paused and then added in a strained voice, "God help me, I believe I've found conclusive evidence that the agency behind Mrs. Ogden's death was supernatural!"

Rogan glanced up in surprise.

"I thought you agreed with Vok that our phantom killer was a trick."

"I did for a time. After I had recovered from my astonishment at the murderer's disappearance, I realized that the disappearance itself was at variance with the idea of a spectral slayer. To borrow Mr. Vok's suggestion: it might be necessary for a living man to break out a window to escape, but it was most unnecessary for a ghost, who presumably could have vanished from the bedroom as easily as from the rail. However, the prints on the roof troubled me. Hobnailed boots are far from ghostly, but for that very reason the idea that anyone masquerading as a ghost would have chosen such footgear was more fantastic than the phantom itself."

"That bothered me, too," Rogan acknowledged. "Those boot marks didn't seem either natural or supernatural."

"What if it were both!" Ambler challenged. "What if the murderer did not vanish when he leaped the rail. What if he flew!"

Rogan cocked his head on one side.

"Don't tell me you credit this little whimsy?"

"I've confirmed it." The little man turned and began pacing back and forth before the fireplace, making jerky gestures with his right hand as if it held a piece of chalk. "The idea of flight had been present in each of the earlier episodes, so it was not safe to ignore it. In no instance did it seem to be particularly well developed, more like levitation than true flight. I thought a wider circuit of the house might disclose footprints where our murderer had landed. We found them—in the middle of a patch of bare snow. There isn't a tree or bush within twenty yards, and the first print is over a hundred feet from the place he took off!"

XV

The Seven Mirrors

I have several times had the opportunity of observing personally these cases of possession. . . . I once had a possessed woman in my university clinic at Tokio for four weeks.
    —E. BÄLZ in *Verhandlungen der Gesellschaft deutscher Naturforscher und Aerzte*

"We began by examining the snow on the north side of the house near the edge of the lake," said the professor. "Then we saw a light. My own instinct would have been to proceed cautiously, but Miss Daventry shouted, 'It's Jeff!' and started to run. Naturally I ran after her."

Rogan smiled. "Old habits die hard."

"They never die." Some of the humor came back into Ambler's eyes. "When we reached Jeff and Mr. Vok everyone started talking at once."

"Out loud, too," Rogan observed. "Sherry and I heard you from here. We thought at first it was our ghost."

"In a way it was. Jeff had been following the main path to the lodge, keeping an eye out on both sides. About a hundred feet from this house he noticed a trail that ran in at an angle but stopped eight or ten feet from the path. When he went over to it he recognized the prints and realized they had been made by the murderer on his way here."

"I thought you said you discovered the tracks he made when he *left*."

"We did later, but we found the incoming trail first. Jeff pointed it out to us. Then because his torch was getting dim, we turned off our lights to save the batteries. Standing there in the dark arguing about a ghost was an uncanny experience."

He took out another cigarette and lighted it.

"Vok claimed a man could have jumped from the end of the track to the main path, but there was no sign of the killer's boots on the path. Jeff and Vok had walked along it, of course, but they could hardly have destroyed every print. On the other hand, it was even more difficult to believe anyone could have flown from the place the track ended to the porch over a hundred feet away. It was Miss Daventry who settled the matter. She suggested that if the murderer had left tracks on the way to Cabrioun he must have made another set when he escaped. We started searching, and five minutes later Vok found the escape trail. This time there was no room for doubt. It started from nowhere, as a bird's track does."

Ambler tossed his cigarette into the fire.

"Imagine it—a sweep of bare snow, a hundred feet from the house and over half that distance from the nearest bush. Suddenly a line of footprints begins. The first few are smudged a bit, as if whoever made them had landed after a glide and taken a few steps to catch his balance. Then the tracks go on as normally as any you'd see in a day's hunting—tracks made by someone who had not touched the ground since he had vaulted the rail a hundred feet away."

"Did Vok offer any solution?"

The professor shook his head. "Oh, he insisted it was a trick of some kind, but he didn't even guess how the trick had been worked. How could he?"

Rogan struck a match, and it was not until his pipe was fully lit that he spoke.

"I gather you have a theory."

"Yes. You agree that the hobnailed boots could have been worn only by a living man, but that they would not have been chosen by one. There is one explanation which will reconcile that discrepancy. Suppose a man's body to have been invaded by a hostile entity which was able to endow it with the power of flight. Suppose the body to belong to Frank Ogden and the spirit to be Grimaud Désanat. Then for the first time the events of the evening fall into a complete pattern and the reason for each incident becomes clear."

"Even the reason why a real ghost should have appeared at a fake séance?"

"The point is that it wasn't a fake séance. Undoubtedly Mrs. Ogden intended it to be, but her husband and Luke took matters out of her hands. If spirits exist at all, the conditions for calling them up are fairly well known. It was the anniversary of Désanat's death. He was summoned by two men whose faith was unquestioned and whose need of him was urgent."

"He was buried here, too," Rogan contributed.

"Yes, so if he were in any sense bound to this spot, tonight was the first time since his death that his wife had put herself in his reach. For one fatal instant during the séance her defenses were down. Désanat took advantage of that weakness to break through the barrier which separated him from this life. Don't forget he hated her. Even beyond the grave there might be no rest for him until he could glut his hate with vengeance. For that her mere death would not suffice. It must take a uniquely horrible form. Désanat found one. He decided that his wife should die at the hands of the only being on earth she loved—Frank Ogden."

"You make him sound even worse than Sherry does."

"Perhaps he has made progress in malice since Sherry knew him." Ambler moved restlessly from the hearth and threw himself into a chair. "In any event, he did not remain in possession of his wife for long. He left her almost immediately to become what Vok's peasant friends would call a powerless wraith—but with tremendous potentialities for evil."

"When do you think he got control of Ogden?"

"When Ogden and Vok went outside to look for tracks. Ogden claimed Désanat did not catch up with him, but he was obviously lying. Certainly his behavior seems to have been influenced by Désanat from the time he returned to the house."

"Your idea is that Ogden was inoculated in some way when the ghost chased him, but that he didn't entirely abandon control of himself until he fell asleep?" Rogan asked. "And that then Désanat used Ogden's body just as I might use a pair of fire tongs to pick up a red-hot coal or to do anything else I could not do myself?"

"That's it exactly. Désanat soon found, however, that the possession of a living body had disadvantages as well as advantages. He could take charge of Ogden, but he couldn't get him through Mrs. Ogden's locked door. The attempt to shoot Vok seems to have been mere frustrated spite. No doubt the old gun was employed because it was the only one in the place that had belonged to Désanat."

Ambler dug in his pocket for another cigarette and lighted it before he continued.

"The first attack lasted only a short time, which I am told is usual in such cases. Apparently Désanat was not powerful enough to overthrow Ogden while he was awake. However, as soon as he went to sleep again, Désanat resumed control and made another, and successful, attempt to reach his wife through an open window and kill her."

Rogan eyed the little professor keenly. "How much of this do you really believe?"

"I wish I didn't believe any of it!" Ambler rose and resumed his restless pacing. "I am more afraid of belief than of the ghost itself. It isn't that I dread the idea of the supernatural. I've always believed in that to a certain extent. But a supernatural that includes Grimaud Désanat—a supernatural of which he is perhaps the type—revolts my very soul. He makes me feel that if I am not very careful an abyss will open before my feet, and abominable things will crawl out of it."

"Désanat was no advertisement for Hell," Rogan conceded, "if you believe in him."

Ambler threw out his hands. "What else can I believe? Every trade marks a man. Mine is science. If that means anything at all, it means becoming the slave of logic. An honest scientist spends his days fighting the will to believe, until at last he ceases to have any control over his own opinions. He follows logic as inevitably and as helplessly as water runs downhill. He can no longer believe a thing because it is pleasant, or because everyone else does. Neither can he refuse to believe anything because it contravenes the theories on which he has based his entire life. I'd like to deny this thing if I could, I'd like to say it's a trick, but the evidence in favor of it seems inexorable."

Rogan rose. He walked to the fire and knocked the dottle from his pipe. The wind, which had fallen to a whisper, swelled once more and wailed a dirge in the chimney. He took his pouch from his pocket and began to refill his pipe—making a ritual of it and seeing that each pinch of tobacco was packed exactly to his taste.

"Logic is a jealous mistress," he said. "I've tried to be untrue to her myself and never had much luck at it. However, you can't be logical about a thing unless you're familiar with it. You don't know what fallacies to guard against. Vok is an expert spook-spotter and he says ours is a trick."

"As far as Vok is concerned," said Ambler, "seeing tricks everywhere is an occupational disease. Besides, he hasn't found the answer."

"There could be good reasons for that."

"And one is that there isn't any answer. No," the little professor insisted. "This is not a conjurer's trick. There is one factor running through the whole thing which negatives that—the snow. Snow cannot be tampered with. It writes an automatic record of everything that is done to it. When snow is drifting in the wind, as it is now, it makes a time record as well."

"The trick idea isn't likely," Rogan admitted, "but the possession idea is only superstition."

"You can't say that," replied Ambler. "Possession exists, whether it is to be interpreted as an invasion by some spiritual entity or merely as a fanciful name for an obscure mental disorder. I've seen cases myself."

"Calling mental disorders by fancy names doesn't give their victims the ability to fly," Rogan demurred. "The flying is the crux of this whole business. I might admit the ghost. A good many funny things in that line seem to happen. However, according to your theory, Désanat could fly not only when draped tastefully in his own ectoplasm, but also when he was inhabiting a hundred and fifty pounds of Ogden."

"I've thought about that, too. Levitation is the rarest of paranormal phenomena, but well-authenticated cases exist."

"I know there are Tibetan lamas who claim to be able to 'walk through air,'" the gambler acknowledged. "And I have met some hardheaded and completely unimaginative Britishers who swear they've seen it done, but I still don't believe it."

"Admittedly the flying is the most difficult thing to credit," agreed Ambler. "But it is also the thing which is most convincingly proved and the one which would be hardest to fake. A trick depends on certain fixed conditions. With a complicated trick like levitation, those conditions allow very little leeway, but tonight the circumstances in which flight appeared varied enormously. We watched Désanat hovering over our heads in the still air of this room. Vok and Ogden saw him floating behind them in the wind outside. Could both those cases be explained except by the power of flight?"

He caught up a lamp and held it over his head.

"See those forked sticks on the chimney-breast? The flintlock rested in them. They are twelve feet off the floor. The mantel shelf is only a two-inch break in the masonry. No one could climb on that, yet the gun was taken down and put back in the dark. Can that be explained except by the power of flight?"

The professor replaced the lamp on the table.

"There is a track on the roof which leads to the railing. It leaves off only to pick up again a hundred feet away. You, and Jeff, and Mr. Vok, and I have examined the snow between and found nothing. It is simply impossible for *all* of us to have been mistaken. Can that be explained except by the power of flight?

Four instances, four entirely different sets of conditions—there can't be one trick that covers them all."

"Maybe someone knows four different tricks."

"There you run into another snag. Vok might be fooled by one trick or even two, but the difficulty increases in geometrical proportion as each new trick is added. I don't know Mr. Vok well, but I am convinced no man living could fool him with four tricks in succession!"

"That," said Rogan, "suggests a reason why Vok wasn't fooled: maybe he did these things himself."

"Of course it does—just as the idea that Ogden knew Querns suggested that Ogden might have stolen Querns' patent—just as the fact that I left my classes to come up here, where I had no apparent business to be, suggested that I had a secret reason, and that that reason was murder. No doubt a similar suspicion could be built up against everyone in our group—you, Jeff, Luke, even the two girls. The difficulty is that each of those suspicions is contradicted by something which makes it completely untenable."

"You may be right," Rogan conceded, "but I never give much weight to physical evidence. It's too easy to fake. In the old three-shell game, you saw the pea go under a particular shell and you didn't see it come out. That looked like the best sort of physical evidence, but when you lifted the shell, the pea wasn't there. As a matter of fact, on the physical side of tonight's happenings all we really know is that we can't explain the tricks."

"If you don't believe physical evidence," Ambler protested, "what do you believe?"

Rogan smiled. "I don't believe very much. However, I give a good deal of weight to psychological evidence. Why was Mrs. Ogden killed? You say her first husband did it as a method of fiendish vengeance, but her second husband had a motive, too, and a very human one. Before I could believe Désanat was behind this, I'd have to find something for which no ordinary human motive could account."

Ambler stared at him, then made a little gesture of resignation.

"There is one such thing. I haven't mentioned it because I don't like to think about it. Can you imagine a living man crushing a woman's skull with a stone ax, and then staying to gloat over her death agonies until her rescuers were pounding at the door?"

Rogan frowned. "You're hinting that Homer was right about the shades of the dead craving fresh blood."

Ambler was startled. "No. I hadn't thought of that. What I had in mind was . . . even worse—something that carries us out of the horror of dreams and into the ultimate terror of a fairy tale."

The little man paused and stood staring into the fire.

"Has it ever struck you," he resumed, "that no adult narrative is half as gruesome as the stories we tell our children? The brothers Grimm were well named—murder, burning, and cruelty on every page. Or take Mr. Punch. Over the years he is probably the most popular of all characters with children. Yet what is he? A creature who exists only to murder. A fiend who lacks even the tiny grace of a motive. Gilles de Rais and the mass murderer of Dusseldorf were better than that."

Ambler swung around. "Do you know anything of the superstitions connected with mirrors?"

"You don't mean seven years' bad luck?"

"No. I mean the idea that appears in stories like Nathaniel Hawthorne's *Feathertop*—that mirrors always tell the truth, and that no supernatural being dares look into one, because it reflects him not as he appears but as he truly is. That's an idea from a fairy tale, but if you think it over, you'll get some conception of the self-horror of the damned."

"Aren't you letting yourself be carried away by this thing? I saw that Mrs. Ogden's dressing-table mirror had been smashed, but surely that was the natural result of the struggle."

Ambler shook his head.

"There were seven mirrors in that room, including an old one in the closet and a tiny glass in Mrs. Ogden's compact. All seven of them had been hunted out and destroyed!"

XVI

The Broken Footsteps

A man with an unclean spirit, who had his dwelling among the tombs; and no man could bind him, no, not with chains: because that he had been often bound with fetters and chains, and the chains had been plucked asunder by him, and the fetters broken in pieces.

—MARK, V, 2-4

Rogan stared. "Do you mean Désanat hated those mirrors because they reflected him instead of Ogden, and that he stayed even while we were beating on the door because he couldn't rest until they were all broken?"

"Can you think of another reason for smashing them?" Ambler demanded. "Remember, they were not all in full view. They had to be searched for. I wouldn't have found out about them myself if I hadn't looked for one to make absolutely certain Mrs. Ogden's breathing had stopped. Yet there was nothing of value in the room. The mirrors must have been the object of the search."

"Mrs. Ogden was a rich woman. We don't know what she might have brought up here with her—jewels, papers . . ."

"You can't explain it that way. The search was not general. The desk and the bureau weren't touched, only the dressing table and her handbag—places one might expect to find mirrors."

"It's something to think about." Rogan stood. "Now, if you don't mind staying with Sherry, I think I'd like to see the spot where our flying murderer landed."

"You're wise. A thing like that looks different when you see it with your own eyes." Ambler paused a moment and then added, "It isn't so easy to shrug off, either."

Five minutes later, standing beside the track itself, Kincaid remembered the little professor's words. Those prints weren't easy to shrug off.

The situation was just as Ambler had pictured it, and the stark simplicity of the thing made it impressive—an unbroken expanse of snow, and then the prints of booted feet.

Ambler had been right about the trees, too. The nearest was the big pine, and that was fifty feet away. In the back of his mind Rogan had held the idea of a rope suspended from a bough like a sort of giant swing, or stretched from tree to tree. Now he saw that any such solution was untenable. Confronted by those tracks it was hard to remain skeptical. The record of the snow might not be enduring, but it did not lend itself to deception.

The moon had broken through the flying clouds, but its light did nothing to banish his uneasiness. By driving away the darkness, it revealed the desolation of the landscape. The pall of snow which lay on the earth made a background for the dark shapes of the trees as they writhed in the wind.

If Ambler's theory were to be avoided, then some way had to be found to prove that the prints had not been made by Ogden. Mr. Kincaid's knowledge of tracking was restricted to youthful memories of *The Last of the Mohicans*, but he recalled that Cooper's heroes could recognize a print as easily as another man might identify a face. Perhaps Madore shared their ability. He hesitated a moment, realizing that the guide was more likely to confirm the little professor's ideas than to upset them. Then shame at this unaccustomed reluctance swept over him, and he turned his steps resolutely in the direction of Madore's cabin.

Rogan found it without difficulty, as a light still burned in the window. He peered in. The half-breed sat hunched on his bunk with Jeff's dueling pistol clenched in his right hand, and the medal of Saint Benoit in his left.

Before announcing his presence, the gambler flattened himself against the log wall near the door. The half-ounce silver ball might not be effective against a spirit, but it would pierce a very convincing hole in Kincaid.

He rapped on the door and identified himself. Then without giving Madore time to form any ideas of his own—and perhaps organize a windigo hunt on the spot—Rogan told of Irene Ogden's murder and ended by saying, "The man who did it got away. We need you to help trail him."

"How you know it was man?"

Kincaid laughed. "It wasn't your old friend the windigo. This fellow was very human. He wore hobnailed boots. You needn't be afraid."

"Who's 'fraid?" the guide shouted. "Me no more 'fraid of windigo dan me 'fraid of baby. Madore, he no 'fraid of not'ing."

"Come on then."

The half-breed thrust his barricade aside and pulled open the door. "You show me tracks, eh? Me, I ketch dis feller plaintee quick." He moved off, testing the priming of his pistol.

Finding the tracks, however, was not easy. The walk to the cabin had upset Rogan's sense of direction. They wandered too near the house and so missed the start of the escape trail. He realized this when they stumbled over the main path, but kept on, sweeping in an arc to the right. For Rogan's purpose the prints made by the murderer on his way to Cabrioun would do as well.

He brought Madore to the trail at a point some yards before its end. The guide stopped.

"Dis track she run to house."

"Yes, I know." Rogan seized the first excuse he could think of. "Mr. Vok and Jeff are following the other trail. I thought we ought to cover both."

Madore grunted and bent over the prints again. Kincaid caught himself holding his breath. Then his eyes left the guide and sought the tracks themselves. He stared in disappointment. The rising wind had already blown so much of the powdery snow into them that the patterns of the hobnails were filled, and even their outer edges were blurred. The prints were no longer recognizable.

Madore rose to his feet. "We backtrack. Fin' w'ere feller come from, eh?" They set out, but a minute later the guide stopped with a snort of surprise. "Look! Trail she is lead up from lake. Feller he walk right 'cross ice."

"You mean it isn't strong enough to bear him?"

"Ice strong 'nough, is only bad on reever. But feller he don't come from 'cross lake. Come from dere." He gestured east. "Dat way point she ees stick out into lake lak your nose. If feller he be on dat point, is more easy walk 'round by pat'. Don't see w'at mak' heem come dis way."

As they passed from the shelter of the trees, the wind, racing across the ice from the north, struck them with all its strength, cutting through their clothes with a cruelty that seemed almost personal. There were knives in it. Blasts piled the snow into drifts through which they had to stumble. In other places the ice was swept bare, so that the tracks vanished entirely or appeared merely as small patches of packed whiteness. To right and left, always just outside the beams of their torches, gusts lifted the snow in whirling wraiths. As each of these appeared, the guide jerked his pistol at it, only to recognize it for what it was and curse it in mongrel French.

Kincaid began to fear that Madore would mistake the wind itself for a phantom hand clutching at his coat. If he did, he might turn and let drive with his pistol, and on that empty expanse the gambler was the only mark. Rogan turned his light on the ground and moved closer. "Have you hunted with all the men here?" he asked.

"All 'cept you an' de tall feller w'at's got de black cloak lak cure, and no wan from you be mak' track lak dis. 'Specially tall feller. He's w'at you call 'loose foot.' Walk dis way." Madore broke into a startlingly vivid imitation of Vok's shuffling gait. "Clumsy feller, dat wan. He drag hees feet so don' never get dem all de way out de snow."

"You mean that you can recognize a man's track by the way he walks?"

"Sure t'ing. Good tracker lak me don't need clear print. Every feller he walk differen'. Jus' lak write hees name."

"Huh," scoffed Rogan, playing his man, "a walk's too easy to imitate. If you can do it, anyone can."

"You t'ink?" The other was stung. "'Sides even Madore can't fool anywan w'at look at de groun'."

"But," Kincaid persisted, "even if a man couldn't imitate someone else's track, he could disguise his own."

"*Non!* Ev'ry feller he got walk w'at ees natural to heem. He mak' false step for feefty feet maybe. Den he's forget jus' wan tam, an' I know heem."

"But if he'd had experience in the woods, say he was a hunter like Mr. Ogden . . . ?"

The half-breed laughed. "M'sieu Ogden he not mak' dis track. Everyt'ing 'bout it is differen'—de way he put his feet down, de way he poosh off when he pick dem up. *Non!* M'sieu Ogden he not mak' walk lak dis if he try for honder year."

Rogan trudged on, letting the information sink in. He had no doubt that Madore's reading of the prints was correct. The half-breed was obviously speaking from conviction based on deep experience.

Knowledge that Ogden had not made the tracks disposed of Ambler's theory. It also reminded Rogan that the little professor's explanation of his presence at Cabrioun had left many points untouched. For instance, he had spoken as if Querns were a stranger, yet in his question at the séance Ambler had addressed the chemist as 'Walter' and referred to some mutual friend as 'Gene.' Then, too, if the professor had waited fourteen years to discover a possible connection between Ogden and Querns, why had that discovery coincided with Irene Ogden's death?

A discreetly worded inquiry drew from Madore the information that the trail was completely unlike any that could have been left by Ambler, or, for that matter, by Latham or Jeff. That line of marks in the snow seemed to fascinate the guide. The more he studied it, the more its peculiarities troubled him. Finally he shook his head.

"Dees is mos' funny prints. Dat's de trut'. Me, I don't t'ink I never see feller w'at mak track lak dis."

"You think they were made by a woman?"

Madore laughed in scorn. "Not 'less she's plaintee beeg woman. Dees step she is seex inch more long dan yours."

"The prints aren't very big."

"Dey ees beeg for woman. Mos' beeg as mine." The guide planted his moccasins beside the track for comparison.

"Then you don't think either of the young ladies could have made them?"

"Dose young ladees dey no got feet at all hardly." Madore tossed a noisy kiss from the tips of his fingers. "Dey don't mak' track half beeg's dis wan."

Rogan needed certainty. "You're positive you never saw anyone who walked like this?"

"*Non.*" Madore shook his head. "I don't t'ink, me. No wan w'at's here now mak' dem, dat's sure t'ing. Is look lak I remember . . ." He broke off and then growled something indistinguishable in bastard French.

They left the lake and began climbing the slope of a little beach. In the darkness Rogan could barely make out the top of the ridge ahead, humped against the sky. The ground did not rise sharply, but the murderer seemed to have raced down it, taking great leaps. As Rogan and Madore climbed, the strides lengthened ominously. Then, suddenly, there were no more prints!

If the trail's beginning had been uncanny, this was far more so. There the full isolation of the track had been disguised by the marks the other men had left when they had examined it. Here there was nothing but the snow field and the track itself, starting with bewildering abruptness.

The slope itself was not entirely bare. A few bushes pushed naked stems through the snow, while here and there a scrub evergreen rose to a height of two or three feet. None of these were near the track itself, and certainly none of them offered an explanation. They were covered with a silvery coating of snow, so that if they had been even touched, the result would have been as obvious as a splash of red paint.

A muffled oath from Madore brought Kincaid's head around. The ground rose more steeply on the right to form a little hill some six feet high, and the guide stood halfway up the slope with his pistol pointed at something ahead of him. Four strides brought Rogan's eyes above the level of the ridge, and he saw a light flicker through the trees thirty yards away.

Madore screamed something halfway between a curse and a prayer and leveled his pistol at the gleam. Rogan's gloved hand dropped over the weapon, seizing it by the hammer so that it could not be fired. He twisted the trigger guard against the man's finger until he writhed in agony and released his grip.

"Some day," Rogan prophesied, "you'll let your superstitions get the better of you and shoot something you'll be sorry for. If there's to be any windigo-hunting, I'll do it."

Anger at Kincaid's interference drove every other thought from the guide's mind. His hand slipped inside his coat and reappeared bearing a hunting knife that gleamed wickedly in the moonlight. Then, with an oath he charged down the hill at Rogan. The gambler side-stepped, and knocked the knife aside with the barrel of the pistol. When Madore's rush carried him past, Rogan caught his foot as it left the ground. The man flew through the air to land twenty feet away. He scrambled to his feet still venomous, and limped up the slope.

Before he could reach Rogan, lights appeared over the brow of the hill. Madore's eyes darted to them in superstitious terror. Rogan took advantage of this to step in, catch the half-breed's wrist and twist it behind him until he dropped the knife. Rogan thrust the pistol into his coat and shouted.

Six heads showed over the hill above. A flashlight picked out Madore and then swung to Rogan. Jeff's voice called:

"Hello, where did you come from?"

"We backtracked the other trail."

"Good God, don't tell me it's down there!"

"It stops down here. Dead."

"Where?"

Jeff came down the slope with Thor at his heels and Vok close behind. Kincaid caught the Dane's collar.

"Whoa, boy. You'll mess up the track."

He pointed with the flash in his free hand. Jeff and Vok went over and stared. Then the Czech turned slowly, letting his light play over the snow around him.

"It is the same," he said.

"What happened to the trail you followed?" Rogan inquired.

"It stopped, too."

"Right there on top of the hill," Jeff added. "That's what Uncle Luke and Mr. Ogden are looking at now."

Rogan climbed the little slope to the others. Ogden's face showed that he had been told of his wife's death. Latham's normally cheerful countenance was drawn and gray. Even Barbara, huddled in her fur coat, seemed impressed. They exchanged a few words and then bent over the end of the return trail. Ogden and Latham stared at it only half believing, but to Rogan it had become a familiar story—a commonplace row of tracks, then the lengthening of the strides, then unmarked snow. He looked up to see Jeff and Vok beside him.

"Where are we?" he asked.

For answer Jeff pointed with his flashlight, and Rogan made out the low bulk of the lodge sprawled on the crest of the ridge a hundred feet away, its blind, lightless windows staring down at them.

"This has me beat," Jeff admitted. "Why the Hell did he pick this spot? There must be some reason, because the point where he stopped on the way back isn't twenty feet from where he started. But damn it, the hill here is as bare as the back of your hand. What makes it a specially good place to vanish from?"

"I don't think we were intended to believe he did vanish." Vok swung to Ogden. "Did you hear anything?"

Ogden murmured a negative which Latham amplified.

"What was there to hear? Might have *seen* something if we'd been looking out. Our rooms face this way, but we were both asleep, at least I was."

"I was asleep, too," Ogden asserted with unnecessary fierceness.

Vok stared at him, his black brows knotted in a puzzled frown. Then he turned to Latham.

"Could we not compare boot prints, as the police do fingerprints?"

"Could, if we had the boots that made these tracks. Needle in a haystack, though. These are about half an inch longer than my feet and about an inch shorter than yours. Mine are sevens. Don't suppose you know what size you take in American shoes?"

"He takes elevens," said Jeff. "At least they're a half-size bigger than mine. The tracks must be eights."

Latham looked at Vok. "You see? Eights are medium. Million pairs like 'em. Prints will be gone by morning."

"That won't matter," Jeff announced. "These shoes are easy to identify by the hob patterns. You can see for yourselves, if I can find a print that hasn't drifted full of snow. God, we've tracked this place up. It was bare as the one down below when we first saw it."

Barbara pointed. "Here are some sharp prints."

"Good girl." Jeff squatted on his heels. "That's funny. Wonder how the wind missed these. See what I mean about the boots? There's a hob gone from the middle of the right toe and two from the outside line of the left. The real payoff, though, is that the shoes aren't a pair. They're the same size, all right, but the nail patterns are different."

"You're absolutely sure," Ogden insisted, "that the man who made that print killed my wife?"

"Absolutely."

Ogden drew a deep breath.

"That isn't the track you followed here. It's one I just made."

XVII

The Badge of Murder

Lurancy was a young girl of fourteen, living . . . at Watseka, Ill.,
who . . . declared herself to be animated by the spirit of Mary
Roff . . . who had died . . . twelve years before. . . .

My friend, M. R. Hodgson, informs me that he visited
Watseka in April, 1889, and cross-examined the principal witnesses
of this case. . . . Various unpublished facts were ascertained which
increased the plausibility of the spiritualistic interpretation of the
phenomenon.

—WILLIAM JAMES, *The Principles of Psychology*

THEY WALKED slowly back to the lodge, each deep in his own
thoughts. Ogden's head drooped on his chest. He moved like a
man in a dream, so that Vok took his elbow to guide him. When
they were inside, and Kincaid had bolted the door, Vok piloted
Ogden to the sofa.

"I'm cold." Ogden chafed his hands. Then the significance of
the gesture swept over him. He wrenched them apart and thrust
them into the pockets of his jacket.

Vok caught his eye. "You mustn't believe such things!"

"How can I help it? Oh, I know you'll say it was another trick,
but you don't believe that yourself. You couldn't!"

"Damn it," Jeff flared angrily. "There's no sense in letting ourselves be stampeded by an ersatz spook like—"

Ogden snarled at him. "It's all right for you to talk. No spirit has taken possession of you in your sleep and made you a murderer! I don't want to argue about it." He looked up at Latham. "Can you give me a room?"

"Sure. Same one you had before."

"No, I want one where the windows can be barred this time. Locking the door isn't enough."

"You don't really—" Jeff burst out.

Ogden turned on him fiercely. "Will you never come to your senses? If I had been barred in the first time, my wife would be alive now."

Jeff grew surly. "Have it your own way, but I don't know what room would be better. Even if we nailed the windows shut, that wouldn't keep you from smashing . . ."

He stopped short. The awkward silence which followed was broken by Madore.

"Maybe gun room do, eh?"

"Might," Latham agreed. "It's got a day bed. Extra guide sleeps there when we have a full house."

"What about the windows?" asked Ogden.

"Only one. Move the gun rack in front of it. Place is just a cubbyhole, though."

Ogden waved that aside. The gun room opened off the hall wing of the living room. Its door stood between the stairs and the passage to the kitchen. Ogden made an inspection and pronounced himself satisfied.

"You'd better take the guns out with you," he added significantly.

"They're not loaded," Jeff told him. "Madore can move the ammunition, if you like."

Ogden said, "Please!" and proceeded to check the guns himself.

The cartridge boxes were in a small cupboard built into the space under the stairs. While the guide carried them into the living room, Latham found a hand ax and drove nails into the woodwork of the window, allowing only an inch of air space at top and bottom. Moving the gun cupboard proved a difficult task. It was of heavy oak, and the combined strength of Rogan and Jeff was barely enough to lift it.

They bade Ogden good night. Rogan noted with grim amusement that everyone made a point of watching Jeff lock the door and pocket the key. That ceremony completed, the tension relaxed. Latham turned to the others.

"Some of us better go back to Cabrioun. Get Sherry and Peyton."

"Take Mr. Vok," Barbara begged. "I want Jeff and Rogan to stay here with me."

"I guess that's best." Latham looked from Barbara to the guide. "Come along, Madore."

The half-breed grunted, but made no objection. It was obvious that he did not relish remaining in the same house with Ogden. Latham called Thor and they set out.

Jeff took Kincaid's coat and his own and disappeared into the closet. Barbara dropped into the saddlebag chair near the end of the sofa. She kicked off her galoshes and drew her feet under her for warmth. Rogan stooped to build up the fire.

"I s'pose we all ought to have gone back after Sherry," said Barbara guiltily.

"What good would it have done?" Rogan threw a final log on the blaze and stood, dusting his hands. "There was no point in your going out in the cold again."

"It wasn't exactly the cold," she confessed. "Cabrioun is sort of shuddersome at night. The floor squeaks, and the plumbing bangs, and the wind makes nasty noises as if its throat had been cut." Her glance flickered to the left and she stared past him into the hall wing. "What's happened to Jeff?"

Rogan peered into the closet. "He's probably in the kitchen."

"I didn't see him go."

Kincaid shut the closet door and called down the passage.

"With you in a minute," Jeff answered.

The gambler strolled back to Barbara. "He's all right. You mustn't let this get you jumpy, too."

"I guess it has, a little." She huddled back in her chair. "It wasn't really scary before Mrs. Ogden was killed. I didn't know what the ghost was exactly, but I had some pretty good ideas. I mean, anybody could have done the raps that frightened Mrs. Ogden, and it would have been easy to make her scream by touching her with a stuffed glove on the end of one of those reaching sticks. The cold wind wasn't hard either, 'cause all Mr. Ogden had to do was open one of the upstairs windows."

Jeff came then, bearing a tray loaded with a steaming pot of cocoa, cups, and a box of little cakes. He seemed glad to be back with the others. "Well, have either of you had any ideas?"

"I haven't," Rogan admitted, "but my friend Philo Holmes"— he indicated Barbara—"has favored me with a few deductions."

"I've got more, too." She regarded him over the rim of her cup. "Remember the ghost thing that scared Mr. Ogden and Mr. Vok and Thor when they went hunting for tracks? Well, suppose an owl really did fly out at them, and they all jumped—just like anybody would. And then Mr. Ogden saw his chance to turn it into a mystery."

Jeff snatched at the idea. "He could have worked it that way. Horned owls are scary as Hell if you've never seen one before. All Ogden had to do was shout 'It's Désanat!' and start running. Vok would have run too, unless he's a better man than I think he is."

Rogan took a rubber pouch from his pocket and began to fill his pipe.

"What about Thor?"

"Pooh," said Barbara. "Thor's an old 'fraidy-cat. Look how he behaved when we tried to get him to go down the hall."

"That's what I'm thinking about," Rogan assured her.

Jeff frowned. "I don't know why Thor was scared in the hall, but there's nothing queer about the way he acted over this owl business. Take that dog outside any time and start to run. He'll run too. And he'll run by you because he can go faster." The frown deepened. "I'm not so sure about Mr. Ogden, though. He's a believer. I can't picture him faking spooks."

Miss Daventry waived the point. "All right, then, maybe he saw an owl and *thought* it was a ghost. Anyway, I'm not so sure Mr. Ogden *is* a believer. He didn't act like one. You said yourself nobody could talk a believer out of believing, even when they showed him how he'd been fooled. Well, as soon as Mr. Vok explained about the alcohol and things, Mr. Ogden stopped believing right away."

"People are different. If Mr. Ogden hadn't been sure his wife was a genuine medium, he'd never have taken a chance on having Vok expose her."

Barbara sniffed. "Maybe he wanted her exposed."

"Why should . . . ?" Jeff broke off as a new thought struck him. "By God, he might have at that!" He glanced around the corner of the fireplace toward the gun-room door. When he spoke again it was in a voice lowered almost to a whisper. "Babs' idea clears up something that's been bothering me all evening. It was dark as Hell at the séance. *How did Ogden know that what touched him on the shoulder was a moccasin?*"

"He could feel it, couldn't he?"

"With what?" Jeff walked over to the girl. "Close your eyes."

Obediently she screwed them tight. Jeff took Rogan's pouch and touched her on the shoulder. She tilted her head and pressed her cheek against the rubber.

"Jeff, that's mean!"

The blue eyes flew open, but Jeff tossed the pouch over her shoulder before she could see it.

"Well, what was it?"

"One of my galoshes." She rubbed her cheek. "Of all the dirty tricks!"

"Wrong. It was Rogan's tobacco pouch." Jeff retrieved it and tossed it to the gambler. "You see, Mr. Ogden couldn't have known it was a moccasin *unless he felt it with his fingers.*"

"But," Barbara objected, "Rogan and Mr. Ambler were holding him."

"They just thought they were. Remember Mr. Vok showed you how a medium could get one hand loose? What'll you bet Mr. Ogden didn't know that trick all along?"

"He could have, couldn't he?" Barbara rose half out of her chair in her excitement. "If he'd wanted to make certain Mr. Vok exposed his wife, Mr. Ogden could have kept one hand free to help out. Maybe he pulled that star off the reaching stick so we'd be sure to find evidence."

Rogan laughed. "You can't have it both ways. If Ogden played the ghost he didn't need a trick to find out what kind of shoes he was wearing. Besides, imagination runs riot at séances. Ogden might have thought a moccasin touched him, even if it were only that stuffed glove his wife had. Barbara's other explanations may be true, but none of them point to any particular person."

Barbara's mouth formed a little 'O' of surprise. "But the prints *prove* Mr. Ogden did it."

"I'm afraid," Rogan told her, "that this isn't a case where anything *proves* anything else."

"But," she persisted, "he was the only one who had a motive. He was awfully tired of his wife. She said herself he married her for her money. Now he's got the money and he doesn't have to sit around and watch her take on weight."

"Ogden obviously had a motive," Rogan conceded, "but so did other people."

Jeff scowled. "Who, for instance?"

"You, for instance."

"Me?"

"Of course. Your interests are bound up with your uncle's. Mrs. Ogden's plans for Onawa threatened him with bankruptcy."

"But that was all settled before she was killed."

"True, but you had a taste of how dangerous she was. She might try something else equally serious tomorrow. You knew you'd never be safe so long as your whole future was at the mercy of a silly woman's next brain-storm. You had a good chance to kill her under cover of the ghost business."

Jeff exploded. "You're crazy! And you're crazier still if you think I wanted Mrs. Ogden dead, or that Uncle Luke did, either. She wasn't always easy to deal with, but her husband's going to be a Hell of a lot worse."

"Of course. So now you're trying to have Ogden hung for murdering his wife. Then you'll be rid of them both."

"Why, you . . . !" Jeff strode forward.

Barbara jumped from her chair and caught his arm. "No, Jeff, please! He doesn't mean it. I'm sure he doesn't!"

"Furthermore," said Rogan, "never hit a man when he's sitting down. He might kick you in the shins."

Jeff glowered. "Do you really think I killed Mrs. Ogden?" he demanded belligerently.

"I didn't, but I'm beginning to. However, the only point I'm making at the moment is that you had a motive."

"It's the only point you could make."

"Not at all. One of the big mysteries in this business is how the ghost at the séance managed to vanish while you were in the hall and I was standing at the mouth of it. If you were the ghost you could have 'disappeared' by merely taking off your make-up. Frankly, I don't see how anyone else could have worked the trick at all."

Jeff's fists clenched till his knuckles showed white. "Go on. What else did I do?"

"I haven't the faintest idea, but for all I know you could have done everything."

"No, by God! I'll tell you one thing I couldn't have done—not possibly. I couldn't have made those tracks we saw in the snow."

"True," Rogan conceded judicially. "Your feet are as large as mine and nearly as large as Vok's. None of us could have squeezed into the boots that made the tracks—particularly as Ogden appears to have been wearing them at the time."

Jeff's expression was a curious mixture of relief and bewilderment. "What the Hell do you mean by that?"

"I'm not quite certain. However, it occurs to me that if you didn't vanish after the séance, no one else could have—except Désanat."

Feet crunched on the snow outside. Rogan crossed to the door and opened it.

"Hello, we didn't expect a butler." Sherry entered, followed by Ambler and the magician. "Babs darling, I picked out some things for you, and Mr. Vok brought them. I hope I got the right ones."

Barbara thrust her feet into her galoshes and clumped over. "Anything so I can get this fur coat off. I'm frying, Egypt, frying." She tilted her head and looked up at Jeff. "Where does a girl change her clothes?"

"There are six rooms upstairs, but the kitchen's warmer."

"Home is where the hearth is. Will you carry my bag, please?"

Jeff picked up her suitcase and followed the girls down the passage. Ambler hung Vok's cloak and his own mackinaw in the closet and then sat in the saddlebag chair Barbara had vacated. The Czech had already taken his place before the fire.

"Luke insisted that someone should remain at Cabrioun with Mrs. Ogden's body," the professor told Rogan. "Mr. Vok offered to do it, but Luke felt it ought to be an old friend, and that both Mr. Vok and I should come here with Sherry."

"I gather," observed Rogan, "that Madore isn't sharing his vigil?"

"He is not. If he were, I wouldn't have left Luke. We bundled Madore off to his own little nest and I hope he stays there."

Jeff returned from the kitchen, glanced doubtfully at Rogan, and threw himself on the sofa. "I don't suppose you found out anything else at Cabrioun?" he asked Ambler.

"I'm not sure there was anything to find. I've been over the whole business in my mind several times and I'm beginning to fear that no solution will stand up which does not include Désanat."

"My dear Professor," Vok protested. "All through the ages people have felt that because they could not explain a thing in natural terms they were forced to accept a mystical interpretation. Savages, unable to realize that the sun was a fiery ball, argued that therefore it must be a god. Even the Christian Fathers were equally credulous. Tertullian said, 'I believe because it is impossible,' which was another way of saying he believed that anything he could not comprehend must be supernatural. Can you not see that you are doing the same thing? As soon as I showed how Mrs. Ogden read your question tonight you accepted it, but before that, when you could find no possible solution, you were inclined to credit her with clairvoyance. Do not make now the same mistake. Do not conclude that because no one has hit upon a rational explanation for the happenings of tonight, possession is proved."

"It isn't so simple as that," replied Ambler. "This hasn't been my only experience with the inexplicable. When an anthropologist has done as much field work as I have, he loses a large part of his skepticism. In any event, possession is far more than a trick. The evidence is too circumstantial to be dismissed. Hundreds of cases have been studied by competent psychologists."

Vok's black brows arched. "Even a psychologist may be deceived."

"I'm talking about cases where deception in any ordinary sense was out of the question. William James, for instance, reports an example from Illinois in which a fourteen-year-old girl was possessed by the spirit of a woman who had died when the girl was only two. The girl took on the personality of the dead woman completely. She remembered everyone the woman had known, recognizing them and calling them by name. She spoke of hundreds of incidents in the dead woman's life. James went to a great deal of trouble to verify his facts, and there seems no possible reason to doubt them."

"If they are as unusual as that," Vok retorted, "I should say there was every reason to doubt them."

"They are not unusual. They merely aren't written up in places where the ordinary person is likely to run across them. Oesterreich has collected enough instances to fill a large volume. I've seen two cases myself."

"Are you sure they weren't ordinary schizophreniacs—what most people would call 'split personalities'?"

"If they were," Ambler replied, "it is a name—not an explanation. That suggestion is far from new. C. G. Jung, who was Freud's best-known pupil, and Hans Friemark both tried to account for their cases that way, although the symptoms they describe are obviously beyond the powers of any sane mind, let alone a disordered one. I suppose the split-personality diagnosis sounded scientific. Certainly the two cases of possession I saw could not have been explained so easily."

"Tell us about them," Jeff demanded.

"One was in China," responded Ambler. "The victim was a sickly-looking boy of twelve. When his fits were on him it took five husky men to hold him. The other case was in southern France—the eleven-year-old daughter of an innkeeper with whom I stayed. I saw two of her attacks. Both times she spoke in the deep voice of a man, a full octave below any tone she could normally make. More remarkable still, she spoke in excellent classical Greek. When things like that happen, most psychologists don't try to explain them. They save their arguments for the easy cases."

"I guess you're right," Jeff acknowledged ruefully. "I don't mean I believe in possession, but calling Mr. Ogden a mental case wouldn't account for what's happened. Maybe a split personality could make him strong. Maybe it could make him talk Greek, or Algonquin, or Provençal French. But nobody can tell me that because a man is lightheaded he can 'float through the air with the greatest of ease.'"

"Come and get it." Barbara emerged from the passage with a pot of coffee in her right hand and a precariously balanced stack of cups in her left. Sherry followed, bearing a huge plate of sandwiches. Jeff took the coffee from Barbara and began to fill the cups.

"I was going to make more cocoa," she explained, "but Sherry said you'd rather have coffee. Have you men figured things out yet?"

Jeff snorted. "It gets worse all the time. Nothing seems to fit except the ghost idea, and Mr. Vok and I can't take any stock in that."

"I wish I couldn't either," Sherry said, "but I can't help it. There's too much evidence."

"Everything that has happened tonight—" Vok began.

"It's not only tonight," Sherry interrupted him, "but there's so much else. If there weren't *something* back of spiritualism so many successful men wouldn't believe in it. I don't mean just people like Luke, but scientists like Sir Oliver Lodge and Sir William Crooks—men who are really famous."

"In their own lines," Jeff emended. "They weren't used to being hoaxed, so they didn't know how to protect themselves."

"He is right, Miss Sherry, believe me," Vok assured her. "One may make a mistake in a laboratory, but test tubes do not lie awake at night planning ways to deceive."

"Besides," contributed Barbara, "all the famous men who fall for spiritualism are so old they owe the undertaker money."

"Yeah," Jeff agreed. "They know they'll be dead soon, but they want to think they'll survive in some way, even if they can't do anything more dignified than push a ouija board around."

"That's not true," protested Sherry, "not about all of them, anyway. There's a celebrated English magician named Will Goldston. You must have heard of him, Mr. Vok. He believes in spirits."

"There is also Harry Price," said Ambler, "head of the London Society for Psychical Research. He has written a number of books describing his scientific investigations of things which cannot be explained by ordinary laws. Then there are the Rhine experiments in extrasensory perception, the Sinclair experiments in clairvoyance, and Dr. Alexis Carrel's expressed belief in thought transference. You'll find more evidence in Seabrook's *Witchcraft,* and every now and then magazines like *Coronet* and *Reader's Digest* publish a number of well-authenticated experiences with the unknown. You might deny one story, or a dozen stories, but when you are faced by all the cases in which well-known men, with nothing to gain except perhaps the scorn of their neighbors, have put themselves on record as witnesses to supernatural happenings, you certainly cannot dismiss those happenings as mere tricks."

Vok said, "There is also such a thing as hallucination."

"Are you suggesting that Mrs. Ogden was murdered by an hallucination?" Ambler retorted.

"I am suggesting that we were deceived."

"Which," observed Rogan, "brings us right back where we started."

"Gracious," Barbara exclaimed, "I'm glad Sherry made the coffee. It doesn't look as if any of us will get much sleep tonight."

Ambler smiled at her. "Don't tell me you need coffee to keep you awake?"

"Good heavens," Sherry gasped. "I almost forgot. Frank will go crazy if he lies there thinking about what's happened. I found Irene's veronal and brought it over for him."

"He's been doing all right on brandy," Jeff assured her.

"No doubt, but he ought not to have any more. He isn't used to it. This is better." She held up the bottle.

Rogan stood. "Come on. We'll give it to him." He held out his hand to Jeff for the key, and then walked with Sherry to the gun-room door.

The girl put her ear against the wood. "I can hear him moving." She rapped lightly.

Ogden's voice asked, "Who's there?"

"Sherry. I was afraid you'd stay awake, so I brought you some veronal."

Rogan turned the key. The door opened and Ogden's drawn face appeared in the crack. He held out his hand for the bottle.

"Irene's legacy. Thanks. I don't suppose I'll ever sleep again without this." His eyes flickered to Rogan. "Don't forget to fasten the door."

As the latch clicked, Kincaid twisted the key in the lock. Sherry caught his arm.

"Did you . . . ?" She broke off and dragged him back to the others. Her face was white, and her gray eyes were wide with terror.

"It *was* Frank! He killed her. He'd taken off his coat, and just now when he put his arm out, there was dried blood on his shirt sleeve."

XVIII

The Turned Stone

The eyes with which he looks forth are not his own eyes.
—FLAVIUS PHILOSTRATUS

Ambler looked at Rogan for confirmation. "Sherry's right about the stain," the gambler told him. "It's on the outside of the forearm where Ogden can't see it. Of course it may be blood from the deer you killed."

"No," replied the professor. "From where I sit I could see Ogden's sleeve when he held out his hand for the bottle you gave him. He's changed his shirt since we came back from our hunt—so if there is blood on the one he is wearing now, it is not deer blood."

"Whew!" Sherry let out her breath and dropped on the sofa.

Jeff exulted. "I guess that proves Ogden did it."

"There you go again," said Rogan. "Find a fact and you start building a gallows. How did the blood get on Ogden's sleeve? While his wife was being killed he was locked in his room here. How did he get to Cabrioun and back without touching the hundred feet of bare snow at either end? Don't fool yourself. The

180

stain doesn't prove Ogden's guilty. So far we haven't found a bit of indisputable evidence against anyone."

Jeff's anger returned. "The Hell we haven't! What about the boot tracks? They're Ogden's. And what about the fingerprints on the gun?"

"You saw those, then?" Vok asked.

"Yes, and checked them, too—with a lens."

"We may not be learning much, Mr. Vok," said the professor, "but at least we aren't leaving any stone unturned."

Vok smote his forehead. "Oh, but we are!" He sprang to his feet and raced around the corner of the fireplace. A moment later he was back. "What did I do with my cloak?"

"I hung it in the closet." Ambler pointed. "Right there, between the end of the fireplace and the corridor. But don't tell me you're going out?"

The Czech put a finger beside his nose. "Of course, and when I come back I shall bring with me the stone we have not turned—unshakable proof of the murderer's guilt!" He pulled open the closet door and disappeared within.

Jeff stood. "Get my coat, too," he called.

Vok's head popped around the edge of the door.

"But why?"

"You can't go by yourself."

"Of course I can." Vok emerged with his cloak, which he flung around his shoulders with a gesture that was more theatrical than ever. "The path is plain now. It has been tramped many times." He kicked the closet door shut.

"I guess," said Sherry, "Jeff wasn't thinking about the path."

"My dear young lady, every living person within five miles, except Madore and the excessively harmless Mr. Latham, is in this house." Vok strode across the room, caught up a small chair, and wedged it under the knob of Ogden's door. "You see?" He whirled back, picked a flashlight from the side table, and dropped his voice to the stage whisper of melodrama. "And if the living cannot hurt me, neither can the dead."

Sherry bit her lip. "I can talk like that too, here by the fire, but outside . . ."

"Outside the dead cannot harm me even if they would." The magician flung out a long arm and pointed to the gun room. "Not while their mortal instrument is locked behind that door!"

He muffled himself in his cloak as he turned, and a moment later the outer door crashed shut behind him.

" 'Dracula X. Vok in *Gore and Gumdrops.* Come and bring the kiddies.' " Miss Daventry's tiny shoe tapped disapproval. "Maybe he can't help looking like a skeleton from the family closet, but that's no reason he should clank his chains."

"I'm inclined to believe," declared Ambler, "that his theatrical background is responsible for his manner. Probably even his uncanny appearance is due more to his clothes than to the man himself."

"Maybe," Barbara conceded. "I admit he looks as if his suit belonged to two other fellows."

"No doubt it did. Refugees are often forced to wear clothes they did not select."

"To Hell with Vok," said Jeff. "Let's see if we can't clear up this Ogden business. His prints are on the gun." He glared at Rogan. "Nobody can deny that."

"The musket was twelve feet off the floor," Ambler reminded him. "The fact that Ogden touched it is meaningless until we can explain how he was able to reach it without either making a noise or being seen by Vok."

"Oooh, I know!" In her excitement Barbara held up her hand like a schoolgirl. "Lookit! He didn't have to touch the old gun tonight. He could have put the fingerprints on it any time—just so nobody was around, and he could use the ladder without being seen."

"Yeah!" Jeff crowed. "There's your explanation."

Ambler shook his head. "Ogden had the musket tonight. Vok saw it."

"Maybe Ogden fooled him with a deer rifle. Vok couldn't have told the difference."

"I wouldn't bet on it," said Rogan. "I wouldn't bet on the tracks either. Troudeau the Tracker claims—"

"What?" Ambler sat bolt upright. "Say that again."

"Madore claims—"

"No, no!" The professor waved a hand. "You mentioned a name."

"Troudeau? It's Madore's last name."

"Sure," Jeff put in. "Didn't you know? What's so funny about that?"

"Simply," Ambler informed him, "that the guide who was with Querns and Désanat when they were lost was named Troudeau."

"You mean Madore was Father's guide?" Sherry asked incredulously. "That's fantastic."

"I don't see why," Barbara protested. "You always did claim it was queer Mr. Ogden practically pensioned Madore by giving him a job up here."

"But that would mean Father and the Querns man didn't really get lost at all. Madore deliberately abandoned them."

"Uh-huh, and that Mr. Ogden paid him to do it—you know, like Uriah Heep in the Bible or somebody." She smiled at the professor. "Isn't that what you think?"

"I certainly agree that the possibility deserves serious consideration." He paused and then added slowly, "As a matter of fact, I have other information which ties in so perfectly with this new idea that I feel the time has come to bring it up. As most of you know, Mr. Ogden's personal income is from patent royalties on a wood-pulping process. However, he had no special training in chemistry. He used to be a patent lawyer. Walter Querns, on the other hand, was an industrial chemist. Ogden applied for his patent six months after Querns' death."

Jeff whistled. "That ties it!"

"Shhh!" Barbara whispered fiercely. "He'll hear you!"

Jeff dropped his voice. "Say Ogden was Querns' lawyer and knew the Désanats. That gave him a perfect setup. If he could put both Querns and Désanat out of the way he could steal Querns' patent, marry Désanat's widow for her money, and at the same time get control of big timber interests so he could exploit the patent instead of just peddling it around."

"The fact that two people happen to be named Troudeau," Rogan argued, "doesn't mean they're the same person. It's a common name in Canada."

"Still," said Barbara, "when both a woman's husbands have guides with the same name I suspect at least a family resemblance."

"Yes," Ambler agreed. "And when one Troudeau loses his party in the snow and the other turns out to be a brute like Madore, it's at least likely that there is only one Troudeau between them."

Rogan glanced at the professor. "You seem to have changed your mind."

"At least I'm beginning to believe Mr. Vok is right in holding the possession hypothesis was the result of logical despair. Certainly you'll admit that we should prefer a normal explanation to a paranormal one."

"I'd prefer the right one. Ogden doesn't strike me as the type to choose such a spectacular method of murder."

"He may well have counted on that line of reasoning." Ambler's eyes sought the gun-room door. "As the dead woman's husband he could not avoid suspicion, and he was almost certain to be found out unless he adopted some unusual method of disguising his crime. Apparently he decided that he would not deny killing his wife, but would claim he was possessed and prove it by pointing out that the murder could not have been accomplished by normal means. Such a scheme presents three important advantages. We, as witnesses, were led to watch for ghost details instead of murder details. As a result we saw all the wrong things and our testimony is nearly worthless. Furthermore, the situation is new, and therefore certain to bewilder the official mind. Finally, the prosecuting attorney must introduce all the ghost evidence. That will confuse the jury and give Ogden's lawyer an unlimited opportunity for sarcasm, which will confuse them still more. Under such conditions it will be almost impossible to secure a conviction."

"But," Sherry protested, "that doesn't explain things. Take the gun trick, for instance. That points straight at Frank, but it didn't help his plot."

"On the contrary. If this hypothesis is correct, the gun trick was the key move. It established the idea that Ogden could fly when he was possessed. It gave him an excuse to come here to the lodge so he would apparently be locked up when the murder was committed. Most important of all, it forced us to go outside where we could see the evidence he had prepared for us."

"How do you figure that?" Jeff asked. "For all Ogden knew we might have gone straight to bed."

"I think not. Under the circumstances he could be quite certain that we would not leave the girls with an unknown and rather *outré* foreigner like Vok."

Jeff turned triumphantly to Rogan. "That ought to satisfy you."

"Far from it. Let's stop trying to fool ourselves into thinking that a psychological impossibility is easier to get around than a physical impossibility. It isn't."

"Phooey! If a thing's physically impossible *no* one can do it. What you call a psychological impossibility is something anyone can get over by changing his mind."

"No one can really change his mind," Rogan insisted. "He must make out with the mind he has. If I could change my mind in the way you mean I might write poetry like Shakespeare or paint pictures like Rembrandt."

"Maybe you can't make your mind better," Jeff conceded grudgingly, "but you can certainly make it different."

"You can't even make it worse. Could you believe that the world is flat, or that the Germans are God's chosen people?"

Jeff grew surly. "What's this got to do with Ogden?"

"A great deal. Consider his mind. He's a frozen, secretive sort, but he's obvious enough. I've met hundreds just like him. You accuse that man of two crimes. One of them is a double murder by remote control. Ogden does not appear at all. Even his tool, Madore, makes no direct move, but leaves the actual killing to chance. Mrs. Ogden's death was the exact opposite. Her murderer is visible at every step. According to your theory he even plants evidence against himself. He welcomes a trial. Those simply are not two pictures of the same man. I wouldn't believe it if Ogden signed a confession."

"To Hell with psychology!" Jeff growled. "Stick to the facts!"

"All right. There's physical evidence in Ogden's favor, too. He couldn't have made the tracks. His method of walking is entirely different. Madore was positive of that. Furthermore, he said the trail wasn't like any he could remember. I pressed him, but all he would admit was that it reminded him of something."

Sherry drew a quick breath. "Rogan! Don't you see? That's it. Frank was wearing the boots, but he didn't walk like Frank. He walked like someone Madore had almost forgotten—Father!"

There was an uneasy silence. Ambler placed a hand on the girl's arm.

"I don't think that follows, my dear. Madore might have been misled if the boots were worn by someone who didn't fit them."

"Damn it!" Jeff exploded. "I don't care what Madore says. Nobody but Ogden could have worn the boots. All the rest of us were together while the tracks on the roof were being made."

"That's not strictly true," Ambler corrected him. "You were downstairs, presumably looking for the ax, and we have no information at all about your uncle."

"Latham might have had access to the boots, too," added Rogan.

Jeff gasped indignantly. "Say, what is this? Are you two trying to pin this on Uncle Luke and me?"

"My dear boy"—Ambler endeavored to pacify him—"Kincaid and I merely wish to be precise about the facts. Without that we shall get nowhere. Certainly we aren't trying to pin anything on anyone."

"You'd better not!" Jeff was still smarting from his earlier encounter with Rogan. "You aren't exactly in the clear yourself."

Sherry's frayed nerves snapped under the mounting tension in the room. She lashed out at Jeff.

"Don't be an idiot! Mr. Ambler didn't have anything to do with it. Can't you see it was Father?"

Attack from a new quarter was too much for Jeff. He struck back automatically.

"My God, you talk as if you *wanted* to believe your father did it. This ghost business is all bunk, I tell you. Don't be too sure about Mr. Ambler, either. The rest of us are too tall to have played the ghost we saw at the séance."

"What about Barbara?"

"You keep her out of this," Jeff stormed.

"Then you keep the rest of us out of it. We didn't do it. It was Father, I tell you."

"You're a fine one to say that, aren't you! Maybe you aren't so innocent yourself—trying to blame it on a dead man."

"Jeff!" Rogan's tone was ominous.

Jeff whirled on him.

"There are a lot of things you don't know about her. I haven't said anything before, but I'm damned if I'm going to have her dragging Babs into this. The Ogdens adopted Sherry, didn't they? She probably gets half of Mrs. Ogden's money. And don't think she couldn't use it. Her coming up here was funny, too. She never hung around the Ogdens if she could help it, and she never went to séances if she could help it. Ask her why she came this time."

Sherry jumped to her feet and faced him squarely.

"If you must know, I'll tell you. It was because your precious

Barbara asked me to bring her so she could see you, you big overgrown ninny!"

Barbara gasped. "Why, Sherry Ogden, that's a downright lie!"

"It is not!" Sherry flared. "You begged and begged, and because I was softhearted and gave in, this is the thanks I get."

"I think," Ambler said quietly, "that we'd all better sit down and count a hundred before we speak again."

Jeff was too furious to listen.

"You'd like that, wouldn't you? Suppose you tell us why you came up here. I don't believe you'd cut classes for a week just on the off chance that Ogden was pulling a fast one."

Ambler kept his temper. "As a matter of fact, I had a secondary reason. I have a sister in Providence and it seemed an excellent opportunity to spend Thanksgiving with her."

Out of the corner of his eye Rogan saw a flicker of conjecture draw Barbara's brows together, but before he had time to guess at its cause Sherry returned to the attack.

"Since coming up here seems to be suspicious, and Barbara says she didn't come to see Jeff, I'd like to know why she did come. She hasn't any sister in Providence!"

"I have a sister in Paradise," Barbara reproved her piously. "I hoped to get a message from her." She gazed at the professor with a rapt expression. "What's *your* sister's name?"

"Imogene. Why do you ask?"

"'Cause I thought it might be something like that. What's her last name?"

There was a dead silence. Then Ambler drew a long breath.

"I don't know why I should make a secret of it. Her name is Querns. Walter Querns was my brother-in-law."

"I sort of thought he might be," said Barbara. "You see, after the séance I gathered up the questions everybody had asked and opened them and I saw you'd called Mr. Querns 'Walter' and somebody else 'Gene,' and of course I thought of Gene Tierney. Then when you spoke about Providence, well, Mr. Latham had told us Mrs. Querns lived in Rhode Island, and Providence is about all there is to Rhode Island, isn't it? So I couldn't very well miss it—about your sister, I mean."

"I suppose you couldn't," the professor admitted. "You see," he explained, "Walter Querns was very close-mouthed. When he left on his last hunting trip, he told my sister nothing about his business affairs except that he had just completed work on a new manufacturing process and that the papers relating to it were in the hands of a patent attorney. Unfortunately, he forgot to add the attorney's name."

Ambler gave a tired smile. "Sherry doesn't remember me, but I knew her father fairly well. After his death I lost track of Mrs. Désanat and did not learn of her remarriage until Luke spoke of it in a letter about his Onawa difficulties. The letter also mentioned that her second husband held a patent under which Luke's firm had been operating for twelve years. Well, Désanat had left a widow and my brother-in-law had left a chemical patent. I investigated and discovered that Ogden had been a patent lawyer and had applied for his patent shortly after Walter Querns' death. With that much to go on, I felt that a trip up here was justified, particularly as I had grave doubts about Mrs. Ogden's good faith in the Onawa matter."

"That explains a lot of things," said Jeff, "but it doesn't explain why you kept so quiet about it."

Sherry flared again. "Stop being a fool! Professor Ambler is trying to get the patent back for his sister. Naturally he'd have a better chance of learning things if he kept quiet."

"Maybe. But he could have had other reasons, too. This patent business gives him a pretty good motive."

"For what?" she scoffed. "You don't seem to have noticed that it isn't Frank that's dead—it's Irene. That's why all these accusations are so silly. The professor had nothing to gain by killing her. I didn't either, because she and Frank made wills leaving everything to each other. You and Luke will probably be better off without Irene around to throw monkey wrenches, but it won't do you any real good unless you get rid of Frank, too. That's the whole situation. As long as my dear step-stepfather is alive, none of us gains by Irene's death."

Before anyone could reply, the door opened and Vok stamped in. It had started to snow, and his head and shoulders were covered with white.

"Did you get what you went after?" Jeff asked.

"Of course. However, I had trouble finding my way back. There is not only snow. There is wind, too, and the tracks we made have almost disappeared."

He advanced to the center of the group.

"Ladies and gentlemen, the celebrated entertainer and magician, Svetozar Vok, late of Czechoslovakia and once idol of all Europe, will now surpass himself and produce"—he thrust out his lips and gave a remarkably realistic imitation of rolling drums—"the evidence!"

Vok made no visible move, but from his hand, supported by its leather thong, dangled the tomahawk.

Barbara shrank back. "Is . . . is that what killed her? I don't want to see it."

"But our fingerprint expert will." Vok held the tomahawk out so Jeff could take it by the thong.

"You're right about that," Jeff assured him. "How's Uncle Luke bearing up?"

"Very well. However, I thought it best not to show him the stone ax. Instead, I told him I had gone after some sleeping medicine for Mr. Ogden."

Jeff glanced at the tomahawk. "This is sleeping medicine," he said grimly. "But it was Mrs. Ogden who took it. It's our job to find out who gave it to her." He turned to Barbara. "Babs, you're the custodian of the tool kit. Does it happen to contain any loose powder?"

"I have some." Sherry offered her compact.

While Jeff shook half of the powder into the palm of his left hand and returned the case, Vok removed his cape with the usual flourish and hung it in the closet. He watched Jeff place the tomahawk on the desk and bend over it, and then wandered to the gun room and inspected the chair wedged under the knob. Frowning, the Czech pressed his ear against the door. His face changed and he came back to the others.

"Ogden's not in his room!"

Ambler stared at him. "What makes you think that?"

"There's no sound of breathing."

"That hardly proves anything. Ogden may breathe very softly. You saw us nail the window shut and move the gun rack in front of it."

"Perhaps he left through the door before I blocked it with the chair."

"No, I'd thought of that," said the professor. "At one time I rather expected some other manifestation and I wanted to be sure where Ogden was, so I kept an eye on the door."

"Can you see it from there?"

The Czech's insistence nettled Ambler. "I can't see the door it-self, but because this room is L-shaped I can look along the wall of the hall wing. Nothing could have come out of Mr. Ogden's door without my noticing it."

"You hardly stood guard the whole time—like a cat at a mouse hole."

"It was less than five minutes," the professor informed him stiffly, "from the time I saw Mr. Ogden's hand and sleeve until you put the chair under the knob. I won't say I watched every minute of those five, but I did keep my face turned in that di-rection and the light is excellent. Even a slight movement must have caught my attention. I assure you Mr. Ogden is still in his room. Why are you making such a point of this?"

"Because," Vok retorted, "Mr. Ogden doesn't breathe softly, and right now he is not breathing at all."

Sherry's compact fell to the floor with a tinkle of breaking glass.

"Good Lord, the veronal! When I gave it to him he said something about its being Irene's legacy, and about never sleep-ing again without it. Do you suppose . . . ?"

"I certainly don't suppose it was a suicide threat," Ambler as-sured her.

"It will be well to make certain." Vok held out his hand for the key.

Instead of giving it to him, Rogan rose and crossed to the gun room. Silently he removed the chair. He unlocked the door and pushed it open. Light fell upon Ogden's pillow, but there was no head on it. Kincaid slipped through the door and flipped the switch.

The room was empty.

XIX

The Curse of the Hrosta

Then he dies a second time and forever.
          —ELIPHAS LÉVI, *Dogme de la Haute Magie*

"He's gone!" Sherry gasped.

Jeff called, "How?" and came running up, followed by Ambler and Barbara.

"Out the window," Vok pointed.

Jeff's jaw dropped. "He couldn't have."

"See for yourself."

The heavy gun rack had been shifted to one side. The nails in the lower part of the window frame had been drawn, and the sash lifted. Jeff stared in amazement.

"Well, I'll be damned!" He turned to Rogan, who had pulled open the door of the ammunition cupboard under the stairs and was staring at its empty shelves. "Looks as if your psychology was a little off. Ogden must have heard us talking and realized the game was up, so he crawled out the window and beat it for the border."

The gambler shook his head. "There's no use trying to clear up an impossible situation with an impossible solution."

"What other solution is there?" Jeff demanded. "Ogden handled the tomahawk, and he's the only one who did. You can check that for yourself if you like. Nobody in God's world could forge clear prints like those."

"Mr. Ogden made the prints on the musket too," Barbara added, "and that was a trick."

"I doubt it." Rogan swung to Vok. "Ogden told us you claimed that the gun he pointed at you was an old-fashioned flintlock. Was it?"

"Of course." The Czech was puzzled. "But I do not comprehend."

"Jeff thought Ogden might have fooled you with a deer rifle," Kincaid explained.

"But why . . . ? Oh, yes, I understand now. No, that was not the case. I had lighted a match before Mr. Ogden entered the room. I could see the musket quite plain—the hammer with the flint in it, the ramrod, everything. I remember it well because it surprised me."

Rogan swung back to Jeff. "There you are."

"Damn it!" Jeff boiled over again. "What difference does it make? Maybe Babs and I were wrong about the trick. But it had to be *some* kind of trick. Anyway, the prints on the tomahawk prove Ogden killed his wife."

"No. All they prove is that his hand struck the blows. There hasn't been much doubt about that for some time. How did Ogden manage to open the window? Why did he leave? I can think of one answer. He was asleep when he handled the musket. He was asleep when he used the tomahawk. Half an hour ago he took a dose of veronal."

"And I suppose every time he drops off to sleep Désanat takes charge!" Jeff sneered. "Good God, don't tell me you really believe that fairy tale?"

"Mr. Ambler will tell you that fairy tales aren't always funny," replied Rogan. "In any event, your picture of Ogden as a conscious murderer won't work. When we went to Cabrioun we saw Mrs. Ogden being killed while we were still thirty yards away. Once she was dead the murderer's job was finished. Yet he stayed in her room, shouting French curses and smashing mirrors although we were actually banging on the door. Ogden hasn't that much nerve. I doubt if any sane man has."

"Maybe he's crazy then," Jeff conceded. "Maybe Mr. Ambler's right about split personality making people a lot stronger than usual. It would have taken something like that for Ogden to have moved that cupboard when you and I could hardly lift it between us."

"No matter how crazy he was," said Rogan, "he couldn't have pulled the nails out of the window with his bare hands."

"The nails weren't driven all the way home," Vok reminded him. "Circus performers pull nails like that with their teeth. I can do it myself."

"No doubt, but I hardly think Ogden shares your talent. However, he has one of his own. He can fly." Rogan pointed to the window. "Ogden didn't crawl over the sill. The snow on it hasn't been touched. You take a look too, Vok. Could any of your circus friends manage that one? Diving head first won't work, because it's a fifteen-foot drop onto rocks outside. Also, five will get you a hundred that there aren't any prints on the snow down there."

Jeff scowled at the band of white on the window ledge. Then he marched into the living room and returned with a flashlight. He thrust his head through the opening and a moment later they saw the glow of his torch reflected on the falling flakes. For several minutes he persevered in his search. When at last he gave up and turned back to Rogan his face was grim.

"You're right about the tracks," he acknowledged. "There aren't any, but Ogden got out that window somehow, and I still don't think he flew."

They drifted back into the living room. Jeff pulled open the closet door and took out his coat. Barbara gazed at him in surprise.

"Where are you going?"

"Out after Ogden. Rogan can say what he likes, but I know Ogden killed his wife. I can't just sit here and let him get away."

"He won't get far in this snow," Vok remarked. "And you won't either, I'm afraid."

"I can try." Jeff turned to Rogan. "You're so keen on psychology. Doesn't the fact that Ogden's gone prove he's guilty? What else would take him out in this blizzard?"

Sherry caught her breath. "That's it, Jeff. Don't you see? He went after Luke!"

Vok rapped out a fearsome Czech oath and started for the coat closet. Jeff whirled.

"Good God! You don't believe that, do you?"

From the depths of the closet Vok shouted, "I do not." He reappeared with his cloak. "But I shall believe it still less when I find Mr. Latham alive and well."

Jeff dove for the main door, opened it, and swung round to face Rogan.

"I think this is crazy as Hell, but we can't be sure till we see Uncle Luke. I'll make better time alone. Follow me as fast as you can. I'll pick Madore up on the way. We may need him!"

He plunged through the door. Vok caught up two flashlights.

"Come on," he said impatiently. "Professor Ambler will guard the young ladies."

It took Rogan less than a minute to find his coat and struggle into it. Even that delay nearly proved disastrous. As they passed through the door, they stepped into a snowstorm so thick that it was like plunging into cotton wool. Jeff had already vanished. Even the glow of his flash was hidden, but Vok picked up the trail and started ahead. The gambler, misliking this mission, misliking the snow, and with a new uneasiness in his heart, followed.

Even in clear weather the journey would have been a test of nerves, but the snow turned it into a nightmare. The heavy flakes made a white wall into which their flashlights could barely penetrate. They were absolutely without protection. Anything might swoop out of that falling cloud to strike without warning. Every few yards the gnarled shape of some tree would loom out with a suddenness that set the strongest nerves jumping. Somewhere dawn was breaking, but in this snow-filled world there was no east—only the whiteness at the end of their flashlight beams took on a false transparency.

As they moved forward, Rogan became conscious of a growing sense of oppression—a feeling that something in the woods had changed. They had been struggling through the deepening drifts for five minutes before he realized what it was. The wind had stopped! All night he had grown accustomed to its presence, first sinking to a whisper, then rising to a shout. Now the air was utterly still. The snow floated softly down, a blanket of silence. There was no sound anywhere. Even his clumsy boots fell noiselessly.

A light appeared in the grayness ahead. Vok stopped and put out an arm.

"What is it?"

"We must be catching up to Jeff," said Rogan.

"I do not think so. The light is not moving. Besides, it is the wrong color."

Silently they crept forward. A dark blur appeared, grew more distinct, and a moment later Rogan made out the snow-streaked logs of a cabin.

"It's the guide's," he whispered. "I thought we were headed for Cabrioun."

"No. I've been following Jeff's trail. He said he was going after Madore. Remember?"

"Then why is the lamp still burning?"

Motioning Vok to stay where he was, Rogan moved to the window and peered in. Despite the coming of dawn, the room was still so dark that a lamp was needed, and by its light the half-breed was feverishly stuffing his belongings into a pack basket.

Kincaid waved Vok back and walked to the front door. The prints on the low stoop told their own story. Jeff had evidently knocked, asking for the guide's help, and been refused. He had apparently stood there arguing for some minutes, and then—convinced that he was wasting time—had hurried on.

A few seconds' thought gave Rogan a plan, and he proceeded to put it into execution. Standing well to one side, in case the half-breed took it into his head to shoot through the door, Rogan rapped sharply and at the same time called out:

"Madore, this is Mr. Kincaid. I'm on my way to Cabrioun and I thought it wasn't fair to leave you alone without your pistol."

Apparently he had chosen the right bait. There was a sound of furniture being thrust aside, bolts were shot back, and the door was opened far enough for the guide's face to appear. He held out his hand. As Madore's fingers closed on the pistol butt, Kincaid casually put his foot in the door.

"There's another thing, too," he remarked. "We've found out that Mr. Ogden killed his wife, but he's escaped. We need you to help us hunt for him."

The half-breed's face grew dark. *"Non!* Wat I care w'at M'sieu Ogden do?"

"Do you come out willingly?" Rogan demanded in French, "or must I take you by the collar to drag you?"

Madore's finger found the trigger, and the barrel swung up until it covered the space between the gambler's eyes.

"Maybe is better I shoot you now."

Rogan laughed. "You'll have need of that silver bullet for the windigo. Besides, the gun won't go off. I blew the priming out of the pan."

Madore pulled the trigger. Sparks flew, but there was no explosion. He tried to slam the door. Then realizing Rogan's boot made that impossible, he turned and ran to the far end of the cabin.

Kincaid threw his weight against the door. It gave only an inch or two. He drew back for a run when Vok stepped in front of him.

"No. Let me."

"Get out of the way," Rogan commanded. "He's priming that gun."

"We need his aid. You cannot force him to help us, but I can," Without waiting for a reply Vok twisted his gaunt body sidewise and slipped through the narrow opening like a shadow.

Rogan ran at the door, gained another two inches, and wriggled after the Czech. When he got his head into the room, he saw that Madore had his back to them and was bent over a shelf in the far corner. A moment later the guide tossed the extra powder into the fire, where it went off with a flash, and whirled with the leveled pistol in his fist.

"Now, by Gar . . . !"

The sight of the towering Czech, when he had expected Rogan, threw Madore off balance for a moment and gave Vok the opening he needed.

"Fool!"

The word rang like struck iron.

"Do you think that stupid toy can harm me? Fool! I could blast you where you stand. You, who are afraid of the windigo, would be wiser to fear me, for I am a wolf compared to whom all the windigos in the world are but silly sheep. I am a great magician of the Czechs. If you do not guide me, I shall launch against you the curse of the Hrosta. Once cast, that can never be withdrawn, and ten generations hence your descendants will revile your name. Their blood shall rot in their veins. Their eyes turn back in their sockets. Their wives shall give birth to living monsters, while the ghosts of their grandsires sit on their hearths gnawing their own bones."

It grew worse as it went on. The guide was visibly shaken. He drew back against a corner of the rough fireplace, and the dirty copper of his face turned the color of ashes. He still held the pistol thrust out in front of him, but it was evident that he no longer thought of it as a firearm. Instead he seemed to use it as a stick to ward off some invisible danger.

Vok threw back his head.

"Very well, I have warned you. Now I shall curse you."

He raised his gaunt arms until the sides of his cloak flapped like the wings of a giant bat, and began the incantation itself. It was in Czech, and Vok delivered it like an archbishop of Hell.

"Don't . . . don't . . ." Madore babbled. "Me can't go. Me can't go, I tole you!"

Vok chanted on. He played every stop in his actor's voice, so that it was now harsh like a raven, now sonorous as a bronze gong. Rogan had not believed any curse could live up to the description Vok had given, but this did. It was vitriol—and blood. The unknown words dripped foulness from all the charnel houses of the world.

> Šla Nanynka do zeli,
> Do zeli, do zeli,
> Natrhat tam jeteli,
> Jeteli, jetelicka
> Přšel za ni Pepicek,
> Rozdupal ji kosicek
> Ty, ty, ty, ty, ty, ty . . .

Sweat broke out on the guide's forehead, and rolled down into his eyes. He dashed his sleeve across them as if he were wiping away tears. The movement appeared to break his nerve, for almost instantly he was on his knees sobbing out prayers and entreaties.

"Non! Non! I do w'at you lak. Madore work for you—work lak nigger-horse . . . do anyt'ing you say . . . anyt'ing, but you no mak' heem go out w'ere M'sieu Désanat hees get me."

Vok paid no attention. The guttural periods of his anathema rolled forth as if the guide had not spoken.

Madore wept. "Torieu! Me can't go out dere . . . Me can't!"

Then his story came out. He had been Désanat's guide, as Ambler had guessed. Ogden had shown up at camp just before a blizzard. Madore had been cooking supper and waiting anxiously for his master and Walter Querns to return. Apparently the guide had recognized Ogden and been afraid of him. Madore gave no reason, but Rogan guessed that Ogden knew things which the half-breed preferred to keep secret.

Ogden, after learning that Désanat and Querns were absent, had told Madore that he came from them—that Querns had been hurt, and that Madore was to strike camp and bring tent and equipment to the fork of Bear River. Ogden pretended he was bound for the mission station after medical supplies.

Madore swore by every saint that he had suspected nothing until he reached the river and found no trace of the others. Then he had realized that Ogden was deliberately planning to abandon Désanat and his friend without supplies or shelter. He realized, too, that he would be accused of deserting the hunters. He swore—more to Désanat than to Vok—that he was innocent. However, by that time the storm had struck and night had fallen. Only the tent had saved Madore himself from death.

Vok gave no sign of having heard. His voice grew louder and his expression more intense. His black brows no longer arched across his mummy's face but came down until the eyes under them seemed to be evil animals watching from their lairs. His voice rose to a shriek, and the rough Czech consonants clashed together in a rhythm that was more than the guide could endure.

Afterward, Kincaid was never sure whether Madore surrendered or whether he merely fled in terror. He charged blindly for the door, pulled it open, and dashed through—with Rogan on his heels and Vok close behind.

"Stop him!" Vok shouted. "He's headed for the river. The ice there won't bear him!"

Madore may have heard. He looked back over his shoulder, then gave a strangled cry and pointed. Rogan turned and saw that something was following them—something that flew.

The dawn, shining through the snowflakes, filled the air with a fantastic light that blurred his vision. For a moment he thought the dark shape was the great horned owl of which Vok had spoken. Then he knew he was wrong. This was the size of a man.

He had barely time to make out the clawing hands on the ends of its up-crooked arms when he turned and ran. Before he could catch his stride he tripped over a root and fell. As he scrambled to his feet he saw Vok plunge past, with the soaring horror behind him. The Czech's panic-stricken voice was screaming:

"Madore . . . the silver bullet. . . . Shoot, man, shoot!"

From somewhere ahead came the crack of the guide's pistol.

Silence settled down—a silence which was harder to bear than any sound. For seconds that seemed eternities Rogan stood there, peering about him and wondering if he could follow his own trail back through the frozen death which surrounded him. Suddenly a huge black shape came bounding through the snow. He whirled to face it and sighed in thankfulness as he recognized Thor.

The dog circled him once, then sat and howled. Rogan shouted and heard an answering shout from his right. He turned to see a man's form emerge from the wall of whirling flakes. It was Latham.

"Did you see it?" he panted, his round face almost as white as the snow on his shoulders. "Did you see it? By God, Frank was right. I only half believed him, but he was right."

"Jeff may argue it, but we won't," Rogan responded. Then, "Do you think you can follow Vok's trail? He and Madore were headed toward the river."

"Then we'd better get after him." Latham searched the snow. "Yes, here are his tracks."

The three set out, Latham in the lead, with Thor crowding against him.

"Maybe Jeff saw the thing himself," Latham called back. "We were together until a minute ago. Got separated in this double-damned snow. Like swimming in a bowl of milk."

"Why did you leave Cabrioun?"

"You didn't come soon enough to please Jeff. He was all for getting back to the lodge. Had some tale about Frank killing Irene. Said Frank heard you talking about it and escaped. Wanted to set out after him. Left a note for you on the table and started. Hell's grate-bars! We couldn't even find the lodge. Jeff came around by Madore's, so he tried to cut across going back. Result: we got lost."

"If you hadn't, I'd have been here till spring."

"Watch it. Here's ice. Can't tell whether it's lake or river. If it's river and Vok's blundered onto the thin part, God help him."

"Maybe our flying friend got to him first."

Latham grunted. "If it did, he'd be better off in the river."

They picked their way gingerly across the snow-covered ice. Latham stopped and pointed.

"What's wrong?" Rogan asked.

"Trail breaks off to the right. Wait. What's Thor found?" Latham caught the Dane by the collar and pulled him back. "Blood!"

The two men stared at each other.

"Do you suppose it's . . . ?" Latham left the sentence unfinished.

Rogan shrugged. "We'd better find out."

They pressed forward. Every few steps there was a spot of red beside the trail. Thor pressed still closer to his master and whined.

"Look!" Latham pointed to the track. "He fell here. Didn't stop him, though."

"He can't be much further, now."

Another ten yards and Rogan made out a crawling figure, which the black cloak identified as Vok. Latham called and the Czech answered. As they came up he stopped and pointed to a dark shape on the snow some eight feet ahead.

"Thing . . . that flew," Vok gasped. "Whatever it . . . is. Madore must . . . hit it when . . . fired. I don't know . . . which one of us . . . it was following. After I saw it . . . didn't dare . . . look back. Just . . . kept . . . running."

"Are you hurt?"

"No . . . wind gave out and I fell."

"But the blood!"

"Came from him, I think." Again Vok pointed, pausing to regain his breath. "I saw drops of fresh blood . . . followed them. . . . Thought the guide had been wounded. The snow blinded me. I didn't see this till just before I heard you shout. . . . Then I realized . . . that although I had found bloodstains . . . I hadn't seen any footprints!"

Latham's eyes grew round. "You mean this thing got here without leaving any tracks?"

"Only the blood."

They circled it slowly. The body lay at right angles to the direction from which they had come, and the snow around it was unbroken. Thor sat on his haunches and began to howl.

"Think it's Ogden?" Latham's question was an awed whisper.

"It's certainly a man," Rogan replied. "We'd better have a look at him."

They knelt by the body.

"It's Ogden's coat," Latham announced. "He can't have been

here more than a minute or two. Snow's hardly begun to stick to his clothes. And look!" He pointed to the outstretched left hand, the index finger of which was twisted at an impossible angle.

Rogan caught the figure by the shoulder and rolled it over. There was a red hole in the chest, and the face was set in an expression of inhuman malice. Vok crawled on hands and knees to touch the cold wrist.

"It's Mr. Ogden's body," he said, "and it's empty."

XX

The Silver Bullet

After this scene I was as if transformed. I had come there as an unbeliever . . . to study . . . superstition. The experiences of an hour had sufficed to overthrow like a house of cards the independent ideas which I had acquired by years of study.
—JACOB FROMER, *Ghetto-Dämmerung*

WITH A sigh, Barbara turned from gazing through the frost-etched glass and dropped on the broad window-seat. Thor, who had been standing behind her, nudged her elbow with his nose. She took him by the ears and stared gloomily into his face.

"Why don't you give one of those nice mean barks of yore, huh?—the kind you give when Jeff's coming." They had carried Ogden's body back to his own house, and then Latham had gone on to the lodge for Ambler and the two girls. They were now gathered around the fire in the high living-room of Cabrioun. In spite of Ogden's death, and although all of them shared some measure of Barbara's anxiety for Jeff, the spirits of the group had revived. They seemed to feel that the danger was over, as if Ogden's death had made the pattern complete. Even the cheerless light of a gray dawn could not hold back their rising mood.

The reaction was greatest in Sherry, perhaps because she had felt the events of the night before more keenly. She moved about the room, telling Latham how Barbara had discovered the professor's relationship to Querns, and explaining the reasons for thinking that Ogden had stolen Querns' patent. Before she had quite finished, Thor began barking furiously, and a moment later they heard Jeff stamp the snow from his boots as he came along the porch. Barbara rushed to open the door, and he greeted her with a shamefaced grin.

"Jeff, where have you been?"

"Round and round. I got separated from Uncle Luke in the snowstorm and was trying to find him again. Then I heard a shout, and here comes Madore running like Hell. Vok's owl was flying after him and he was frightened out of his wits. I suppose he thought it was Ogden or somebody playing windigo. Anyway, he turned and took a crack at it with his precious silver bullet. He didn't wait to see if he'd hit anything—just dug in his toes and kept running like a greased jackrabbit."

Jeff turned to Latham.

"I was pretty well lost by that time, and I knew it wasn't any use hunting for you, so I concentrated on trying to find the lodge. It took quite a while. By the time I got there you'd all left, so I came on back. I suppose nobody found Ogden's tracks?"

"No," his uncle answered shortly, "but we found Ogden. He's dead."

"Dead! How?"

"You saw Madore shoot him."

"When? You mean . . . ? Why, that's insane."

"Unfortunately," Vok observed dryly, "that doesn't keep it from being true."

"Are you trying to tell me that what I saw was Ogden—flying?"

"Did you get a good look at it?" asked Rogan. "Madore did. That's why he used his silver bullet."

"So you all believe it now. That's fine. I suppose the next move is for you to clear out like Madore."

Sherry stared at him. "You mean Madore's gone?"

"For good. I guess he felt the atmosphere around here was so stiff with ghosts it stifled him. I wanted to find out what had happened to him so I stopped by his cabin on my way back. He'd taken everything he could carry and lit out."

"But how can he travel in this snowstorm?"

"He's half Indian. Besides, the snow's letting up. Getting out of this won't trouble Madore."

Ambler sighed. "I wish it wouldn't trouble us."

"What do you mean?" demanded Latham.

"Do you realize," the professor answered, "that we have two dead bodies on our hands, and that we can't possibly give the police a reasonable explanation of how they were killed?"

"But," said Sherry, "why can't we tell them exactly what's happened? Certainly they'll believe all of us."

Ambler shook his head. "I doubt if anyone outside our own group believes *any* of us for a long time to come."

"You mean they'll think one of us did it?" asked Barbara.

"Wouldn't you?"

"Surely," Sherry protested, "they couldn't convict any of us?"

"It would almost be better if they did. One chance in seven of being hung might not be as bad as the certainty of being covered by the cloud of this thing until we die. The only story we can tell is incredible. Because of that, everyone—even our nearest and dearest—will feel sure that we are partners in a murder pact, and the fact that they can't even guess at our motives will make them certain it's something diabolical."

"But they couldn't *do* anything," Barbara insisted.

"They wouldn't need to. We'll suffer just the same. For instance, I'll have to give up my chair at the University."

"But"—Sherry was aghast—"that will seem like a confession!"

"Of course, though people will be so convinced of our guilt, anyway, that a confession more or less will hardly matter. However, I couldn't drag the University into a scandal, even if it would save me. Which it wouldn't."

"Do you really think it will be as bad as that?" Barbara demanded.

"I think," Ambler told her, "that when you are an old, old woman some people will still be leery of you because you are 'Barbara Daventry—the one who was mixed up in those awful murders in New England . . . some sort of devil worship or human sacrifice, you know. They say the police never did get to the bottom of all the dreadful things that went on. . . .'"

Jeff scowled furiously. "What's the idea of trying to scare Babs?"

"I'm not," the professor assured him. "But we are in a very nasty position and the sooner we all realize it, the better."

"Maybe, but there's no sense weeping about it. Let's get busy and finish solving this case before we tell the police."

"Look, Jeff," Rogan put in. "Get it out of your head that this is something to be solved. It isn't. Somehow Désanat, or whatever it was, got loose at our séance and took possession of Ogden."

"I'm afraid there's no way of avoiding that conclusion now," Ambler agreed. "Désanat worked off his spite against his former wife by making Ogden kill her. Then he revenged himself on Ogden and obtained his own release by deliberately flying at Madore so that Ogden would be shot."

"Hell!" Jeff swung to Vok. "For God's sake, talk 'em out of this nonsense."

"I can't," replied the Czech. "You see, I found Ogden's body."

"You too? Last night you laughed at the idea."

"I have stopped laughing."

Jeff sneered. "I'd never have believed hardheaded men like you and Rogan would fall for this stuff."

"There's a difference between being hardheaded and being pigheaded," Kincaid retorted. "You're dodging the facts. Vok and I prefer to face them and not refuse to believe something that has been abundantly proved, merely because we neither understand it nor like it."

"Believe anything you please," Jeff stormed. "The police will believe the fingerprints."

"You think so? After we've carried the gun and the tomahawk over to the lodge and played around with them?"

"There are lots more prints," Jeff protested. "I went upstairs here before Uncle Luke and I started out. Ogden's prints are marked in blood on his wife's nightgown. The police can't get around that."

Rogan smiled. "You've led a sheltered life. The police will point out that we had Ogden's body and plenty of time to work. We could have put his prints anywhere we chose."

Sherry laid her hand on his arm. "What can we do, Rogan?"

"I don't know yet. Obviously our problem is to convince the coroner along some definite line and avoid an inconclusive investigation. That will be a difficult job, but at least Madore has run away and can't upset any story we choose to tell."

"Suppose," Barbara suggested, "he calms down in a few days and comes back?"

"I can promise you he won't." Vok raised his gaunt arms and chanted:

> Nanynka went to the cabbage patch,
>> Cabbage patch, cabbage patch,
>
> To pick a peck of clover,
>> A peck of pretty clover.
>
> Pepi followed after her
>> And kicked her basket over.

Rogan grinned. "I fear the Curse of the Hrosta loses some of its effectiveness in translation."

Miss Daventry became severe. "What in the world are you two talking about?"

"Madore," Rogan informed her solemnly. "During M. Troudeau's last few minutes among us, our friend here put the fear of Vok into him. Besides, we gathered a few excerpts from Madore's biography which will make him prefer to keep as many miles between himself and us as possible."

"You see," Vok explained, "we persuaded the guide to confess that he had caused the deaths of Miss Sherry's father and Mr. Querns by abandoning them. Also, that Mr. Ogden had forced him to do it."

Jeff caught at that. "Then, by God, I was right all along! If Ogden killed Désanat, he must have murdered Mrs. Ogden, too."

"I'm afraid that doesn't follow," said Ambler. "If Ogden was consciously responsible for his wife's death, then his own death is not merely inexplicable, it is incomprehensible. However, I doubt if that matters much to us now. Certainly the fact that Madore can't upset our story doesn't matter. We haven't one to tell."

"Maybe," Barbara offered hopefully, "the police would just take it for granted that Mr. Ogden killed his wife and then shot himself. I mean, if we fixed things to prove it, sort of."

Latham grunted. "Never get away with it. Nobody who ever knew Frank Ogden would believe he committed suicide—not if fifty witnesses swore they saw him do it. I wouldn't myself."

"Neither would I," Sherry agreed. "But there's one thing Frank *would* have done. He'd have stolen Mr. Querns' invention if he got the chance. We have proof of that anyway, even if it isn't the kind of proof that would stand up in court." She smiled at the professor. "Frank spent his patent royalties as fast as he got them, but I want to fix it so everything that comes in from now on will go to your sister."

Ambler thanked her. "You are very kind. If the police would be as generous about dispensing with legal proof, our troubles would be over."

"Huh!" Latham snorted. "'Tisn't proof we need for the police—it's plausibility."

"Even that won't help us," said Rogan. "We must avoid any investigation at all."

"Hell," Jeff groaned. "There's bound to be *some* investigation."

"I fear so," the professor acknowledged gloomily, "and if there is, even a good story wouldn't help. The police would trip one of us in some way."

"Exactly," said Rogan. "Therefore, it's best for most of us not to have any story."

Sherry's eyes brightened. "You mean you've got a plan?"

"Yes, but I warn you it isn't a pretty one. The snow's almost stopped now—enough for you to travel, anyway. Jeff told me yesterday that there's a place called Hall's Junction which isn't much further than Lynxhead, if you cut across country. The down train from the junction leaves this afternoon. I suggest that Mr. Ambler and Barbara decide to catch it. They'll make the trip on skis, leaving their luggage to be sent on when the roads are cleared. Latham, Sherry, and Jeff will go along for company. Vok and I will stay behind because we aren't up to a fourteen-mile round trip on skis."

"The rest of us aren't either," Latham grumbled.

"True, but you won't find that out till you get there. That will give you three an excuse to stay in the village overnight. By the time you get back everything will be over."

"What," asked Sherry, "are you going to do in the meanwhile?"

"Vok and I shall be preparing a skiing accident for the Ogdens. For that we'll make a toboggan out of a pair of skis and load the bodies onto it. I'll put on snowshoes, push the toboggan out on the river ice, and let it go through. The corpses will be carried under the lake ice and stay there until spring. By that time no country coroner will be able to tell they weren't drowned, even if he does an autopsy."

"Ours won't," Latham assured the gambler. "He isn't a doctor. He's an undertaker. Don't know I like the idea, though—treating the Ogdens' remains that way. What do you think, Peyton?"

"I don't like it either, and I daresay Kincaid likes it least of all, as he has to carry it out. However, I see no alternative. We have the girls to consider as well as ourselves. Even as concerns the Ogdens, Kincaid's plan seems desirable. If I had to choose between suffering a few indignities to my corpse, and having my character discussed in whispers for years afterward, I'd choose the former."

"Guess you're right," Latham conceded doubtfully. "What do you say, Jeff?"

"Oh, I'm for the plan, only it won't work. It leaves Rogan

standing on the edge of a hole in the ice. How's he going to get back without leaving a herringbone trail up the bank, and what's supposed to have happened to Madore?"

"Those two difficulties cancel out," Rogan responded. "I carry a pair of skis with me. I throw the snowshoes into the river and put on the skis. Vok tosses me a rope and pulls me up the bank, so I leave what looks like a downhill trail."

"The idea is, I take it," said Ambler, "that the Ogdens skied onto the river ice and it broke under them. Then Madore, on snowshoes, went to their rescue and was pulled in."

The gambler nodded.

"It ought to work," Jeff admitted. "Only I'll need the ski boots Rogan's wearing now, and all the skis up here have cable bindings, so he can't use 'em with ordinary boots."

"That's another reason why I can't go to Hall's Junction with you," Kincaid pointed out. "However, as far as the job here is concerned, I can stick my shoes into the toe plates of the skis. That will hold well enough for Vok to pull me up the bank."

"What is your plan after that?" inquired the Czech.

"You and I walk into Lynxhead for help. We say we went over to visit the Ogdens and found the trails leading down to the broken ice. We aren't woodsmen enough to be certain what's happened, but we fear the worst. It's hunting season, so the police—state and local—will be out in the woods. We pick up the likeliest-looking native we can find and bring him back with us. On the way we ply him with strong drink and the power of suggestion. I don't think we'll have any trouble in getting him to report an accident."

Jeff gave a short laugh. "You're a Hell of a guy. First you say the things that happened here weren't tricks. Then you work out a trick yourself to fool the police."

Rogan shrugged. "Only because the police will think we're liars if we *don't* fool them. It isn't just a matter of proving our conclusions. We can't even prove our facts. We've seen a dozen things with our own eyes that no one else will ever believe."

"I'm not so sure I believe 'em myself," Jeff replied with a wry grin. "I may not be able to explain the things I saw, but damn it, they were the sort of things that *could* have been faked."

"Not all of them," said Rogan. "You saw what Madore shot at, didn't you?"

"Yes, but not close enough to tell what it was. I thought it was a bird, though I'll grant you it was pretty big. Still it might have been a piece of dark paper blown by the wind."

"There wasn't any wind, but never mind that. The point is you know Madore shot at the thing. You saw him yourself."

"Oh, there's no doubt about *that.*"

"If I can prove to you it was Ogden that Madore shot, would you be convinced?"

"I couldn't help myself—but you can't prove it."

Rogan rose. "I can try. Come on." He led the way to the store-room where Ogden's body lay on a long table.

Jeff flinched at the expression on the dead face. "What have you brought me here for?"

"Because you saw Madore load his pistol—with a silver bullet. Later you saw him fire that bullet. Judging by the wound there's a bullet in Ogden now. If it's silver, and you saw it fired at something flying twenty feet in the air, then . . ." Rogan left the rest of the sentence unspoken.

"Maybe." Jeff stared dubiously at the body. "How are we going to find out?"

"By digging the bullet out of him." Rogan displayed a slender knife he had picked up on his way through the kitchen.

Jeff drew a deep breath, and held out his hand. "No, let me. I'd rather take a beating than touch him, but I've got to be sure. If you did it, I'd always be asking myself if you hadn't switched bullets just to convince me."

The task took ten ghastly minutes. Jeff was dripping with perspiration when he finally coaxed the metal ball to a place where he could reach it with his fingers. Gingerly he carried it to the kitchen where he doused water over it. It was silver, and Madore had scratched its surface with the initials J-M-J.

XXI

Exorcism

No less is proposed, therefore, than a universal solution of all problems.
　　　　　—ELIPHAS LÉVI, *Dogme de la Haute Magie*

THREE DAYS later Mr. Kincaid followed Sherry out of the diner of the southbound train. The girl entered her compartment and then turned in surprise as she realized he had halted in the doorway.

"Don't tell me you need an invitation?"

He winked. "I must return to my guest."

"I can't make you out. Why did you share your compartment with Mr. Vok?"

"Among other admirable qualities, the Czechs are fanatical about accepting favors they can't repay. Vok hasn't a cent. I told him American trains work somewhat like a hotel on the American plan, and that transportation goes with the compartment. He thinks he is occupying an upper berth which cost me nothing. As a matter of fact, it didn't. Now that Latham can log Onawa, he can afford to lose at poker." Rogan turned away. "I'll be back, but don't wait up for me." Sherry smiled wisely. "I won't, but hurry." When Mr. Kincaid reached his own compartment he found the Czech staring out at the white drifts as they flashed by in the light of the train.

Vok's welcoming smile was more Egyptian than ever.

"I scarcely expected you."

"Between beauty and duty I never hesitate." Rogan threw himself on the seat. "You see, I have a confession to make. That pistol I gave Madore—it wasn't the one I took away from him."

"I do not understand."

"The pistols were a pair. I didn't trust our guide to know a windigo when he saw one. I thought a good bang might satisfy Madore without hurting anyone else, so I put a little powder in the pistol I handed him. I didn't count on having to face it at close range."

Vok shook his head. "You must have given Madore the wrong one. Otherwise how did the silver bullet get into Ogden?"

"I put it there."

Vok blinked. Then: "Would it be indiscreet to inquire why?"

"I hoped it might induce the others to let me wind up the case without police interference. It did."

"But . . . how did Ogden get shot?"

"He didn't. He was stabbed."

"Who stabbed him?"

"You did."

Vok's smile faded, became a puzzled frown, and then returned—with a difference.

"May I ask where you obtained such an idea?"

"From Sherry's vanity case. You see, Ambler had suggested that the mirrors in Mrs. Ogden's room were smashed because ghosts don't like them. I didn't like his explanation, but I couldn't think of a better until Sherry dropped her compact and broke the mirror in it. Then I remembered that mirrors are made of glass. When you drop one it sounds exactly like a window-pane breaking. That reminded me that when I first searched Mrs. Ogden's closet there was no mirror in it, but after her death Ambler found a broken one on the closet floor. I decided that the extra mirror was important, and that the others had been smashed to avoid calling attention to it."

"Ah!" said Vok, "and you then recalled how, in my divination trick, I had dealt the whole pack to disguise the fact that only ten cards were significant. Your reasoning becomes clear. However, I trust that all my poor attempts to explain what happened at Cabrioun were not 'taken down in writing to be used in evidence against me.'"

"As a matter of fact," Rogan told him, "your pretense of trying to explain things was all that kept me from suspecting you at the start. You seemed so sincere and so genuinely baffled. It wasn't until I began checking that I realized you hadn't contributed one valid suggestion which we weren't about to think of for ourselves."

Vok shook his head. "I confess you disappoint me. All this is oversubtle. After your direct accusation, I expected some crushing evidence, or at least an explanation of how I might have performed the marvels at Cabrioun."

"I can supply both." Rogan's smile was as inscrutable as the Czech's. "Will a chronological treatment suit you?"

"Perfectly." Vok leaned his head back and let his eyes fall almost shut.

"During the first part of the séance," Rogan began, "Jeff sat on the arm of Barbara's chair because there were not enough places for all of us. Later, after we shifted, no one sat on the chair arm, yet all had seats. Obviously someone had stayed out of the circle so he could impersonate Désanat."

Vok opened one eye. "Not me. I am nearly a foot taller."

"We had no real means of judging the ghost's height," Rogan reminded him. "It looked short, but we thought in terms of people who stood on the landing. Difference in height is largely a matter of length of limb, and all we saw of the ghost was the luminous face and hands. By keeping your hands close to your face you disguised the length of your arms. Also, by leaning far over the rail with your face held vertically, you cut a foot off your apparent height and at the same time seemed to hang in space outside the balusters. To make the ghost's imaginary body appear to pass through the rail, you had only to draw back your head. When you straightened up to your full height the ghost, which Jeff believed to be very short, seemed to float a foot off the floor."

"The analysis is ingenious, but why apply it to me?"

"Because of the way the disappearance was worked. You circled through the bath into Ogden's room and bolted the connecting door after you. The darkness made it possible for you to cross the hall behind Jeff's back and slip into your room without being seen. Of course the door was only bolted on the bedroom side when Barbara tried it. You bolted it on the bathroom side when you pretended to try it. Getting the makeup off presented no problem, for it must have been a gauze or rubber mask with wig and beard attached. No doubt you possessed other masks which you hid in case we searched your trunk. The hands were probably phosphorescent gloves with the left index finger cut off. The bare finger under it would have been invisible in the dark. As a matter of fact, your statement that the make-up would have required some time to remove should have made me suspect you at once, for you must have seen a dozen quick-change artists who could shift make-up, costume, and all in twenty seconds. The tremendous impression of supernatural evil was due to your acting, but after hearing you deliver the Curse of the Hrosta I am no longer surprised."

Vok smiled gravely. "I am beginning to see myself in an unexpectedly sinister light. Is there more of this imaginary reconstruction?"

"The flintlock trick," said Rogan, "was entirely imaginary. Ogden never went to your room. You merely told him he had."

"No doubt the fingerprints on the gun were also imaginary."

"No, but they weren't Ogden's. They were yours. The prints on the card were yours, too. You substituted your card for the one that carried Ogden's prints. The idea back of the gun trick was to get Ogden out of the house and bring us there as witnesses for your star turn. And that takes us back to the broken mirrors."

"I am glad. I was beginning to think you had forgotten them."

"The whole charade in Mrs. Ogden's room was staged as a conjurer's alibi," Rogan went on. "You began by breaking the bathroom window and raising the sash. You'd found an old mirror somewhere. You stood the glass on the closet shelf and looped a length of black thread around it. You brought the thread out the crack of the closet door, and led it through the handle of the half-open door to the bathroom. When the glow of Jeff's flash told you we were coming, you made the shadows on the blind. I should have realized that those shadows were a little too opportune. You smashed things and cursed in French till you heard us pound on the door. Then you stepped backward out of the open bathroom window and lowered the sash. To maintain the fiction of the ghost's presence until the last moment, you stuck your head in the broken window, so you could shout and toss bric-a-brac through the doorway into the bedroom."

Rogan took his pipe from his pocket and began to fill it as he talked.

"By taking five steps backward you created what I thought was the incoming trail. That brought you in front of your own window, which was open. Even a high-school gymnast could have dived over that low sill without touching the snow, and I know you were an ex-acrobat because I saw your pictures of yourself in tights. Half a minute after the last crash in Mrs. Ogden's bedroom you appeared at your own door across the hall. When you broke into Mrs. Ogden's room you yanked the thread that pulled the mirror off the shelf and set the bathroom door in motion. With that you shouted, 'There he goes!' and dashed through the doorway. The deception was complete. It never occurred to any of us that we hadn't just missed seeing an escaping murderer crash through the window."

"Does your reconstruction," Vok asked, "include an explanation of how I could have made the tracks that ran to the rail, and how I happened to be wearing Ogden's boots at the time?"

"The tracks were part of the stage setting. You made them by vaulting the rail and re-entering the house through a kitchen window. As for the boots, Ogden was in such a dither that when he put on his hunting boots he took two from different pairs. You used their mates to make the tracks."

"Sketchy," Vok complained. "And offhand I would pronounce the kitchen-window stunt impractical. However, this is no time to interpose objections. I await breathlessly to hear how I made the tracks on the ground. Or did your ingenuity fail you at that point?"

"That was the easiest part of all," Rogan assured him, "once I realized that the tracks led from Cabrioun to the lodge and back, instead of the other way around. Ogden told us you went part way to the lodge with him. When you turned back, which must have occurred somewhere near the big pine, you took off your own shoes and left them in the path. You changed into the boots, which you'd carried under that magician's cloak of yours, and walked out to the middle of a nice patch of snow. Call your trail from the path to that point the 'feeder' trail. From the end of that feeder trail you jumped eight or ten feet and landed at what then became the beginning of the 'escape' trail, headed toward the lodge. Somewhere along your route you'd picked up a pole, possibly the boat hook I saw in the storeroom. When you reached the lodge end of the escape trail, you used the pole to make a downhill vault which automatically turned you half around and landed you twenty feet away—headed for Cabrioun. You walked back across the lake, passed the big pine, and jumped the last eight feet to the path. There you took off the boots and wiped out the prints they'd made. Finally you went back to where you'd left your own shoes, put them on, and finished your original trail to Cabrioun."

"You made it sound quite easy."

"The real trick came not so much in laying the trails as in 'finding' them. Jeff's discovery of the trail from which you'd jumped to the path gave you an excuse to leave him and go 'hunting' for the escape trail. You 'found' it by walking along your original feeder trail and scuffing that out of existence as you went. It never struck any of us as a coincidence that the 'finding' took place at the exact spot where the escape trail began."

"Ah, yes," said Vok, "and of course I obliterated the mark of the vaulting pole at the lodge end by planting a foot on it as I went down to look at the start of the lower trail. However, your 'track theory' is less good than your earlier standard, because the prints seem to have been made by the actual boots Ogden was wearing at the time. Jeff's identification was positive."

"And quite correct," Rogan agreed. "When you went to Ogden's room at the lodge to tell him of his wife's death, you still had on that convenient cloak. Under it you carried the boots with which the tracks had been made. It was easy for you to put them on the floor beside Ogden's bed and to pick up those he had originally worn. Naturally when he dressed he put on the ones you'd used."

Vok sighed. "After that it seems a positive shame to upset your beautiful theory with a hard fact." His feet rested on the seat beside Rogan. He waved them. "Alas, my feet are an inch longer than Ogden's. I could not possibly have squeezed them into his boots by any stretch of either imagination or shoe leather."

Rogan smiled. "I've been waiting for you to bring that up. You'll notice I've been using your own tactic of making a suggestion obvious and then waiting for the other fellow to offer it. Your shoe-size is what clinches the whole thing. It's a fair guess that you left Europe half a jump ahead of the Gestapo—probably in the middle of a performance, for you kept your magician's cloak and equipment but had to wear whatever street clothes you could pick up. Your shoes *must* have been too large, for no acrobat normally walks with a loose-footed shuffle. However, the real proof is that you went skiing with Sherry *before Jeff arrived and at a time when the only ski boots available were Ogden's.* No doubt they were a snug fit, but if you managed his ski boots you could manage his hunting boots too, and they changed your walk so much even Madore couldn't recognize it."

Kincaid placed a finger on the toe of Vok's shoe.

"Let's play it this way. Take this off. If your foot fits it even fairly closely I'll apologize."

Vok stared into the gambler's eyes. There was a long silence broken only by the roar of the train as it drove through the night. Finally the Czech shrugged.

"What do you want me to do?"

"Tell me the rest of your part in it. I can guess, but I'd rather be sure."

"Why not?" Vok made a gesture of resignation. "I went to Cabrioun intending to expose Mrs. Ogden. It was obvious from the start that she planned to simulate her first husband's ghost at the séance and make it support her refusal to have Onawa logged. Believers cling to their folly with amazing tenacity. If I wished to disabuse Ogden and Mr. Latham I should have to force the medium to confess."

"So you decided to turn the tables on her and impersonate Désanat yourself."

Vok nodded slowly. "I picked up a good deal of information about him from Ogden, and of course I saw the pictures on the walls. Then by good luck I heard Mrs. Ogden practicing her role. She had gone into the woods for privacy, but I happened to be out on the lake and she had forgotten how sound travels over ice. Miss Sherry was with me, but I don't think she heard and I gave no sign."

"The accent must have been easy for you, since you seem to have played a number of Provençal cities."

"So you knew that too?" Irony was never far from the Czech's tone but now it was tinged with bitterness. "I should have locked my trunk—or wouldn't that have mattered? Another thing I learned on the lake was that a well-known folk song was in some way connected with Désanat. That enabled me to give Mrs. Ogden a preliminary fright by imitating Miss Sherry's accordion on an harmonica."

"I heard you."

"That's right. I remember. It was immediately before I came downstairs with the note I had found in front of Mrs. Ogden's door. I confess I had taken that note at its face value, and when Miss Sherry laughed I was piqued. To bolster my dignity I wrote on the back of the card while I was pretending to scrutinize its face." He demonstrated with an inch-long stub of pencil, held point up between the tips of his first two fingers. "The message itself was chosen to be mildly mysterious, in the hope that Miss Sherry would repeat it to her stepmother."

"Your real masterpiece was the Dane. How did you persuade him to co-operate?"

"Ah"—Vok brightened for a moment—"that is sheer genius, but alas not mine. I learned the trick from a gypsy dog-trainer. Listen." He compressed his lips. "You hear only the faintest hiss, but to a dog it is a shrill squeal. The sound is too high-pitched for our ears. Possibly Thor had been trained on one of those whistles they call 'silent.' However, it is more likely that he was merely made nervous by a sound he did not understand."

The conjurer's enthusiasm faded. "As for the impersonation of Désanat, I am afraid I let myself be carried away. I desired to make sure of terrifying Mrs. Ogden, and at that time I had no idea Miss Sherry was Désanat's daughter. Perhaps it is as well I did not work the last trick I had planned. My intention was to set off the old musket as a climax. As you guessed, I had that afternoon loaded it with powder and looped a fish line around the trigger. However, just as I was about to fire it I heard Jeff's foot on the stair and realized I was being stalked. In exposure work, one learns to devise impromptu effects, and I realized that a convincing vanish was possible if I could lure Jeff to the end of the hall. I did, and the rest you know."

"All but one thing. What made Ogden think Désanat's moccasin had touched him?"

Vok frowned suddenly. "Because Désanat's moccasin *did* touch him. A pair of them served as a wall decoration in my room. I stuffed one with a towel and used it on my reaching rod."

The gaunt Czech seemed to have arrived at the end of his resources. His whole body sagged. Then he straightened again and faced the gambler squarely.

"I learned while in Canada that a magician does not easily earn a living in a strange country these days. I am at the end of my rope, so perhaps it does not matter that there is a noose in it. What do you intend to do with me?"

Kincaid opened his suitcase and drew out an unsealed envelope which he gave to the Czech. Vok read with growing surprise the letter it contained.

"But I do not understand. This is a recommendation to a theatrical booking agent in New York."

Rogan nodded. "Yes. I happen to know he needs a good magic act. Judging by your extemporaneous performance at Cabrioun I think you're his man."

"But if you think I murdered Mrs. Ogden . . . ?"

"I don't." Rogan blew a careful smoke ring. "Ogden did that. However, I wasn't absolutely sure you weren't an accomplice until you told me that what touched Mr. Ogden was really a moccasin. If it had been something else—a hand, say, or a padded glove—then Ogden was merely guessing and the incident was unimportant. However, if it were actually a moccasin, Ogden wasn't guessing—he knew, and he could only have known if he'd kept one hand free by a trick. That proved he'd lied about his belief in spiritualism, and had planned for you to expose his wife. You, of course, knew it was a moccasin and recognized the significance of the incident at once."

"I was furious," Vok said fiercely. "I had gone to Cabrioun in good faith to save Ogden from being imposed upon. The moccasin episode showed me I had been his dupe."

"I was fairly certain you felt that way. Before Ogden mentioned the moccasin you exposed everything that came up. Afterward you were baffled, a little too baffled."

"Yes," Vok admitted. "You see, my original plan had been to climax my exposures by exposing myself as the ghost. Now I decided to omit that. The Onawa situation had been covered, so Mr. Latham was safe. If I kept the ghost 'alive,' I thought I might protect Mrs. Ogden from whatever plan her husband had and punish him at the same time."

"At least the punishment was effective. The ghost that chased Ogden from the boathouse was too much for his nerves. What was the thing—some sort of kite?"

"Yes. My trunk contained a collapsible Chinese kite made in the form of a man. I decided to use that. In my stage séances it hangs in a box on the balcony rail and floats down over the audience at the climax of the performance. At Cabrioun I made Ogden fly it himself by attaching the thread to his coat with a small hook. When he ran up the outside steps the kite soared over the porch roof and broke the thread. Fortunately it swerved to one side and fell on the ground where I was able to recover it."

Rogan grinned. "For Madore's benefit, and mine."

Vok nodded. He was still a little unsure of himself, and at the moment the expression on his face was curiously reminiscent of a naughty child who thinks he has been funny and hopes his opinion is shared.

Rogan's grin broadened. "Your kite didn't trouble me too much. By then I had guessed what was going on and had decided my best plan was to play up to your magic. Also, I had begun to see the significance of some tangible evidence that I held." He took another envelope from his suitcase. "Sherry found this under the edge of the bed where Ogden must have flipped it."

Rogan handed the envelope to the Czech, who drew out the card it contained and stared at it with a bewildered frown.

"But this is a suicide note!"

"Perhaps. Nevertheless, it was written weeks or months before Mrs. Ogden's death. Unfortunately for her, her husband saved it."

"How can you know that?" Vok demanded.

"Look at the round blurs on the writing. They are tearstains where the ink ran, but *on the night of Mrs. Ogden's death she had only one pen, and that wrote in waterproof India ink.*"

Vok stared at the note. "This is proof of murder," he agreed, "but how did you reconcile the idea of a false suicide letter with Mrs. Ogden's wounds?"

"I reasoned that all the grisly trappings in the bedroom were part of the side issue you raised and not directly connected with Ogden's scheme. His plan wasn't hard to figure out. The Désan-at-Querns affair gave Ogden's recipe for murder: *Take advantage of a favorable opportunity; make someone else do the dirty work; avoid all suspicion that murder has been committed.* The situation at Cabrioun had all those features. Mrs. Ogden was an habitual suicide. Ogden knew you could be depended upon to expose his wife's mediumship. Once you did, a quarrel was inevitable and no one could blame him for it. Mrs. Ogden probably wouldn't try suicide again, but no one would be surprised if she did. In any case, the quarrel was certain to make her take veronal to put herself to sleep, and that was all Ogden needed. He procured a duplicate bottle filled with veronal in a concentrated form, so that even her regular dose would contain a lethal amount. At some time before the séance, he substituted the lethal bottle for the harmless one. Then, when he went upstairs to 'apologize' to his wife, he slipped the secondhand suicide note under her door. He had only to switch bottles back the next morning and he would have achieved another perfect crime."

"But how did you account for Mrs. Ogden's wounds—or didn't you?"

"Oh, yes," Rogan replied. "By that time I knew the tomahawk was a false clue. But it was the only reason for thinking the trail of blood ran from the bed to the bath. Suppose the trail ran in the other direction. Then Mrs. Ogden had been wounded near the tub and carried to her bed, dripping blood on the way. Was there anything in the bathroom that could have caused such injuries? Yes—the faucets of the tub itself. The wounds were four inches apart in a vertical line, which is about the distance between the faucet handles of a tub. Presumably Mrs. Ogden knew she was dying and made blindly for water like a hurt animal. She used up her last strength in opening the door and then crashed face-downward into the taps. Such a fall—more than four feet with her whole weight behind it—would have struck a terrible blow. The house was full of night noises, and apparently the plumbing groaned and banged at intervals, so one more bang wasn't noticed downstairs. However, I gather you heard it in the next room and rushed in."

"She lay there with her head hanging over the edge of the tub." Vok winced at the memory. "The amount of blood was incredible."

"Head wounds are gory things."

Vok nodded. "At first I thought her throat had been cut. She was still alive, so I carried her into her room. As I laid her on the bed the flow of blood stopped and I knew she was dead. As I stood there looking down at her, the desperateness of my position swept over me. I had built up an appearance of enmity to the poor lady, and with her blood on my hands I felt no one could credit my innocence. I lost my head completely. I rushed into the bathroom and cleansed the blood from the tub and from myself. It was not until I had nearly finished that I realized I had done the worst thing I could—I had made it impossible for anyone to believe my story."

He drew a small cloth-wrapped package from his pocket and began to unroll it. "You were right about the veronal. I was still on my knees by the tub when I noticed this." Vok held up a small bottle. "It was under the tub, a place one would never normally put anything, yet it was obviously new and half full. Then I remembered I had seen an identical bottle on the bedside table of Mrs. Ogden. Here it is." He held up the second bottle. "It is the one Miss Sherry later took to Ogden at the lodge. I found it in his pocket after he was dead. With the two bottles to go on I reasoned out what had happened just as you have. Then it occurred to me that the supernatural atmosphere I had already created would confuse the police and that I could not do better than to increase it, both to protect myself as much as possible and to make Ogden suffer for causing his wife's death. I never found time to develop a real plan. My ability to improvise had brought me out of Europe, and again I delivered myself to its keeping. The episode of the ghost kite had proved that Ogden was highly suggestible, and since then he'd dulled his wits with a quantity of unaccustomed brandy."

"No doubt the gun trick softened him up, too," Rogan commented. "From the point of view of a man who had just committed the perfect murder by poison, it must have seemed as if Grimaud were trying to avenge himself on Ogden by making him shoot his wife under circumstances in which he was certain to be caught redhanded. There was a fiendish poetic justice behind that which would have frightened anyone. Ogden must have seen through your scheme later, though. What gave you away?"

"From what he said when we met, I gather it was the boots. After we locked Ogden in the gun room, he was like a man in a nightmare. He was convinced that Désanat had controlled him. Nevertheless, Ogden kept searching, against all hope, for some fragment of evidence which would permit him to doubt. Of course the effects of the brandy were then wearing off and he was commencing to recover from the worst of his shock. So it hardly surprises that when he started to unfasten his boots he realized that each of them had a mate in the coat closet of Cabrioun, and that the condition of those mates offered him a test. If the boots at Cabrioun were dry, then he would know that he had worn the same boots all along and that therefore, of a certainty, he was possessed. But there was a chance that the Cabrioun boots were damp. If they were, then Ogden's boots had been switched and he had been tricked. Is it to be wondered that he could not wait for an answer? But if the boots were dry, he did not wish to share that knowledge with anyone. He decided to slip out secretly and see for himself."

"He tried to get away by the window, first, didn't he?" Rogan asked. "By that time I had a fair idea which side I was on, so I decided not to point out that Ogden could have used one of the rifles as a lever to shift that heavy cabinet, and that the hammer or some other projecting part of the gun would have enabled him to draw the nails from the sash."

"Yes," Vok agreed. "He gave up the window idea when he saw what a nasty jump it was. Then he realized that if the key of my lock had fit Mrs. Ogden's door, the key from the ammunition cupboard might open the gun-room door. However, the rest of his escape was most ingenious."

"Not really. Earlier that evening Jeff had disappeared out of the coat closet and down the passage to the kitchen. Ogden no doubt heard Barbara remark on it and must have realized that when the closet door was open, it hid that whole wall from any-one who wasn't actually in the hall wing. When Ogden heard you say you were leaving and going into the closet for your cloak, he knew he'd be screened while he slipped out the gun-room door, relocked it, and took the single step which was all that was necessary to carry him to the passage. There wouldn't have been any mystery if Ambler hadn't happened to be watching. Howev-er, you can hardly blame the professor for being fooled. He could always see nine-tenths of the hall wing, and he had too much on his mind to remember later that the closet door had masked the crucial spot for over half a minute."

"Ogden reached Cabrioun before me," said Vok, "and un-locked the front door with his own key while Mr. Latham was letting me in the back way. Ogden slipped into the coat closet and found the boots, which I had replaced. Of course they were damp, which made it plain to Ogden that he had been tricked. He remembered I had said I was going after 'proof of the mur-derer's guilt,' so when he heard me come downstairs and tell Mr. Latham that I had gone for the veronal, Ogden jumped to the conclusion that I had discovered the second veronal bottle and with it his secret. He found a hunting knife in the closet, and, when Mr. Latham went to let me out through the storeroom, Ogden followed us and hid in Miss Sherry's bedroom until Mr.

Latham passed back through the dining room. Ogden then slipped out the back door and followed me. Mr. Latham had no idea he had been in the house. Ogden told me how he had escaped and said he intended to kill me for my interference."

"It was probably more important to keep you quiet," Rogan observed. "He was in a really fine position for an impromptu murder. He could drop your body through the river ice and your disappearance would pass as another of the inexplicable events of the night. If he could get back to the gun room at the lodge without being seen, he even had an alibi. I take it he tried to kill you with the hunting knife?"

"Yes. Fortunately he held the blade down as they do in the American cinema, so it was easy for me to seize his wrist and turn the point away from myself. However, his rush carried us off our feet and the knife went into his chest as he fell."

"Leaving you with another body on your hands. You rose nobly to the occasion."

"My device was mostly a rehash of the ideas I had already used," Vok said frankly. "Also, as it was beginning to snow, it seemed well to turn that to account. Ogden had left the storeroom door of Cabrioun unlocked, so I slipped in, left the stone ax, and came away with the boat hook and a sheet. I carried Ogden's corpse to one of those bare spots on the lake where the wind had swept the ice free of snow and I would not leave footprints. There I covered him with the sheet, tucking it in so that none of the edge stuck past the body. I left the bare ice by the trail I had made when I entered. The snow was falling thick by then, and I knew I should need a fairly well-marked path if I were to find my way back to the corpse. I planted the boat hook in the snow to mark the beginning of the trail and returned to Cabrioun for the stone ax. The rest you know."

"Yes," Rogan agreed. "Once you got Madore outside his hut it was easy to fly your kite again and scare him into shooting at it. The blood on the trail was yours, of course?"

Vok rolled up his left sleeve and displayed a small half-healed cut near the elbow.

"I stopped about eight feet from the body and lifted the sheet off with my boat hook. I had already tied together the four corners, so when I raised the sheet it formed a bag which caught all the snow that had fallen on the body. I hurled the boat hook away and watched it bury itself in a drift. Then I walked back along my trail, scattering the snow under foot. The sheet I hid by wrapping it beneath my coat. When I heard the dog whine and knew you were following me, I dropped on hands and knees and crawled. In that way I effaced the tracks I had made walking back and forth."

"The illusion was perfect," Rogan told him. "Ogden looked as if he had fallen out of the air and landed in an inch of fresh snow. I hadn't finished working things out then, and for a moment I doubted not only my reasoning but my reason."

"I owe you a great deal for covering all the loose ends I left," Vok said. "When a man has devoted half a lifetime to sleight-of-hand, he can usually depend on it even in the tightest corners. I think I could have disposed of the fingerprints and other evidence before the police came, but it would have been touch and go."

"I'm glad if I helped, but you did a marvelous job by yourself. May I congratulate you?"

"No." Vok shook his head. "I am not a man of blood, in spite of Herr Heydrich's efforts to turn me into one. In the days since Ogden's death I have come to question my reading of his motives. Even your reconstruction does not entirely quench those doubts. The two veronal bottles and the false suicide note leave no doubt that Mrs. Ogden was murdered. However, we have no absolute proof that her husband killed her. It is still possible that someone else planted the poison and the note. If that is the case, by taking a course which drove Ogden to attack me I practically murdered him."

Rogan smiled. "You looked at the suicide note I gave you, but you didn't examine the envelope."

Vok took it from the seat where he had placed it and stared at it.

"But this is a business envelope."

"Nevertheless, Ogden used it to keep the suicide note in—clean and free from fingerprints. I found the envelope empty in his pocket. Somehow it got damp and the ink of the note came off on the inside of the envelope. You can even read a few letters."

"Yes," Vok replied, peering into the open envelope, "but the letters are not the same as the note. This reads 'emit,' then a 't,' then 'net.' Besides, this writing slopes forward, while Mrs. Ogden's leans backward."

Rogan laughed. "I'm glad I wasn't the only one who missed the point that the imprint on the envelope is a mirror image of the writing. The only letters you can read are those which are the same either way. An 'h' or a 'y' reversed is just a meaningless scrawl. Look." He took a small bottle from his bag and rubbed its contents on the envelope. "This is Mrs. Ogden's odorless alcohol." When the paper became transparent and the imprint showed through, Rogan slipped the note inside and adjusted it until the two sets of writing matched exactly.

"You see, 'net' is the 'ten' of 'forgot*ten*' reversed. The 't' forms part of 'wha*t*,' and 'emit' is 'time' read backward."

The conjurer let out a long breath. "My friend, you bring me life. I owe you my peace of mind."

"Sherry needs peace of mind, too." Rogan stood. "That business about her father wasn't too easy to bear."

"Yes, yes, of course," Vok said soberly. "She deserves the truth."

"Truth's precious. We mustn't squander it. However, she has a right to an explanation that makes Ogden a villain and leaves Désanat out of it. I've thought up a splendid one for her."

Rogan's knock on Sherry's door was answered by a soft, "Who's that?" Then, when he had given his name, an even softer, "Come in."

He turned the knob and stepped into darkness. Surprised, he found the switch and flipped it on. The lower berth had been made up. He smiled down at Sherry.

"So you finally got past the pink-silk-pantie stage."

THE END

DISCUSSION QUESTIONS

- Were you able to solve the mystery before the solution was given? If so, how?

- Did anything about the novel surprise you? If so, what?

- How did the cultural history of the era play into the novel? Did anything about the story help date it?

- How did the geographic setting of the novel contribute to its plot?

- How did this compare with other "impossible crime" novels that you've read?

- Did Hake Talbot's writing remind you of any contemporary authors of today? If so, which ones?

- Did you find the solution to the case credible?

All titles are available in hardcover and in trade paperback.

Order from your favorite bookstore or from
The Mysterious Bookshop, 58 Warren Street, New York, N.Y. 10007
(www.mysteriousbookshop.com).

Charlotte Armstrong, *The Chocolate Cobweb.* When Amanda Garth was born, a mix-up caused the hospital to briefly hand her over to the prestigious Garrison family instead of to her birth parents. The error was quickly fixed, Amanda was never told, and the secret was forgotten for twenty-three years … until her aunt revealed it in casual conversation. But what if the initial switch never actually occurred? **Introduction by A. J. Finn.**

Charlotte Armstrong, *The Unsuspected.* First published in 1946, this suspenseful novel opens with a young woman who has ostensibly hanged herself, leaving a suicide note. Her friend doesn't believe it and begins an investigation that puts her own life in jeopardy. It was filmed in 1947 by Warner Brothers, starring Claude Rains and Joan Caulfield. **Introduction by Otto Penzler.**

Anthony Boucher, *The Case of the Baker Street Irregulars.* When a studio announces a new hard-boiled Sherlock Holmes film, the Baker Street Irregulars begin a campaign to discredit it. Attempting to mollify them, the producers invite members to the set, where threats are received, each referring to one of the original Holmes tales, followed by murder. Fortunately, the amateur sleuths use Holmesian lessons to solve the crime. **Introduction by Otto Penzler.**

Anthony Boucher, *Rocket to the Morgue.* Hilary Foulkes has made so many enemies that it is difficult to speculate who was responsible for stabbing him nearly to death in a room with only one door through which no one was seen entering or leaving. This classic locked room mystery is populated by such thinly disguised science fiction legends as Robert Heinlein, L. Ron Hubbard, and John W. Campbell. **Introduction by F. Paul Wilson.**

Fredric Brown, *The Fabulous Clipjoint.* Brown's outstanding mystery won an Edgar as the best first novel of the year (1947). When Wallace Hunter is found dead in an alley after a long night of drinking, the police don't really care. But his teenage son Ed and his uncle Am, the carnival worker, are convinced that some things don't add up and the crime isn't what it seems to be. **Introduction by Lawrence Block.**

John Dickson Carr, *The Crooked Hinge.* Selected by a group of mystery experts as one of the 15 best impossible crime novels ever written, this is one of Gideon Fell's greatest challenges. Estranged from his family for 25 years, Sir John Farnleigh returns to England from America to claim his inheritance but another person turns up claiming that he can prove he is the real Sir John. Inevitably, one of them is murdered. **Introduction by Charles Todd.**

John Dickson Carr, *The Eight of Swords.* When Gideon Fell arrives at a crime scene, it appears to be straightforward enough. A man has been shot to death in an unlocked room and the likely perpetrator was a recent visitor. But Fell discovers inconsistencies and his investigations are complicated by an apparent poltergeist, some American gangsters, and two meddling amateur sleuths. **Introduction by Otto Penzler.**

John Dickson Carr, *The Mad Hatter Mystery.* A prankster has been stealing top hats all around London. Gideon Fell suspects that the same person may be responsible for the theft of a manuscript of a long-lost story by Edgar Allan Poe. The hats reappear in unexpected but conspicuous places but, when one is found on the head of a corpse by the Tower of London, it is evident that the thefts are more than pranks. **Introduction by Otto Penzler.**

John Dickson Carr, *The Plague Court Murders.* When murder occurs in a locked hut on Plague Court, an estate haunted by the ghost of a hangman's assistant who died a victim of the black death, Sir Henry Merrivale seeks a logical solution to a ghostly crime. A spiritual medium employed to rid the house of his spirit is found stabbed to death in a locked stone hut on the grounds, surrounded by an untouched circle of mud. **Introduction by Michael Dirda.**

John Dickson Carr, *The Red Widow Murders.* In a "haunted" mansion, the room known as the Red Widow's Chamber proves lethal to all who spend the night. Eight people investigate and the one who draws the ace of spades must sleep in it. The room is locked from the inside and watched all night by the others. When the door is unlocked, the victim has been poisoned. Enter Sir Henry Merrivale to solve the crime. **Introduction by Tom Mead.**

Frances Crane, *The Turquoise Shop.* In an arty little New Mexico town, Mona Brandon has arrived from the East and becomes the subject of gossip about her money, her influence, and the corpse in the nearby desert who may be her husband. Pat Holly, who runs the local gift shop, is as interested as anyone in the goings on—but even more in Pat Abbott, the detective investigating the possible murder. **Introduction by Anne Hillerman.**

Todd Downing, *Vultures in the Sky.* There is no end to the series of terrifying events that befall a luxury train bound for Mexico. First, a man dies when the train passes through a dark tunnel, then it comes to an abrupt stop in the middle of the desert. More deaths occur when night falls and the passengers panic when they realize they are trapped with a murderer on the loose. **Introduction by James Sallis.**

Mignon G. Eberhart, *Murder by an Aristocrat.* Nurse Keate is called to help a man who has been "accidentally" shot in the shoulder. When he is murdered while convalescing, it is clear that there was no accident. Although a killer is loose in the mansion, the family seems more concerned that news of the murder will leave their circle. *The New Yorker* wrote than "Eberhart can weave an almost flawless mystery." **Introduction by Nancy Pickard.**

Erle Stanley Gardner, *The Case of the Baited Hook.* Perry Mason gets a phone call in the middle of the night and his potential client says it's urgent, that he has two one-thousand-dollar bills that he will give him as a retainer, with an additional ten-thousand whenever he is called on to represent him. When

Mason takes the case, it is not for the caller but for a beautiful woman whose identity is hidden behind a mask. **Introduction by Otto Penzler.**

Erle Stanley Gardner, *The Case of the Borrowed Brunette.* A mysterious man named Mr. Hines has advertised a job for a woman who has to fulfill very specific physical requirements. Eva Martell, pretty but struggling in her career as a model, takes the job but her aunt smells a rat and hires Perry Mason to investigate. Her fears are realized when Hines turns up in the apartment with a bullet hole in his head. **Introduction by Otto Penzler.**

Erle Stanley Gardner, *The Case of the Careless Kitten.* Helen Kendal receives a mysterious phone call from her vanished uncle Franklin, long presumed dead, who urges her to contact Perry Mason. Soon, she finds herself the main suspect in the murder of an unfamiliar man. Her kitten has just survived a poisoning attempt—as has her aunt Matilda. What is the connection between Franklin's return and the murder attempts? **Introduction by Otto Penzler.**

Erle Stanley Gardner, *The Case of the Rolling Bones.* One of Gardner's most successful Perry Mason novels opens with a clear case of blackmail, though the person being blackmailed claims he isn't. It is not long before the police are searching for someone wanted for killing the same man in two different states—thirty-three years apart. The confounding puzzle of what happened to the dead man's toes is a challenge. **Introduction by Otto Penzler.**

Erle Stanley Gardner, *The Case of the Shoplifter's Shoe.* Most cases for Perry Mason involve murder but here he is hired because a young woman fears her aunt is a kleptomaniac. Sarah may not have been precisely the best guardian for a collection of valuable diamonds and, sure enough, they go missing. When the jeweler is found shot dead, Sarah is spotted leaving the murder scene with a bundle of gems stuffed in her purse. **Introduction by Otto Penzler.**

Erle Stanley Gardner, *The Bigger They Come.* Gardner's first novel using the pseudonym A.A. Fair starts off a series featuring the large and loud Bertha Cool and her employee, the small and meek Donald Lam. Given the job of delivering divorce papers to an evident crook,

Lam can't find him—but neither can the police. The *Los Angeles Times* called this book: "Breathlessly dramatic … an original." **Introduction by Otto Penzler.**

Frances Noyes Hart, *The Bellamy Trial*. Inspired by the real-life Hall-Mills case, the most sensational trial of its day, this is the story of Stephen Bellamy and Susan Ives, accused of murdering Bellamy's wife Madeleine. Eight days of dynamic testimony, some true, some not, make headlines for an enthralled public. Rex Stout called this historic courtroom thriller one of the ten best mysteries of all time. **Introduction by Hank Phillippi Ryan.**

H.F. Heard, *A Taste for Honey*. The elderly Mr. Mycroft quietly keeps bees in Sussex, where he is approached by the reclusive and somewhat misanthropic Mr. Silchester, whose honey supplier was found dead, stung to death by her bees. Mycroft, who shares many traits with Sherlock Holmes, sets out to find the vicious killer. Rex Stout described it as "sinister … a tale well and truly told." **Introduction by Otto Penzler.**

Dolores Hitchens, *The Alarm of the Black Cat*. Detective fiction aficionado Rachel Murdock has a peculiar meeting with a little girl and a dead toad, sparking her curiosity about a love triangle that has sparked anger. When the girl's great grandmother is found dead, Rachel and her cat Samantha work with a friend in the Los Angeles Police Department to get to the bottom of things. **Introduction by David Handler.**

Dolores Hitchens, *The Cat Saw Murder*. Miss Rachel Murdock, the highly intelligent 70-year-old amateur sleuth, is not entirely heartbroken when her slovenly, unattractive, bridge-cheating niece is murdered. Miss Rachel is happy to help the socially maladroit and somewhat bumbling Detective Lieutenant Stephen Mayhew, retaining her composure when a second brutal murder occurs. **Introduction by Joyce Carol Oates.**

Dorothy B. Hughes, *Dread Journey*. A bigshot Hollywood producer has worked on his magnum opus for years, hiring and firing one beautiful starlet after another. But Kitten Agnew's contract won't allow her to be fired, so she fears she might be terminated more permanently. Together with the producer on

a train journey from Hollywood to Chicago, Kitten becomes more terrified with each passing mile. **Introduction by Sarah Weinman.**

Dorothy B. Hughes, *Ride the Pink Horse*. When Sailor met Willis Douglass, he was just a poor kid who Douglass groomed to work as a confidential secretary. As the senator became increasingly corrupt, he knew he could count on Sailor to clean up his messes. No longer a senator, Douglass flees Chicago for Santa Fe, leaving behind a murder rap and Sailor as the prime suspect. Seeking vengeance, Sailor follows. **Introduction by Sara Paretsky.**

Dorothy B. Hughes, *The So Blue Marble*. Set in the glamorous world of New York high society, this novel became a suspense classic as twins from Europe try to steal a rare and beautiful gem owned by an aristocrat whose sister is an even more menacing presence. *The New Yorker* called it "Extraordinary … [Hughes'] brilliant descriptive powers make and unmake reality." **Introduction by Otto Penzler.**

W. Bolingbroke Johnson, *The Widening Stain*. After a cocktail party, the attractive Lucie Coindreau, a "black-eyed, black-haired Frenchwoman" visits the rare books wing of the library and apparently takes a head-first fall from an upper gallery. Dismissed as a horrible accident, it seems dubious when Professor Hyett is strangled while reading a priceless 12th-century manuscript, which has gone missing. **Introduction by Nicholas A. Basbanes**

Baynard Kendrick, *Blind Man's Bluff*. Blinded in World War II, Duncan Maclain forms a successful private detective agency, aided by his two dogs. Here, he is called on to solve the case of a blind man who plummets from the top of an eight-story building, apparently with no one present except his dead-drunk son. **Introduction by Otto Penzler.**

Baynard Kendrick, *The Odor of Violets*. Duncan Maclain, a blind former intelligence officer, is asked to investigate the murder of an actor in his Greenwich Village apartment. This would cause a stir at any time but, when the actor possesses secret government plans that then go missing, it's enough to interest the local police as well as the American government and Maclain, who suspects a German spy plot. **Introduction by Otto Penzler.**

C. Daly King, *Obelists at Sea*. On a cruise ship traveling from New York to Paris, the lights of the smoking room briefly go out, a gunshot crashes through the night, and a man is dead. Two detectives are on board but so are four psychiatrists who believe their professional knowledge can solve the case by understanding the psyche of the killer—each with a different theory. **Introduction by Martin Edwards.**

Jonathan Latimer, *Headed for a Hearse*. Featuring Bill Crane, the booze-soaked Chicago private detective, this humorous hard-boiled novel was filmed as *The Westland Case* in 1937 starring Preston Foster. Robert Westland has been framed for the grisly murder of his wife in a room with doors and windows locked from the inside. As the day of his execution nears, he relies on Crane to find the real murderer. **Introduction by Max Allan Collins**

Lange Lewis, *The Birthday Murder*. Victoria is a successful novelist and screenwriter and her husband is a movie director so their marriage seems almost too good to be true. Then, on her birthday, her happy new life comes crashing down when her husband is murdered using a method of poisoning that was described in one of her books. She quickly becomes the leading suspect. **Introduction by Randal S. Brandt.**

Frances and Richard Lockridge, *Death on the Aisle*. In one of the most beloved books to feature Mr. and Mrs. North, the body of a wealthy backer of a play is found dead in a seat of the 45th Street Theater. Pam is thrilled to engage in her favorite pastime—playing amateur sleuth—much to the annoyance of Jerry, her publisher husband. The Norths inspired a stage play, a film, and long-running radio and TV series. **Introduction by Otto Penzler.**

John P. Marquand, *Your Turn, Mr. Moto*. The first novel about Mr. Moto, originally titled *No Hero*, is the story of a World War I hero pilot who finds himself jobless during the Depression. In Tokyo for a big opportunity that falls apart, he meets a Japanese agent and his Russian colleague and the pilot suddenly finds himself caught in a web of intrigue. Peter Lorre played Mr. Moto in a series of popular films. **Introduction by Lawrence Block.**

Stuart Palmer, *The Penguin Pool Murder*. The first adventure of schoolteacher and dedicated amateur sleuth Hildegarde Withers occurs at the New York Aquarium when she and her young students notice a corpse in one of the tanks. It was published in 1931 and filmed the next year, starring Edna May Oliver as the American Miss Marple—though much funnier than her English counterpart. **Introduction by Otto Penzler.**

Stuart Palmer, *The Puzzle of the Happy Hooligan*. New York City schoolteacher Hildegarde Withers cannot resist "assisting" homicide detective Oliver Piper. In this novel, she is on vacation in Hollywood and on the set of a movie about Lizzie Borden when the screenwriter is found dead. Six comic films about Withers appeared in the 1930s, most successfully starring Edna May Oliver. **Introduction by Otto Penzler.**

Otto Penzler, ed., *Golden Age Bibliomysteries*. Stories of murder, theft, and suspense occur with alarming regularity in the unlikely world of books and bibliophiles, including bookshops, libraries, and private rare book collections, written by such giants of the mystery genre as Ellery Queen, Cornell Woolrich, Lawrence G. Blochman, Vincent Starrett, and Anthony Boucher. **Introduction by Otto Penzler.**

Otto Penzler, ed., *Golden Age Detective Stories*. The history of American mystery fiction has its pantheon of authors who have influenced and entertained readers for nearly a century, reaching its peak during the Golden Age, and this collection pays homage to the work of the most acclaimed: Cornell Woolrich, Erle Stanley Gardner, Craig Rice, Ellery Queen, Dorothy B. Hughes, Mary Roberts Rinehart, and more. **Introduction by Otto Penzler.**

Otto Penzler, ed., *Golden Age Locked Room Mysteries*. The so-called impossible crime category reached its zenith during the 1920s, 1930s, and 1940s, and this volume includes the greatest of the great authors who mastered the form: John Dickson Carr, Ellery Queen, C. Daly King, Clayton Rawson, and Erle Stanley Gardner. Like great magicians, these literary conjurors will baffle and delight readers. **Introduction by Otto Penzler.**

Ellery Queen, *The Adventures of Ellery Queen*. These stories are the earliest short works to feature Queen as a detective and are among the best of the author's fair-play mysteries. So many of the elements that comprise the gestalt of Queen may be found in these tales: alternate solutions, the dying clue, a bizarre crime, and the author's ability to find fresh variations of works by other authors. **Introduction by Otto Penzler.**

Ellery Queen, *The American Gun Mystery.* A rodeo comes to New York City at the Colosseum. The headliner is Buck Horne, the once popular film cowboy who opens the show leading a charge of forty whooping cowboys until they pull out their guns and fire into the air. Buck falls to the ground, shot dead. The police instantly lock the doors to search everyone but the offending weapon has completely vanished. **Introduction by Otto Penzler.**

Ellery Queen, *The Chinese Orange Mystery.* The offices of publisher Donald Kirk have seen strange events but nothing like this. A strange man is found dead with two long spears alongside his back. And, though no one was seen entering or leaving the room, everything has been turned backwards or upside down: pictures face the wall, the victim's clothes are worn backwards, the rug upside down. Why in the world? **Introduction by Otto Penzler.**

Ellery Queen, *The Dutch Shoe Mystery.* Millionaire philanthropist Abagail Doorn falls into a coma and she is rushed to the hospital she funds for an emergency operation by one of the leading surgeons on the East Coast. When she is wheeled into the operating theater, the sheet covering her body is pulled back to reveal her garroted corpse—the first of a series of murders **Introduction by Otto Penzler.**

Ellery Queen, *The Egyptian Cross Mystery.* A small-town schoolteacher is found dead, headed, and tied to a T-shaped cross on December 25th, inspiring such sensational headlines as "Crucifixion on Christmas Day." Amateur sleuth Ellery Queen is so intrigued he travels to Virginia but fails to solve the crime. Then a similar murder takes place on New York's Long Island—and then another. **Introduction by Otto Penzler.**

Ellery Queen, *The Siamese Twin Mystery.* When Ellery and his father encounter a raging forest fire on a mountain, their only hope is to drive up to an isolated hillside manor owned by a secretive surgeon and his strange guests. While playing solitaire in the middle of the night, the doctor is shot. The only clue is a torn playing card. Suspects include a society beauty, a valet, and conjoined twins. **Introduction by Otto Penzler.**

Ellery Queen, *The Spanish Cape Mystery.* Amateur detective Ellery Queen arrives in the resort town of Spanish Cape soon after a young woman and her uncle are abducted by a gun-toting, one-eyed giant. The next day, the woman's somewhat dicey boyfriend is found murdered—totally naked under a black fedora and opera cloak. **Introduction by Otto Penzler.**

Patrick Quentin, *A Puzzle for Fools.* Broadway producer Peter Duluth takes to the bottle when his wife dies but enters a sanitarium to dry out. Malevolent events plague the hospital, including when Peter hears his own voice intone, "There will be murder." And there is. He investigates, aided by a young woman who is also a patient. This is the first of nine mysteries featuring Peter and Iris Duluth. **Introduction by Otto Penzler.**

Clayton Rawson, *Death from a Top Hat.* When the New York City Police Department is baffled by an apparently impossible crime, they call on The Great Merlini, a retired stage magician who now runs a Times Square magic shop. In his first case, two occultists have been murdered in a room locked from the inside, their bodies positioned to form a pentagram. **Introduction by Otto Penzler.**

Craig Rice, *Eight Faces at Three.* Gin-soaked John J. Malone, defender of the guilty, is notorious for getting his culpable clients off. It's the innocent ones who are problems. Like Holly Inglehart, accused of piercing the black heart of her well-heeled aunt Alexandria with a lovely Florentine paper cutter. No one who knew the old battle-ax liked her, but Holly's prints were found on the murder weapon. **Introduction by Lisa Lutz.**

Craig Rice, *Home Sweet Homicide.* Known as the Dorothy Parker of mystery fiction for her memorable wit, Craig Rice was the first detective writer to appear on the cover of *Time* magazine. This comic mystery features two kids who are trying to find a husband for their widowed mother while she's engaged in sleuthing. Filmed with the same title in 1946 with Peggy Ann Garner and Randolph Scott. **Introduction by Otto Penzler.**

Mary Roberts Rinehart, *The Album*. Crescent Place is a quiet enclave of wealthy people in which nothing ever happens—until a bedridden old woman is attacked by an intruder with an ax. *The New York Times* stated: "All Mary Roberts Rinehart mystery stories are good, but this one is better." **Introduction by Otto Penzler.**

Mary Roberts Rinehart, *The Haunted Lady*. The arsenic in her sugar bowl was wealthy widow Eliza Fairbanks' first clue that somebody wanted her dead. Nightly visits of bats, birds, and rats, obviously aimed at scaring the dowager to death, was the second. Eliza calls the police, who send nurse Hilda Adams, the amateur sleuth they refer to as "Miss Pinkerton," to work undercover to discover the culprit. **Introduction by Otto Penzler.**

Mary Roberts Rinehart, *Miss Pinkerton*. Hilda Adams is a nurse, not a detective, but she is observant and smart and so it is common for Inspector Patton to call on her for help. Her success results in his calling her "Miss Pinkerton." *The New Republic* wrote: "From thousands of hearts and homes the cry will go up: Thank God for Mary Roberts Rinehart." **Introduction by Carolyn Hart.**

Mary Roberts Rinehart, *The Red Lamp*. Professor William Porter refuses to believe that the seaside manor he's just inherited is haunted but he has to convince his wife to move in. However, he soon sees evidence of the occult phenomena of which the townspeople speak. Whether it is a spirit or a human being, Porter accepts that there is a connection to the rash of murders that have terrorized the countryside. **Introduction by Otto Penzler.**

Mary Roberts Rinehart, *The Wall*. For two decades, Mary Roberts Rinehart was the second-best-selling author in America (only Sinclair Lewis outsold her) and was beloved for her tales of suspense. In a magnificent mansion, the ex-wife of one of the owners turns up making demands and is found dead the next day. And there are more dark secrets lying behind the walls of the estate. **Introduction by Otto Penzler.**

Joel Townsley Rogers, *The Red Right Hand*. This extraordinary whodunnit that is as puzzling as it is terrifying was identified by crime fiction scholar Jack Adrian as "one of the dozen or so finest mystery novels of the 20th century." A deranged killer sends a doctor on a quest for the truth—deep into the recesses of his own mind—when he and his bride-to-be elope but pick up a terrifying sharp-toothed hitch-hiker. **Introduction by Joe R. Lansdale.**

Roger Scarlett, *Cat's Paw*. The family of the wealthy old bachelor Martin Greenough cares far more about his money than they do about him. For his birthday, he invites all his potential heirs to his mansion to tell them what they hope to hear. Before he can disburse funds, however, he is murdered, and the Boston Police Department's big problem is that there are too many suspects. **Introduction by Curtis Evans**

Vincent Starrett, *Dead Man Inside*. 1930s Chicago is a tough town but some crimes are more bizarre than others. Customers arrive at a haberdasher to find a corpse in the window and a sign on the door: *Dead Man Inside! I am Dead. The store will not open today.* This is just one of a series of odd murders that terrorizes the city. Reluctant detective Walter Ghost leaps into action to learn what is behind the plague. **Introduction by Otto Penzler.**

Vincent Starrett, *The Great Hotel Murder*. Theater critic and amateur sleuth Riley Blackwood investigates a murder in a Chicago hotel where the dead man had changed rooms with a stranger who had registered under a fake name. *The New York Times* described it as "an ingenious plot with enough complications to keep the reader guessing." **Introduction by Lyndsay Faye.**

Vincent Starrett, *Murder on 'B' Deck*. Walter Ghost, a psychologist, scientist, explorer, and former intelligence officer, is on a cruise ship and his friend novelist Dunsten Mollock, a Nigel Bruce-like Watson whose role is to offer occasional comic relief, accommodates when he fails to leave the ship before it takes off. Although they make mistakes along the way, the amateur sleuths solve the shipboard murders. **Introduction by Ray Betzner.**

Phoebe Atwood Taylor, *The Cape Cod Mystery*. Vacationers have flocked to Cape Cod to avoid the heat wave that hit the Northeast and find their holiday unpleasant when the area is flooded with police trying to find the murderer of a muckraking journalist who took a cottage for the season. Finding a solution falls to Asey Mayo, "the Cape Cod Sherlock," known for his worldly wisdom, folksy humor, and common sense. **Introduction by Otto Penzler.**

S. S. Van Dine, *The Benson Murder Case.* The first of 12 novels to feature Philo Vance, the most popular and influential detective character of the early part of the 20th century. When wealthy stockbroker Alvin Benson is found shot to death in a locked room in his mansion, the police are baffled until the erudite flaneur and art collector arrives on the scene. Paramount filmed it in 1930 with William Powell as Vance. **Introduction by Ragnar Jónasson.**

Cornell Woolrich, *The Bride Wore Black.* The first suspense novel by one of the greatest of all noir authors opens with a bride and her new husband walking out of the church. A car speeds by, shots ring out, and he falls dead at her feet. Determined to avenge his death, she tracks down everyone in the car, concluding with a shocking surprise. It was filmed by Francois Truffaut in 1968, starring Jeanne Moreau. **Introduction by Eddie Muller.**

Cornell Woolrich, *Deadline at Dawn.* Quinn is overcome with guilt about having robbed a stranger's home. He meets Bricky, a dime-a-dance girl, and they fall for each other. When they return to the crime scene, they discover a dead body. Knowing Quinn will be accused of the crime, they race to find the true killer before he's arrested. A 1946 film starring Susan Hayward was loosely based on the plot. **Introduction by David Gordon.**

Cornell Woolrich, *Waltz into Darkness.* A New Orleans businessman successfully courts a woman through the mail but he is shocked to find when she arrives that she is not the plain brunette whose picture he'd received but a radiant blond beauty. She soon absconds with his fortune. Wracked with disappointment and loneliness, he vows to track her down. When he finds her, the real nightmare begins. **Introduction by Wallace Stroby.**